Dance of Obsession

Dance of Obsession

OLIVIA CHRISTIE

BLACK
lace

Black Lace novels are sexual fantasies.
In real life, make sure you practise safe sex.

First published in 1996 by
Black Lace
332 Ladbroke Grove
London W10 5AH

Typeset by CentraCet Limited, Cambridge
Printed and bound by Mackays of Chatham PLC

ISBN 0 352 330101 1

Chapter One

The cold glass of the window was damp. With the tip of her finger Georgia traced the path left by a drop of condensation and stared out at grey swirls of mist drifting over frosty lawns. Autumn was beautiful here at Lusigny, but this was the weather she liked least. Rather than go for a ride as she had promised, she would prefer to spend the day in front of a blazing fire.

Olivier's warm hands on her shoulders surprised her. 'You're cold. Come back to bed,' he said. Georgia shivered as she felt his fingers slide round to stroke her breasts, but it was the hard length of his naked body against her back that caused her to tremble, not the chill of the morning.

'It reminds you of England?' he asked.

She nodded. 'A little. The cold. The mist.' But she hadn't been thinking of England. Her home was here in France with Olivier now. The wiry, dark curls on his chest tickled her bare shoulders as she swivelled round to face him. Lifting her hands up to his face, she stroked the rough stubble on his unshaven cheek. Her meticulous, usually immaculate husband was even more desirable in the early morning, she thought.

'Won't you let me take you to London?' he asked. 'You

can't hide away for ever. Think of it as a celebration of our anniversary.'

Georgia shook her head and pressed her face against his chest. She knew that most of her friends would have forgotten the old scandal, but she had no wish to revive painful memories. And this year there would be an endless round of parties following the Silver Jubilee of King George and Queen Mary. She would be a constant source of gossip if she returned now.

Slithering out of his grasp, she smiled up at him. 'I've had my present, remember?' She still wore the matching pair of sapphire bracelets he had given her the previous night.

She trembled as she felt his warm lips brush the inside of each wrist, an inch above the glittering, jewelled bands. She could feel his desire mount as his teeth grazed against the soft pad of her thumb, and the grip of his fingers tightened on her arms. He looked up into her face, his dark irises staring at her with open lust. The quickening of her breath matched his as he slid his hands down her back, pulling her tight against him, letting her feel the hard, tangible vigour of his erection.

'Olivier,' she murmured, 'again?' Yes, she thought, she wanted him to take her back to bed, even though they had spent the night making love. Her thighs parted instinctively as she felt the heat of his body pressing on her belly. She heard him gasp as she rose on tiptoe to take him between her legs, then his arms caught her shoulders, pushing her back, forcing her down on to the silky fibres of the blue and rose Aubusson carpet. She reached out for him, arching up to meet him as he drove the full length of his thick, powerful penis deep inside her.

There was an urgency in his passion which thrilled her. She could see his need in every harsh line of his face, contorted by passion as he thrust again and again. There was none of the slow, tantalising foreplay at which he was so expert, none of the practised skills which he knew excited her to fever pitch. He cried out with a wild roar as he climaxed, crushing her to him as he sank down on to her. She could not tell where his joy ended and hers began. She felt she was a part of him, sharing his ecstasy, giving and taking his love.

Gently he withdrew and caressed her breasts. He knelt over her, tenderly kissing the moist warmth of her inner thighs, his unshaven jaw teasing her soft flesh. He picked her up in his arms, and grinned sheepishly. 'I promised you could go back to bed,' he murmured, as he laid her on the silk sheets, drawing the thick feather cover over her. She curled up beneath it, half drugged by the lingering sensations of her sated body.

Olivier had been so different the night before when she had sat at the piano in the library, playing the Chopin nocturne he loved. Then, he had slowly aroused her, kissing her bare shoulders and pretending that he was simply admiring the dress she had worn especially for their anniversary. It was an extravagant sliver of midnight-blue velvet, modestly discreet when seen from the front; the back fell in a deep curve below her waist, and Olivier adored it.

She was so lucky to be here and to have this man. His eyes were fixed on her as he tightened a tan leather belt on his jodhpurs, and pulled on his gleaming riding boots. She admired him as he walked over to her, his dark hair scarcely touched with grey, his powerful body youthfully lean. As he bent over her, she nuzzled her face in the soft, black cashmere of his sweater, lazily wishing he would spend the morning here with her. Incredibly she felt her nipples start to tingle again as his hard body pressed down on her.

She looked up into his laughing dark eyes. 'Later ... later,' he said, tucking the sheets around her. 'Think of something special.' He was still laughing as he stood in the doorway, blowing her a kiss. Then he was gone.

The November weather was so cold and dull that Georgia delayed joining Olivier on his ride. She snuggled further down in bed, enjoying the sensation of silk sheets on her bare skin, her body soothed and languid after Olivier's blissful love-making.

There was plenty of time to consider what to do next. She would prefer to lie here, and wait for him to come back to her, hot and sweating from his vigorous exercise. She knew that he would want to make love to her again, and would forgive her for not having accompanied him. But she had given her word and would not disappoint him.

Reluctantly, she slid her legs out of bed and padded over to the window. The mist had lifted now but the sky was leaden. She stared out, past the formal gardens, to the rough pasture and the chestnut woods beyond to see if Olivier was in sight.

He and Dominic were riding together. It was a great pleasure for Olivier that his son had come to live with them, and Georgia was delighted to see her husband so happy. It had been a shock the previous year to find that Dominic was not quite the child she had expected. At eighteen, he was already a man. He had inherited his father's tall, lean figure and dark colouring and, after a childhood spent travelling around the capitals of Europe with his mother, he was unusually sophisticated for his age.

They were just coming out of the woods now. Georgia could hear the two male voices urging each other on. Olivier looked up at the window and smiled at her. She waved and mouthed silent promises to him. She would be down soon.

In summer he would have taken her into the woods after their ride, and made love to her under the leafy, green canopy of the chestnut branches. Instead, she must think of an exciting alternative.

She loved this bedroom, which Olivier had designed to mirror the changing colour of her eyes, ordering the walls to be painted in shades of pale aquamarine and dove-grey. But today she wanted somewhere different.

The library, Olivier's favourite room, with its heavy mahogany shelves and dark panelled walls, would be perfect.

They would come in from their ride, in their dirty shirts and jodhpurs, and she would let him take her as if he were a stable lad having fun with one of the girls from the village. They would pretend to be illicit lovers using their master's château.

She started to dress before ringing the bell. She would order champagne. Then she changed her mind. Not champagne – it was too ordinary and she wanted today to be special. Calvados would be better. That was it.

'Madam?' The voice was still firmly English.

Georgia smiled. It had amused Olivier to train David to become the perfect English butler, although Olivier's idea of one was very different from her family's. David had started off working at Fleur's, their club in Paris, and, at the end of his year there, he had come to the château. He now had a high opinion of his skills, but he was far too young and good-looking. Georgia's father's butler had seemed ancient to her, and he would never have dreamt of entering his mistress's bedroom, especially when she was half-dressed. Briskly Georgia tucked her shirt into her skin-tight cream jodhpurs, and zipped them up before addressing David.

'Please arrange for the fire to be lit in the library and have the curtains drawn. We shall want a bottle of Calvados and two glasses. Kitchen glasses.'

If David was surprised he didn't show it. But then Georgia knew he prided himself on his imperturbability. He did not raise a single objection, and she was confident he would prepare the room for them perfectly, even to the extent of rescuing the dress she had discarded there the previous night. She would make sure her ride was a short one. There were better things to do.

Georgia stopped to take one last look out of the window as she tied back her long black curls with a length of velvet ribbon. Below her she could see the two men riding together, circling a field at the far end of the rose garden. She could hear Dominic's shout of encouragement as his father galloped towards a high stone wall. Nimrod, Olivier's powerful, black stallion was soaring over the jump, perfectly in tune with his master. Georgia watched with pleasure, proud of her husband's horsemanship.

Dominic prepared to follow his father, cantering round to the back of the jump just as Olivier was in mid-air. Then Olivier seemed to lose his concentration. Did she imagine it, or did he look up at her one last time?

Suddenly Nimrod was down, falling heavily on the ground, and she could not see Olivier. He must have been thrown clear. But, as she raced down the wide marble staircase, she went over the terrifying image that filled her mind. Olivier had fallen under the horse. She was sure of it.

David ran towards her in the hall. As she pulled open the heavy front door, Georgia screamed out at him. 'Call the doctor. Get him here now.'

Outside, on the cold ground, her feet seemed to move unbearably slowly. She felt paralysed, unable to go any faster, as she tried to force her trembling legs to run over the frosty grass.

Nimrod was upright, shuddering but uninjured and held by Dominic, who had dismounted and now stood calming both stallions some distance away from his father's motionless body. Georgia knelt beside Olivier, hesitant even to touch him in case she hurt him more. There was no sign of injury; he didn't look as if he had broken any of his limbs, but he was unnaturally pale and cold. She wanted to believe that he might simply be concussed. And she prayed for a miracle.

Gently she stroked his dark hair back from his forehead and looked round to see if help had come. Where was the doctor? Surely he must be here by now? She told herself that Olivier would be all right – he must be all right. Then her fingers curved round the back of his head, and she felt thick, sticky blood congealing on her fingers from the horribly crushed base of his skull, smashed and broken by Nimrod's flying hooves.

Georgia bent over him, pressing her lips on his cheek. He was cold, ice cold, and she felt the chill creeping into her own flesh as she finally understood there was no hope.

She hardly noticed David and the doctor running across the field towards them. It didn't seem to matter any more. She shook off their kind hands, refusing to let go of Olivier until they found a stretcher, brought him into the house and, on her instructions, laid her husband's lifeless body in his favourite room.

She sat beside him in the library, ignoring the sedatives the doctor had prescribed for her. All that day and night she stayed alone in the darkening room, mourning the man she had loved.

And behind him, on the ebony wood of the grand piano, she saw a bottle of rough, peasant Calvados, waiting for them on a tray with two coarse kitchen tumblers.

'What will you do about Fleur's?' Dominic stood in front of the blazing fire in the library, after the last funeral guest had gone home. The damp chill of the day of the accident had grown steadily harsher, until now, a week later, the sky was rose-grey with a threat of snow. Georgia looked at her stepson blankly, her mind numb as her fingers traced the outline of a bronze statuette on the piano. She was tired – deathly tired. And she did not want to think about the club. It had been closed for a week, and for all she cared it could stay shut for ever.

'Dominic, I don't want to make any decisions now.'

'You can't leave it any longer. Your clients will take their custom somewhere else.'

'That's fine by me.' She supposed she should reassure him that they didn't need the money. Olivier had created his exclusive club simply for his own amusement and pleasure. And, however adult Dominic looked, he was far too young to be involved. 'I don't want to run Fleur's without your father,' she said quietly.

'You can't let it go.'

'Why not, Dominic?' Why couldn't he leave her alone? She was in no condition to make any plans.

'It's my inheritance. Father had already begun to train me. Are you going to let it go before I have a chance to take over?'

Georgia filled her glass with cognac and sank into one of the antique, red leather armchairs comfortably placed on either side of the fireplace. She watched Dominic fling himself into the other, and dug her fingernails into the palm of her hand to stop herself shouting at him. That was Olivier's chair. What right did Dominic have to sit there? He wasn't her responsibility. Why couldn't he go home to his mother?

His eyes were cold and hard, blacker than Olivier's. She tried to think clearly but her brain was frozen with pain. Dominic rose to his feet and crossed the narrow space between them, looming over her. 'What else would you do?'

Helplessly, she watched as he picked up the decanter of cognac, refilled her glass, and pressed it to her lips. 'You need to keep busy and you're right. You're in no condition to take any decisions while you're shocked.' His voice was as smooth and persuasive as his father's. 'Wouldn't it be better not to change anything until you feel stronger?'

As Georgia sipped, she felt the spirit hit her stomach, warming her, lulling the sense of apprehension that unnerved her. Dominic's hands were firm and comforting on her shoulders. Perhaps he was right. Maybe this was what Olivier would want her to do. Anything would be better than burying herself here at Lusigny, alone with her memories.

Slowly she nodded. 'Just until the end of the season,' she told him.

She promised to keep on with her evening performances, to maintain her list of rich and influential clients and to run the club exactly as she had done with Olivier, until Dominic was able to take over.

He kissed the back of her hand and gazed into her eyes. She shivered as she stared back into those too familiar depths. She would keep Fleur's in business, but she would never allow him to watch her act, and never work with him as she had done with Olivier. No one else would ever be that close to her again.

After the summer, Dominic would have to manage on his own. Only there was no need to tell him that yet. And how could she say anything, when she had not given a single thought to her own plans for the future?

Chapter Two

Seven months later, on a sweltering June evening, Georgia stood outside Fleur's, looking up at the elegant town house where she had worked for so many years with Olivier. Tonight she was here to give her last performance. The beautiful old building, one of the finest of many such imposing stone mansions in the respectable, residential seventeenth *arrondissement* of Paris, was set on a corner of the wide, leafy Boulevard Berlioz.

Marc, her chauffeur, waited patiently beside her. 'Are you ready?' he asked.

She nodded. During these last months she had missed Olivier more and more. The sharp pain of her grief was transformed into an overwhelming sense of loss. Now, she had to admit, it was the comfort of Olivier's body she missed, longing to feel again his powerful male flesh filling and satisfying her.

'I'm fine, Marc. I'll be all right. Dominic will drive me back to Lusigny when we're through.' She smiled up at him. Marc had been one of the first young men Olivier had chosen for their act. She had seen him develop from a brash, uneducated boy, struggling for work in the docks at Marseilles, into a gentle giant of a man whose concern touched her.

She took a deep breath, opened the door and walked into the richly carpeted hall, nodding an acknowledgement to the clients assembled there before she climbed slowly up to the first floor.

Here the rule was strictly members only. No casual visitors were allowed in the salon where Georgia performed nightly, taunting her team of young men with the erotic movements Olivier had designed for her. It was an act intended to excite the eager group of watching women, and to allow them ample opportunity to select their partners for the evening.

At the end of a long passage, behind the main salon, was Georgia's dressing-room, a small, windowless space in the centre of the house. She had spent many hours in this room with its red damask-lined walls and its polished oak floor, almost entirely covered by a thick Persian rug. Now, she kicked off her shoes and curled her bare toes in the rug's silky fibres, enjoying the feel of it against her skin. Olivier had always chosen this place for them to make love after her show.

Georgia bit sharply on the soft flesh of her lower lip. She must not think of Olivier now, must not allow the memory of his skilful love-making to overwhelm her. There was too much to do. And Olivier was no longer with her – Olivier, her partner, her lover, her husband, would never delight her senses again.

In the salon adjoining this room, the club's most valued members were already seated, impatiently awaiting her entrance. Georgia slipped out of her light silk shirt and slacks, and reached for her costume. Always the same colour, always the same style, it was new every night. By the end of the evening it would be torn to shreds.

As she draped a fragile, burgundy chiffon cloak over her naked body, she looked up at the portrait that dominated one wall of the room. That painting had brought her and Olivier together. It was the one possession of hers that she would take from this house.

11

She took a deep breath. She was ready. Despite her sadness, she felt a familiar surge of excitement as she pulled back a crimson silk curtain and stood in front of the gleaming mahogany door which divided her dressing-room from the salon. She loved this moment, relishing the anticipation, aware of her power to arouse and control her team. For years she had known this thrill, but now, without Olivier to satisfy her maddened senses after her performance, she could no longer continue.

Georgia raised her hand, turned the brass key in the lock and opened the door to the salon. The women invited here tonight were rich; for years they had been her most valued clients. She was determined to ensure they would not be disappointed.

The eyes of twelve young men were fixed on her as she entered the darkened room. Total silence prevailed as she padded softly towards them and paused, waiting to make her choice. Thick beeswax candles gleamed in gilt wall brackets, scenting the air with their honey odour, their glow outlining the faces of women who reclined on soft leather sofas around a circle of almost naked bodies.

Georgia felt the tension heighten as she moved inside the ring. Candle-light flickered over the alabaster sheen of her flesh, barely hidden by the sheer folds of silk chiffon which clung to her shoulders and floated in a dark cloud to her feet.

She needed three men.

Swinging round she looked straight at the boy who had almost lost control last time. His tawny eyes were fringed with thick, black lashes and his blonde hair flopped appealingly forward, inviting women to smooth it back.

Georgia moved one step towards him, forcing her tall figure to appear deceptively relaxed, allowing her full lips to curl slightly at the eager response he was too young to hide. She bent swiftly, her teeth working at the knot of the leather pouch which was his only covering, tearing it away until he stood naked, the well-honed perfection of his body pleasing the watching women almost as much as the size of his erection.

Georgia turned slowly, deliberately delaying her decision. Stepping towards a man whose dark tan contrasted well with her own pale flesh, she bent her head again and released his swollen penis from the constraining leather. She stared fiercely at him, commanding restraint.

She had one more mate to choose. It would not be the southern-looking man who stood behind her now, arrogantly languid; he reminded her too much of Olivier. Spinning on her heels, she darted down and bit into the tight leather thong of the man next to him.

She had made her choice.

Georgia looked into the eyes of the remaining nine, promising, commanding, reminding them who was in control and who paid their wages. Their throbbing erections must remain restricted by the taut leather to excite the watching women.

Her chiffon covering drifted behind her and Georgia could see the men's eyes fix on to the curve of her breasts as they stared at her fully exposed nipples. This was the moment she enjoyed most, when she felt like a lion tamer commanding wild beasts, risking that at any moment they would break free from her domination.

She raised her arms to the dark boy's throat, undulating towards him, reaching out to grasp his massive erection between her thighs. She stared hard into his eyes, forcing his restraint, refusing to allow him permission to pump his juices over her until she was ready.

Rising on the balls of her feet, she parted her legs and, releasing her hold, she turned towards the blonde boy. Georgia watched him carefully; he was very young and perhaps a little too eager. Bending in front of him for the second time that evening, she closed her lips around the swollen head of his penis, relishing his urgent response, rubbing her sharp teeth against his straining flesh to warn him to delay his climax.

She took the whole of his huge shaft into her throat as she slid her hands up round his hard buttocks, pulling him down with her on to the floor. He knelt over her, the long stretch of his heavily muscled thighs straddling her breasts like a young god of love. Georgia felt her discipline falter as her excitement grew, and swiftly she beckoned to the last man of the three.

She struggled to maintain her concentration. Her mind was filled with the image of Olivier, who no longer watched from the room outside. She felt her desire mount as she longed for him and fought to resist her weakness. There was so little more to do. Surely she couldn't fail now.

The last man trod silently across the deep pile of the carpet and bent over her naked belly. His hands tore apart the flimsy chiffon as she raised her long slim legs to his neck. He placed his penis between the curving arches of her feet, and rhythmically rubbed himself between them. He took his time. He would be the last to come.

The blonde boy was losing control. Georgia tried to drown out the sound of his husky groans as she sucked his sweet young flesh, and spread her wine-red, painted nails across his buttocks. She signalled to the others. They turned to face the door, stared arrogantly at the group of eager women, and slowly paced out of the room.

She twisted slightly, breaking free from the urgent grasp of her young man. She heard their audience gasp as he climaxed, and saw a glistening flood of semen trickle off her breast, and fall on to the velvety garnet-coloured carpet in a starburst of pearls.

She licked the last drops from the slackening sac of the blonde boy, teasing his now limp flesh with her teeth and raising her arms high above her head to display the dark amber peaks of her still swollen nipples.

14

Georgia rose swiftly to her feet, dark shreds of torn chiffon floating out behind her. She was trembling. Dominic had asked too much of her. How could any woman bear this sexual frenzy without a man to satisfy her afterwards?

She lingered for a moment in the soft glow from the flaming candles, confident that she looked composed, except for the increased gleam of her warm flesh and a few tears of semen drying matt on her skin. Then she turned on her heel and walked out of the room, leaving the waiting women to choose their partners for the hour before dinner.

They were paying a fortune for the privilege.

Chapter Three

Georgia walked into her dressing-room and sat down in front of the mirror, her body quivering with frustration. If only Olivier were here to take advantage of her arousal. She had a lonely bed ahead of her tonight when her duties were finally at an end.

'Congratulations, stepmother.' Dominic's deep voice startled her. His languid body uncoiled itself from the crimson satin cushions of the chaise longue as he rose to pour a glass of champagne from a bottle chilling in a silver pail. In the oppressive heat of the room the ice was melting fast.

As he handed her the drink, Georgia stared angrily at the obvious bulge of his erection, swelling out the front of his tight black trousers. Dominic was becoming a problem. He might have inherited this house from his father, but he had no right yet to be in this room. She had made it clear this was her private place. No doubt he had taken full advantage of the narrow slit in the door, hidden behind the curtain, to watch her performance.

She pointed to a vivid cerise kimono hanging in her cupboard. 'Pass me my robe, Dominic,' she said wearily. Reluctantly, he handed her the covering.

'I gather from the boys that they've lost their bet,' he said lazily. 'They were sure you'd give in to one of them before the end of the season.'

'They always believe that, Dominic. Every year at least one of them thinks he's irresistible.' Georgia tried to sound casual, but he was too close to the truth. She was still shaking with frustration.

'But now, my darling, it's different,' he persisted. 'This time you don't have a man of your own. And we're all perfectly aware of that. The mere thought of your delicious body lying alone in an empty bed at night is enough to drive us all mad.'

Georgia sipped her champagne, hoping its icy chill would help to calm her temper. She dipped her fingers into a jar of cold cream and calmly smoothed the make-up off her face. She didn't want to argue with him tonight. She knew that she was too strung up and, with the whole summer together ahead of them, she needed to maintain her distance. Already she regretted her decision to help Dominic audition a new team of young men.

She watched in the mirror as he paced the room. His presence unsettled her; he was too like his father. He stopped in front of her portrait, lifted his hand to touch the rough surface of the canvas, and slowly traced the glowing contours of her naked breasts with one finger. 'Who painted this?' he asked.

'Theo Sands,' she said.

Dominic's hand lingered over the cinnamon-tinged swirls of Georgia's clearly defined nipples. 'Monsieur Sands obviously turned you on in a big way,' he said, scowling at her, his dark eyes flashing. 'He was your lover, I presume?'

She pulled her robe more tightly around her, feeling the sweat prickling as it dried on her skin. 'That's none of your business, Dominic.'

'Everything about this club is my business now.'

17

'The painting is mine. I've made arrangements for it to be taken to Lusigny.'

Dominic's dark eyes glittered. 'I'm surprised my father allowed it here.' He walked towards her, eyes fixed on the low cut of her thin robe. 'But then he enjoyed the effect you have on men, didn't he?'

Georgia flushed, aware of his scornful gaze on her thinly covered body. When Olivier was alive, her performance had seemed fun, a prelude to a night of pleasure for everyone. Now she wasn't sure and Dominic's attitude confirmed her doubts. She was glad that it was finally over.

She felt him closing in on her, the heat of his thighs burning through her silk gown as he caught her chin roughly, forcing her to look up at him. 'My father waited for you in here, didn't he? And he watched you as I did tonight. What did he do to you when you came back, excited by all those eager young men?' Dominic laughed and let her go. 'You must miss that, chérie. It's time you let me help.'

Georgia watched, paralysed, as Dominic's hands dropped to the zip of his trousers. She took a deep breath and stood up.

'Get out, Dominic. We run a business here, in case you'd forgotten. Go away and tell Françoise I'm ready. I need to rest before dinner and you're in my way. I'm sure you can find plenty of girls your own age without teasing me.'

'I thought that was your speciality,' Dominic retorted, as he turned on his heel and stalked out to fetch her masseuse.

Georgia lay down on the narrow bed in the corner of her room and closed her eyes. How could he be so unfair? He had asked for her help and she had given it for his father's sake. And sometimes, when she looked at the sweet curve of Dominic's high cheekbones and the curl of his thick, black eyelashes, the resemblance was so strong that she imagined Olivier was back with her.

She was almost asleep when Françoise bustled in, stripping off her white linen uniform and revealing her plump, golden body. There was no false modesty in the club and on this hot night it was more pleasant for her to work naked.

'Three months away for you now,' Françoise murmured, as she dripped soothing, aromatic oil on to Georgia's back. 'You'll miss Fleur's.'

Georgia moaned ecstatically as the young girl's hands rippled over her tense shoulder muscles. Every year until now, she had looked forward with pleasure to her three months' summer break. She used to go with Olivier to their villa on the Côte d'Azur where they enjoyed each other's company while training a new team. This year would be different.

'It's time I gave up,' she said.

'Oh, don't do that.' Françoise sounded shocked. 'It's impossible. You can't mean it.'

Georgia pressed her face on the warm towel. Why should anyone be surprised? She was 36. If Olivier had lived, how much longer would she have gone on? They had always intended to choose someone to take over, but it had still been so much fun that they had delayed looking for a replacement.

Before they left for Antibes, she would find a girl to work with Dominic. Until that was arranged, she had no intention of worrying either him or her staff. 'Maybe I just need a rest,' she said, turning to allow Françoise to work on her front. 'Perhaps I should let Dominic do more.'

The stroking hands stopped their work and Georgia saw a deep crimson flush tinge Françoise's honey-gold cheeks at the mention of Dominic's name. The girl's healthy young nipples were pink and swollen and Georgia closed her eyes, unwilling to embarrass her friend. Damn Dominic, she thought; if he intends to run this club successfully he has to learn to take his fun elsewhere. From the expression on Françoise's face, Georgia

19

was sure that Dominic had already promised her the full benefit of his expert training. Maybe that was how he had gained access to this room.

Françoise's palms pressed deeply on the long curve of Georgia's thighs, releasing the tension from her stiffened muscles, relaxing her body until she felt she was melting into the bed.

'What would Dominic do?' The girl's voice was low and husky.

Georgia thought carefully. It would be up to him to choose his act. Olivier had trained Dominic well and, if her plans worked out as she hoped, all would be fine.

'We'll think of something this summer. I'm sure he'll have plenty of ideas,' she said smoothly.

She felt Françoise's hands quiver over her ribs. 'I'll be back in an hour,' the girl promised. 'Have you decided what you want to wear?'

'Mmm.' Georgia was almost too drowsy to respond. 'The black Chanel, I think. It should be just inside the cupboard. You don't have to worry about that.'

Her eyelids closed. 'But please don't forget to wake me up.' She lay drowsily on the hard bed, pleasurably aware of her soothed and scented body as she drifted off into a deep sleep. Françoise would rouse her in time to change for dinner and, now that she was relaxed, Georgia was almost content to lie like this, rather than indulge in the sexual activities taking place upstairs. Or was she fooling herself? Perhaps she was simply afraid that no one else could satisfy her after Olivier.

Dominic walked to the end of the long passage and opened the door to the deserted salon. All the beeswax candles had been extinguished. He lit a match and held it to the singed wick of one thick stub. The air was heavy with the scent of rich perfumes, dominated by the familiar fragrance of Georgia's distinctive Chaleur and, above all, by the mingled musk of male and female lust.

It would amuse him to make love to Françoise here. Looking out into the corridor, he watched her close the door of Georgia's dressing-room, pause to tie back a loose strand of blonde hair, and fasten the buttons on her crisp, white uniform.

Dominic moistened his lips, realising that Françoise must have been naked while she massaged his stepmother. He visualised Françoise's strong hands kneading the creamy, pale flesh he had seen earlier. He had wanted Georgia since he had come to live with her and his father two years ago, and, now that Olivier was dead, he saw no reason to deny himself that pleasure.

Tonight was the first time Dominic had watched his stepmother's performance, the first time he had seen her naked. Everything else in the club had been carefully taught to him. He understood how to provide all the various pleasures that were offered in the private rooms on the upper floor. Only Georgia's dressing-room and salon had been forbidden to him. No longer! She was the most blatantly sensual woman he had ever seen and it was time that he took his rightful place in her life.

But for the moment he had other things on his mind. Françoise had given him the dressing-room key and she was entitled to her reward. Georgia would disapprove, but she must understand that he intended to lay down the rules from now on.

He breathed deeply, staring into the semi-darkness. As Françoise passed the open doorway, he stretched out one hand and pulled her towards him. Covering her mouth with his lips, he silenced her small yelp of surprise. He pressed his body against hers as he led her into the heart of the salon, pushing her hands inside the waistband of his tight, leather trousers, encouraging her to rip them off him as he parted the low front of her uniform, and lifted out her full golden breasts.

His dark head bent over her and his lips enclosed her stiffened nipples, sucking fiercely as she stripped him naked. He lowered her on to the rich, red carpet, sliding

21

the crisp linen off her shoulders as he pushed between her thighs, seeking the warm opening which waited so eagerly for him.

There was no need for foreplay. He knew only too well how excited she had been before, and how she must have longed for this while her fingers caressed his stepmother's body. He thrust hard up inside her as he kissed the tips of those fingers, taking them deep into his mouth, revelling in their musky odour. Françoise's warmth flowed round him; her young muscles clung sweetly to his thick shaft buried deep inside her. He felt her swollen bud pulsating with each lunge of his body, as he used all his skill to bring her to fulfilment.

When he withdrew from her, she lay beneath him, looking softly content. Gently he pulled her hands towards him, encouraging her to take his stiff, wet cock between her strong fingers, milking his juices in one hot, glorious stream. He shuddered in ecstasy as the pink finger tips worked on his body until he lay prone beside her, stroking her tousled, blonde hair. If only it was Georgia lying beside him now, he knew that he could satisfy her, too.

Too soon he felt Françoise stir reluctantly beneath him. 'I have to go,' she said. 'Will I see you later?'

Dominic tilted one honey-tinged breast with the tip of his finger. He was driving Georgia home. He would need all his strength for that. 'The boys will be jealous,' he murmured. 'Haven't you promised them a massage after their work?'

Françoise flushed. He saw her greedy eyes gaze down at the full length of his naked body as she fastened the final button on her uniform. 'Another time?' she queried hesitantly.

'After the summer,' Dominic promised, suitably regretful. 'We'll have to wait until then.' He blew her a kiss as she closed the door behind her, then he stretched out indolently on the garnet-coloured carpet, and covered his face with his hot palms, breathing in

the heady scent that he had sucked off Françoise's
fingers.

In the dressing-room, airless in the sultry heat, Georgia
felt her energy return as Françoise towelled the oil
briskly off her body and wrapped her in a light cool
gown. She sat in front of her mirror, checking her make-
up while her hair was brushed into glossy curls.

'The ladies will be ready for you promptly at ten
o'clock,' Françoise announced. 'None of them are missing dinner this evening.'

Georgia smiled. 'If you intend looking after the boys
while we eat, Françoise, make sure you don't exhaust
any of those who are booked for later on.'

The girl giggled and Georgia felt relieved that Françoise enjoyed taking advantage of the young men who
would soon be relaxing by the swimming pool in the
cellar. It might take her mind off Dominic.

'I know the rules,' Françoise assured her, 'and a rub-
down is all they'll get if they're working. But it is their
last night and some of them will be finished soon.'

Georgia had seen how Françoise's expert fingers
excited the young bodies she worked on. She sighed,
regretting that she could never use any of her team to
ease her own frustration. Françoise was lucky.

She was satisfied with a light make-up that disguised
the violet shadows under her eyes and the excessive
pallor of her skin. Her dark hair fell in uncontrolled Pre-
Raphaelite abundance down her shoulders, contrasting
with the deliberate severity of a deceptively simple,
black Chanel evening gown. Coco Chanel was her
favourite designer and a personal friend.

Picking up the long string of creamy pearls that Olivier
had given her the first time they made love, she wound
them three times around her throat, allowing the final
strand to swing low and loose. She kissed Françoise
gently on her full lips, sliding one finger under the tip of
the girl's excited nipple.

23

'I won't delay you any longer,' Georgia promised. 'Go and enjoy yourself.' She paused, deciding to try her hand at a little matchmaking. 'Why not see Marc?' she said. 'He's feeling quite left out now that he's not in the team. And he asks about you all the time. He's not driving us home tonight. Perhaps you could help him relax?' Françoise and Marc had seemed to be getting on well together until the last few weeks. It would be a shame if Dominic spoilt their relationship.

Before she left the room, Georgia made one telephone call. She intended to make sure that there would be no more trouble with her stepson tonight.

Chapter Four

*T*he private dining room, like the salon upstairs, was lit only by candles. Georgia surveyed the arrangements. Antique silver and crystal shimmered on the dark polish of the rosewood table. Everything was as it should be. Exotic tropical orchids were arranged as a centrepiece and also filled the fireplace, in the middle of a June heatwave in Paris, in every shade from the palest apricot to a deep topaz.

'Chérie!' A slender doe-eyed woman appeared in the doorway, her arms outstretched. 'I had a wonderful time. Your boys are divine. I only wish I could take one of them home.' Georgia kissed her friend's cheek and handed her a flute of chilled champagne. She knew that Nadine's husband treated his wife like a piece of Sèvres porcelain. Upstairs her favourite partner, Gaston, was instructed to be considerably more forceful.

Georgia admired her friend's quiet elegance. Nadine managed her private life with the utmost discretion. She was a perfect client, as were most of the women invited for this evening's entertainment. They were her most faithful customers, her friends, in so far as she had any. They crowded in now, their faces alight with the glow of women fresh from sexual gratification. Mellow satisfaction softened their mouths and darkened their eyes as they sipped and nibbled on the delicate slivers of fruit and fish which accompanied their champagne.

'Darling, must you really desert us again this summer? It seems such a long time to wait until September,' Marie pouted.

'It's all in a good cause,' Georgia said lightly, unwilling to reveal her decision to leave Fleur's, until her plans for Dominic were finalised. 'In September twelve fresh young men will be eager to meet you all.'

There was no need to let her friends know that she was worried. She had already spent some time looking for a girl to replace her, but so far without success. The strippers in the clubs and theatres were too blasé and lacked the natural enjoyment which gave her act its special excitement.

When she performed, Georgia physically wanted every one of those young men whose bodies she controlled. It was an effort of will to hold back from taking each swollen penis into her aching sex. That fine balance between genuine lust and iron control generated the sexual arousal which no other event provided. That, and the real beauty of all the participants. Fleur's was unique.

'The boys will be available for you privately all summer,' she promised, 'and in September I'm sure you won't be disappointed with the new team.'

'I certainly wasn't this evening,' giggled Marie. 'That beautiful blonde boy is heavenly. She sighed. 'I only wish I could take him back with me.' Georgia was aware that Marie allowed herself total freedom for her own needs here. At home, in an elegant mansion overlooking the Bois de Boulogne, she behaved like a perfect wife to her extremely rich but rather old husband.

The food was kept deliberately light in order not to spoil the pleasure of those women who intended to make it a full night of love, either taking the boys home with them, or returning to the rooms upstairs. By the time the

26

cassis sorbet was served in its brittle shell of spun sugar, Georgia could feel a heightening of tension, a buzz of erotic excitement which flowed through the women as they shifted in their seats, licking the crisp, sweet shreds off their lips in anticipation of their later exploits.

The babble of conversation rose and fell. Georgia had placed her oldest friend on her right. Solange always amused her and tonight she was on sparkling form, smiling sensuously as she dabbed at her rouged mouth with her damask napkin.

'Jean-Paul and I are looking forward to our holiday in the country,' she purred, stretching her small slim body in pleasurable anticipation. Her extremely expensive, low-cut dress made her tiny breasts look positively voluptuous and, in the soft glow of the candle-light, her carefully made-up skin could have belonged to a woman ten years younger. Jean-Paul would enjoy his summer.

'I envy you having Dominic as an escort, chérie,' Solange murmured. 'Will he be on the books next season?'

Georgia knew this was not the moment to announce that Dominic would be running Fleur's in future. She hoped that he would learn to captivate the clients in his own way.

'He's certainly keen, and of course Olivier trained him well.' Georgia smiled noncommittally. 'We'll spend our time planning new acts for you to experience.'

Solange's delicate pink tongue dipped into her champagne glass, savouring the tingling bubbles. 'I look forward to enjoying Dominic,' she breathed, 'he's every inch his father's son.'

Solange had made no secret of the excitement that Olivier had aroused in her, but she had always been content to satisfy her desires with one of the young men on offer. Now Georgia saw her nostrils flare at the prospect of bedding the boy who had inherited Olivier's magnificently lithe body and brooding dark authority. Solange closed her eyes for a moment, then rose swiftly to her feet and bent over Georgia, her cleavage threatening to burst out of the tight bodice of her dress.

'Darling, I must go,' she breathed heavily. 'Jean-Paul and I are driving through the night.'

There was a flutter of laughter around the table. Solange looked as if the trip she planned for Jean-Paul tonight was up between her legs. She rustled from the room, smoothing her clinging silk dress over her youthfully slim hips.

Solange gave them all hope for the future. Although she looked fabulous, she couldn't be a day under 55, and yet all the boys were eager to be chosen for her legendary summer holidays, not only because of her incredible generosity.

There was a general movement around the table as the ladies prepared to leave: some, reluctantly, to return to their homes, most of them eager to resume their earlier activities with the boys.

Georgia smiled at her friends and raised her glass. 'To Fleur's – and to men,' she toasted. 'Ladies, I leave you to your evening pleasures. Let's all look forward to September when you'll be introduced to our fresh team.'

She rose, relieved that at last she could withdraw, the pressure of her final evening almost over. One woman caught her hand, her tall, slightly heavy body just an inch away. Georgia was only too well aware of Yolande's interest in her, but had no intention of breaking her firm rule of never having sex with anyone at the club.

Georgia smiled and raised one arched eyebrow. 'Come with me, I've found someone you should enjoy. I have a new young girl for you upstairs, tall, slim and full-breasted.' She grinned, knowing that it could be a description of herself.

'And you?' Yolande asked as she followed Georgia up the narrow, back staircase to the private rooms. 'Will you find someone this summer?'

Georgia shrugged. 'I have a lot to do. And there's Dominic . . .' Her voice trailed off.

'Yes, Dominic,' Yolande agreed thoughtfully. 'Why not have an affair with Dominic? It's obvious that he's crazy about you.'

'Dominic is Olivier's son,' Georgia said. She was suddenly overwhelmed with tiredness.

'But not yours,' Yolande's calm voice reminded her. 'And he's a very beautiful young man who might just satisfy you for a while. Are you sure anyone else will?'

Georgia raised anguished eyes to the concerned face of her friend, who had voiced her own fears. 'Not Dominic,' she said, refusing to answer the question.

'Then you have to choose someone else very soon,' Yolande warned her. 'How long do you think you can remain like this?'

Georgia felt Yolande's fingers resting on the bodice of her dress, delicately drawing attention to her swollen nipples. 'You weren't made to sleep alone, chérie,' she said, 'and if I'm not what you want, you'd better find yourself a man soon.'

Georgia looked at her friend. 'I know. I know. I'll do something, I promise.'

'I'll be waiting for you if your tastes change.' At the top of the stairs Yolande smiled appreciatively at the girl waiting for her. She kissed Georgia full on the mouth, her lips parting as she held her close. Georgia breathed in Yolande's warm female scent, wishing for a moment that she had agreed to assuage her lust this way. Her friend was right. Georgia had been seven months without a man and she was losing all control of her body.

Chapter Five

*D*ominic enjoyed life in Paris, especially looking after Georgia. He was sure she needed his protection now that his father wasn't around. Their love for each other had surprised him. It was so different from the way his mother behaved. He had lost count of the men she had lived with after leaving Olivier. And she treated them all like dirt. He wanted a woman like his step-mother. No – more than that – he wanted Georgia.

Waiting for her in the quiet street outside Fleur's, he leant against the sleek Bugatti his father had given him the previous year. It was a beautiful machine, the very latest Type 57, light, powerful and fast. He ran his hands over the gleaming chromework, stroking the cool metal as though it were female flesh. This car excited women; he had already proved that on many occasions. Now, waiting to take Georgia back to the château, he felt equally sure that the car's speed would be effective with her.

At this hour in the early morning the Boulevard Berlioz was deserted, and most of the houses were in total darkness. She would not be long now. It had been an enjoyable evening and it was not yet over.

Dominic imagined Georgia's increasing frustration as

she encouraged her clients to indulge their expensive tastes. He had seen her in that severe black dress, looking as prim as any society lady holding a discreet dinner party.

It was time she stopped wearing mourning; it did not suit her. As soon as she permitted, he would take her to Patou and Chanel for a collection of clothes in the sparkling cerulean and azure that only she could wear so well. No, he would not wait. He would speak to Madame Chanel immediately. Between them, they would complete an entire wardrobe to the stage of final fitting. And, for the summer, he would take her to Elsa Schiaparelli's boutique for beach pyjamas.

And lingerie. He would always choose that for her. He knew that beneath her ladylike crêpe de Chine dinner dress, she was wearing fine lace Directoire knickers, a tiny brassière that cupped and lifted her full breasts, and sheer silk stockings secured by delicate satin suspenders. He had played with her underclothes while he waited in her dressing-room, twisting the scraps of flimsy fabric between his fingers as he watched the men fighting for control.

He wanted to slip the strands of silk and lace over her breasts, to see those pouting nipples caught in the carefully designed cups. He longed to fasten the narrow belt round her waist, slide the black stockings on to her legs and secure them to the slim bands circling the thrilling curve of her thighs.

And, more than that, he yearned to be the man who would remove each layer of her clothing at the end of the evening. When he had shown her how good he could make her feel, he would drive her home and order her to take off her pants, roll her dress up her thighs and lie back on the soft leather sofa, exposing her triangle of black curls and the moist, rosy sex he had seen earlier through the slit in the wall.

Dominic's fingers drummed on the chrome panel in front of him. Maybe she would do as he asked. He knew she was aroused, and that there was no other man whom she could use to slake her lust tonight. She was a woman who needed sex; she could not hold out for long. And, once he had made love to her, once she had experienced his power inside her, he was sure she would beg him to take her again and again.

Dominic watched the guests leave one by one, quietly disappearing into chauffeur-driven cars that waited discreetly in narrow side streets. Lights still glowed softly on the top floor of Fleur's where the rooms were occupied throughout the night. As he stared up at the elegant building Dominic felt a deep satisfaction at the knowledge that all this now belonged to him.

At last the front door opened again and he saw Georgia hesitate on the stone steps. He walked around the car and opened the passenger door of the Bugatti for his stepmother. He watched her sink down on to the cream leather seat. After a performance she was used to relaxing in the back of the Phantom while Marc drove her home. In this car there was only the single front seat. He stretched out next to her, sliding the steering wheel through his fingers. He pressed his foot hard on the accelerator as the powerful engine roared into life.

Towards the centre of the city the streets were busier. Empty bottles were clanked noisily together as hotels and restaurants put out their rubbish and closed their doors. From the pavement bins the stench of food, already rotting in the summer heat, nauseated him. Dominic waited impatiently at each delay, his eyes darting sideways as he stared at Georgia's full mouth. He had seen those painted lips distended round one eager cock this evening. When he got her home, he would show her just how much more pleasure she could have with him.

Dominic jerked the car away from the junction as he drove on, increasing his speed when he reached the open countryside. Their headlights shone on the hot dusty road, silhouetting straight columns of stiff poplars that stretched into the distance. Dominic watched Georgia's face, relaxed as she dozed beside him. Her eyelids were closed, but they fluttered occasionally as the engine noise changed. He was not sure if she was asleep.

He stroked her thigh with the tips of his fingers, enjoying the warmth of her skin. He felt her stir at his touch.

'Awake, Georgia?' he asked. 'Not too cold, I hope. Can I warm you up?' He moved his hand back to the smooth, black leather knob of the gear lever.

She looked at him sleepily. 'I'm perfectly comfortable, thank you, Dominic. There's nothing I need.'

As they drove through the main street of the deserted village near the château, the tyres rumbled over the cobbled streets. They were nearly home. A mile further on, Dominic turned through massive, wrought-iron gates and drove along a winding drive between acres of dense woodland. He came to a gentle halt outside the magnificent front entrance of the château, taking care that no spray of gravel shot up from behind his wheels. Quietly, he slid out and stepped softly around the car. He opened Georgia's door and leant over her. She had to touch him now, even if only to push him aside.

He could see that her eyes were soft and dark; she must have been dreaming of sex. Every undulation of her body, every tell-tale curve of her face assured him that there was only one thing on her mind. It was the perfect time to catch her off guard.

As she rose towards him, he leant forward and slid his hand under her arms, supporting her, letting her languid body melt into his. He felt her unmistakable arousal through the fragile silk of her dress, the quick stiffening of her breasts, the sudden heat that met his eager palms.

He lowered one hand, stroking her, reassuring her that he was with her. His fingers trembled as he felt her hips move instinctively closer, and then she raised her face, her lips moist, her breath fast and deep, her eyes dreamily half-closed. Her lashes fluttered against his cheek as he bent down to kiss her, longing to taste those sweet, full lips that seemed to part in an open invitation.

He laid her back on the soft leather seat of the car, raising the sheer folds of her fragile gown, sliding his fingers over the warm flesh of her thighs as he lifted the lace hem of her silky knickers. As she responded to his light touch, her thighs parting and her hips rising towards him, he felt the moist heat of the beautiful mound he had seen so clearly in her dressing-room. He wanted to increase her pleasure, to show her how he could satisfy the need he had seen in her. Now he was sure that she wanted him. But there was no privacy here; already the heavy wooden front door was swinging open and a shaft of light flooded the wide stone steps of the château.

Dominic bent to take Georgia in his arms, to carry her in triumph up the steps to his home and his bed. As his hands slipped down her thighs to lift her, she opened her eyes fully. He saw her pupils dilate in alarm as she felt his body hard against hers, then she struggled free and stood in front of him, breathing heavily.

He blocked her way as she tried to brush past him, enjoying the thrill of her body against his. He almost lost his balance when Georgia struck out at him, her sapphire wedding ring catching his cheekbone.

'Damn you, Dominic. Leave me alone.'

He held up the hand that had stroked her eager sex, his fingers glistening with the juices of her desire. 'Deny that you want me!' he taunted her. 'You can lie to me all you like. We both know your body can't.' She was lying. But why? Why was she refusing him?

He saw Georgia stiffen as he spoke. Icy cool, she pulled away and he cursed his stupidity. This woman was not one of the eager girls he took so easily. He had to go more carefully; that was part of the excitement. But he would succeed – the whole summer at the Villa d'Essor lay ahead of them.

* * *

Georgia smoothed down her crumpled skirt, trembling at her instinctive response to Dominic's clumsy approach. Quite awake now, she fully recognised the danger she was in and struggled to fight with all her strength to protect herself from it.

It had felt too familiar! Her drowsiness had deceived her into believing for a moment that those were Olivier's lips burning on hers, Olivier's fingers which had reached up so deliciously inside her. Olivier . . .

Georgia caught her breath. This wasn't Olivier. Dominic was his son. A boy with his whole life ahead of him. He had to find his own woman. Not his father's. Not her.

'What made you think it was you I wanted?' she demanded. The words stuck in her throat as she recognised the cruelty of her denial. Why was she tormenting the two of them when she knew that Dominic was right? That the arrogance of a virile young male, coupled with his dangerous resemblance to his father, was driving her out of her mind.

What would Olivier have thought? He might even have approved. But she didn't. She wanted to be a mother to this boy, not part of his inheritance.

Holding her head high, she forced her trembling legs to carry her to the open doorway of the brightly lit hall. Thank heavens she had taken the precaution of making other arrangements for Dominic tonight.

'Don't be too long,' she called out, without looking round. 'You have a guest waiting for you.'

She heard his angry gasp as he slammed the car door shut behind him, crunching the gravel underfoot as he strode after her. Swiftly she crossed the marble-tiled floor, and reached out both hands to open the double doors to the library. She breathed a sigh of relief as she welcomed a stunning young woman who rose eagerly to her feet.

Lisette's scarlet slip of a dress should have clashed with her riotous red hair, but it only enhanced the dramatic impact of her beauty. She flung her arms round Dominic. 'How wonderful! I thought you had already left for Antibes,' Lisette purred. 'And now we have another night.' Her plump, pointed fingers stroked the back of his neck provocatively.

Georgia saw him tense, then give a wry smile as he responded to Lisette's enthusiasm. He led her up the stairs, pausing half-way to slip one shoe-string strap off her shoulder. He turned round and Georgia felt his black eyes burn into her as his mocking voice echoed down the staircase. 'Goodnight, mother dear, sleep well.'

When they had gone, she climbed the stairs alone. She was sure that Lisette would enjoy her night with Dominic. For the past year, he had been trained by his father in the art of love-making, and Georgia understood exactly how skilled he must be. She had been wise to invite Lisette here to wait for her stepson.

Dominic had made her aware of her vulnerability, especially tonight with the strain of her final evening at Fleur's. Tomorrow she would be stronger, and better able to resist his sexual attentions.

With a sigh of relief, she opened her bedroom door. She felt some of her tension fade as she looked around her. David had lit the twin bronze lamps which stood on either side of her four-poster bed, their soft glow reflected in the golden threads of the bed's rich brocade drapes.

The small drawing-room off her bedroom was heavy with scent from the baskets of lilies that she always kept there. Olivier had insisted that the room was filled with her favourite flowers and she had kept up the arrangement with the florist since his death, reluctant to change anything in her life which could remain the same. Georgia breathed in their perfume as she stared out of the window into the indigo darkness of the night. She heard a soft laugh echo around the courtyard. Lisette. What was Dominic doing to her now? Georgia shivered as she heard the girl's muffled moan of pleasure.

Her fingers were trembling as she struggled to undo the long row of dainty satin buttons down the side of her dress. She drew a fine lawn negligée over her shoulders, feeling its clinging folds flutter round her legs. Olivier had always loved seeing her in it.

She longed for him now as she sat in front of her mirror, brushing out her thick mane of black curls, enjoying the hard strokes and the rippling caress of the vibrant locks on her skin. She wanted to feel his hands on her shoulders, lifting her hair so that he could brush his lips over her bare neck. He used to come up behind her and slide his hands inside her gown, covering her breasts with his eager palms. He had teased her with his control, until she begged him to tear the light shift off her greedy body.

She had been without a man for seven long months now, and she ached for her dead husband. Since Theo Sands had seduced her when she was seventeen, she had never been without a full sex life and she had not realised how desperately she would miss it.

Involuntarily, she remembered Theo's painting in her dressing-room. What could she do with it? She didn't want to hang it here. Even on these high walls it would dominate the room, but she couldn't leave it at Fleur's for everyone to see.

She paced around the room, her toes curling in the familiar softness of the Aubusson carpet. She lit the wall-brackets, trying to decide on the best place for the portrait. Perhaps it would be better to burn it and put an end to all the memories it held for her. But there were other paintings. What had Theo done with them?

She walked across to the windows and flung them wide open, desperate for some cooler night air, although it was so still that the leaves on the trees scarcely stirred. In the distance, she could hear the night birds and the steady murmur of the river that flowed through the woods.

Dominic's windows were open too; Georgia could see

a shaft of bright light from his room. She moved back quickly into the shadows and tried to close her ears to the increasing sound of his vigorous love-making.

She was sure that his husky groans were partly for her benefit, but there was no doubt about Lisette's enthusiastic response to his attentions. Georgia heard her cry out for him to enter her, and Dominic's low voice respond. 'Wait ... wait. Let me do this. And this. Do you like that?'

The girl was gasping now. The sound of her throaty breaths sent tremors thudding through Georgia's aching flesh. If Olivier had taught Dominic all he knew, there would be no quick release for Lisette tonight. Georgia stood in front of the window, unable to pull back, her hands feathering over her full breasts as she visualised Dominic's mouth encircling Lisette's eager nipples.

She forced her racing pulse to slow down, shamed by the longing which heated her belly. If only he hadn't watched her performance tonight. He must never know how vulnerable she was, conditioned to his approaches in a way that was infinitely more powerful than her reaction to the ardent and obvious lust of her young men.

It was too hot to close the window, but Georgia ran streams of water into her bath to drown out the sounds of their passion. She drenched her heated limbs in the foaming, scented bubbles, desperately trying to control the desire which raged through her. It was no use at all.

She lay on her bed, her thick curls spread out in a black cloud on her pillow, as she squeezed the tip of one aching breast. Her long manicured nails stroked the smooth skin of her inner thighs, prising open her moist sex lips until her fingers nestled on the burning ridges of her inflamed clitoris.

Georgia had learnt over the last months how she could ease the fierce need that washed over her night after night, lying alone in the vast double bed where she and Olivier had loved so passionately. The memory of his male splendour filled her mind as her fingers thrust harder and deeper, feeling her nails dig sharply, forcing herself to come until she lay trembling with relief. It was only a pale shadow of the ecstasy which she had known with Olivier.

Georgia buried her head under the covers when she heard the wild roar of Dominic's final climax – a cry of male domination recalling his father's shout of triumph. She curled up in the bed, clasping her hands round her knees as her flesh responded to that memory. But as she drifted off into sleep, it was Dominic who filled her dreams, and it was his hard, young body that she imagined lying beside her.

Chapter Six

Something woke her. Drugged by the heat of the airless night, Georgia stretched out, uneasily aware, as always now, of disappointment at the emptiness of her bed. She heard a soft knock on her bedroom door. Was it time for breakfast already?

She sat up, fumbling for her gown before she realised that she had left it on the bathroom door. It wouldn't matter. David would place her breakfast tray on the table by the window and leave discreetly. She pulled the silk sheet around her before she called out. 'Come in.'

The cream and gold double doors swung open. Georgia saw Dominic's tall figure poised in the doorway. His loose, black shirt was unbuttoned to the waist, showing a broad expanse of olive-skinned chest. In his hands was a silver tray, laden with steaming coffee and delicious smelling croissants.

'Well, aren't you going to invite me in?' Laughing, he balanced the tray precariously on a delicate, satinwood bedside table and bent over her. She felt his lips press lightly on her forehead. 'Bonjour, Maman,' he murmured. 'Did you sleep well?'

'Dominic, what are you doing in here?' She could feel his body weighting down the mattress as he sat close to

40

her. He was sweating slightly as if he had already taken exercise that morning, and his face was flushed with the vigour of young blood pumping through a healthy body. His breath smelt cool and sweet as he leant over her.

She longed to feel his lips on her mouth, to accept what he was so plainly offering her. One gesture – that was all it would take. At the faintest sign from her, she would have a powerful young lover, eager to serve her.

And what if she reached up for him now? If she allowed her fingers to stray over the tempting curve of his bare chest? It would be so easy to take what she wanted. But then there would be shame for both of them. Perhaps he would be disgusted when he understood what they had done.

Innocently, he brushed a strand of hair from her cheek and tucked it behind her ear. 'David told me you wanted breakfast up here today. I thought I would save him the trouble.'

Georgia forced her unwelcome thoughts out of her mind. 'Thank you. Now please leave,' she said stiffly.

'Surely we have a lot to discuss.' He broke off a piece of flaky, warm croissant, spread it with a thick layer of home-made cherry jam and held it out to her.

She watched his eyes flicker over her tense body, all too clearly naked under the sheet. He put the bread back on a plate and grinned at her. 'Aren't you hungry?'

'Get off the bed, Dominic. If you insist on eating with me you can pass me my robe.' She pointed to where it hung on the bathroom door. 'And take the tray over to the table.'

Expertly, she drew the flimsy gown round her shoulders, tying its narrow-corded ribbons tight across her breasts. Fortunately the voluminous folds made it moderately decent when firmly secured. She slipped out of bed, walked over to the table and poured herself a large cup of strong, black coffee. 'Shouldn't you be with Lisette?' she asked.

Dominic pointed to the blue enamel and gold clock on

41

the mantelpiece. 'It's ten o'clock. I rode home with her an hour ago.' Georgia looked anxiously at the time. They had to be in Paris in three hours, and they mustn't be late. She had far more planned for today than she had told Dominic. What a fool she was to have overslept.

She swallowed the scalding hot coffee in an attempt to clear her brain. She wished that she had explained everything to him earlier, but so far she hadn't found the right moment, and now they would have to hurry if they were not to be late. All Dominic knew was that they had agreed to have lunch at The Ritz with his godfather, Raoul Dufrais.

She watched his strong, white teeth bite into a buttery brioche. 'Are you sure you want to leave here so soon?' he said between mouthfuls. 'Why not rest for a while before we go back to Paris? We can see Raoul next week. I'm sure he'll understand.'

Georgia had no intention of rescheduling her plans. The sooner she was free to distance herself from Dominic, the better. But she had promised to help him take control of Fleur's, and she would keep her word. There was still much to do. They had to choose a new team, and then spend a couple of months in the south of France, training them.

As soon as that was achieved, her task would be over. And for her the château was no longer a place of relaxation. There were too many painful memories. Even sitting here, taking breakfast by this window, with the sweet scent of old English roses drifting up from the garden below, reminded her of the bushes which Olivier had planted in full bloom one night, so that she would wake in the morning and see them. They were a constant joy to her each summer.

Dominic dropped two lumps of pale brown sugar into his cup. She watched him stir his coffee as he waited for her response. She had asked Raoul for a favour, and he had agreed to do everything he could to help her. The trouble was she hadn't told Dominic yet. Damn! Why hadn't she explained all this earlier?

She told herself it would be simpler to do so over lunch. Feeling half-naked and vulnerable in the frothy negligée, Georgia decided that this was neither the time nor place to discuss what she had in mind.

'It's thoughtful of you, Dominic, but I think we should keep to our arrangements. I can relax at the villa later.' She drained her coffee and tried to appear unruffled. 'Now, perhaps you will allow me to dress in peace. Shall we meet downstairs in an hour?'

'If you insist.' Dominic brushed the crumbs off his lips and stood up.

With a sigh of relief she saw him close the doors behind him. He was in an unusually calm mood. Georgia tried to convince herself that she was worrying unnecessarily, and that their lunch would go smoothly, but she couldn't escape an uneasy feeling that Dominic wouldn't be pleased with what she had in mind.

In an hour, they were half-way to Paris. Marc handled the Phantom beautifully, and the speed brought a welcome draught of air through the half-open windows. Dominic was behaving perfectly. Georgia smoothed down the skirt of her navy and white printed silk dress, and wondered how she could make an excuse to be rid of him for half an hour so that she could talk to Raoul alone.

She played with a brooch on her left shoulder. It had been a present for her 30th birthday – a single diamond in the shape of a crescent moon, with outlying stars of diamonds and sapphires on delicate platinum ribs. She pressed on the pin that secured it to her dress, tearing the silk slightly, so that the jewel fell into her lap.

She exaggerated her dismay. 'My favourite brooch! How stupid of me. I've broken it.'

'Let me see.' Dominic twisted the clasp between his strong, brown fingers. 'It'll snap if I try to force it into

shape. It must have been damaged before you put it on.'
He touched the tiny hole in her dress. 'I'll take it back to
Cartiers. They'll fix it immediately for me.' He stepped
out of the car first and offered his hand to help her. 'I'm
sure Raoul won't mind. Give me a few minutes and I'll
join you in the bar.'

She watched him run towards the famous jeweller's
on the corner of the Place Vendôme. Marc was looking
at her very strangely. But, before he could make any
comment on her behaviour, she marched into the foyer
of The Ritz Hotel.

She needed Raoul's help. Who better than Dominic's
godfather to guide her in choosing of a replacement for
herself? Raoul was an old friend and he owned Le Grand
Marquis, one of the most successful night-clubs in Paris.
If anyone could help her, he could. She was sure one of
his dancers would attract Dominic.

Raoul had been one of Olivier's few male friends. As
young men they had scandalised Parisian society, rely-
ing on their titles, their beauty and their youth to keep
them out of serious trouble. But Raoul had not the
money to keep up that life style for long and had refused
to live off any of the women who offered to fund him.
He had chosen to make his own way. Although Raoul
was born an impoverished aristocrat, his night-club had
earned him a fortune.

At 56, but looking ten years younger, with immacu-
lately styled silver hair, laughing grey eyes and an
upright, trim figure he took great care to maintain, Raoul
was famous in Paris. His presence in Fouquet's restaurant, or Maxim's, was a familiar sight. Raoul's clients
included many of the most influential and well-con-
nected people in Paris, and his discretion and charm was
such that his well-born friends relied on him to enliven
their social life without hint of scandal. Nevertheless, he
had warned Georgia, now that she was a widow, it
might jeopardise her reputation to be seen alone with
him.

Georgia's social standing was more precarious than she was prepared to admit. When Olivier was alive, she had been welcomed as his wife. Olivier's background was irreproachable, and the activities at Fleur's were sufficiently discreet for him to maintain the position in society into which he had been born. Paris might well not take a lone woman to its heart in quite the same way.

As she had expected, Raoul was waiting in the cocktail bar where they had arranged to meet. As she approached him, a waiter opened a bottle of her favourite Pol Roger champagne, which was chilling in a silver ice-bucket on his table.

'Georgia! Wonderful to see you!' Raoul welcomed her with an exuberance that drew all eyes. 'You look magnificent.'

She was glad that her appearance pleased him. When she had last seen him, at Olivier's funeral, she had been distraught, with her tear-stained face hidden behind a heavy veil.

'So, where is my godson? I see you trust me alone with you, after all.' He looked at her carefully. 'What is it, Georgia? You want to talk to me first?'

She touched the small tear in her dress. 'Dominic offered to have my brooch repaired. But you're right. I am grateful for this opportunity. I haven't told Dominic what I asked you to do for me.'

She hesitated, sipping her champagne, unsure how to continue.

Raoul helped her out. 'So! I invite the two of you to my night-club tonight and I tell Dominic I'm offering him a gift. Simple!' He looked at her speculatively. 'Why so secretive? Any young man should be delighted.'

'He wants me to stay on at Fleur's.' Georgia felt uncomfortable. She hated having to go through all this. Was it really necessary? Perhaps her jangled emotions had caused her to imagine a problem where none existed. That, and the enervating June heat of the city.

Raoul frowned. 'I thought you told him you would leave at the end of the season?'

'I did.'

'And you've taught him the business as you promised?' he asked.

'He knows it all.'

'He's seen your act?' Raoul put his glass down on the table and stared at her intently.

Georgia half closed her eyes, and said in a whisper, 'Without my permission.'

'And he wants you to stay on with him?'

She felt trapped. She hadn't expected to have to explain all this. Raoul would probably say it was all her fault and refuse to help her. His fingers drummed sharply on the pale ash table-top as he rapped out his next question. 'And at home? What is he like with you outside Fleur's?'

'Demanding.'

Raoul's fingers ceased drumming. She could feel his eyes fixed on her as she played with the floppy bow on the front of her dress.

'Georgia, we don't have much time. Tell me the truth, please. Dominic wants you as his lover?'

She looked up at him then, anguished, unable to put it into words.

He took her hand in his and looked gently into her eyes. 'And you – how do you feel?'

'How can you ask? Of course it's impossible.'

Raoul stroked the palm of her hand, softly tickling it with his thumb until she was forced to give a little smile. 'That's better,' he said, without letting go. 'Now let me tell you something. When we were boys, Olivier was seduced by a beautiful actress. She was many years older than he was, and she gave him great pleasure. Until he married that bitch.'

'Dominic's mother?'

'You're lucky you've never met her.' There was a long pause before he spoke again. 'Maybe Dominic needs

46

you. Why not? You could give him so much. And you would enjoy a younger man. I have no doubt that Olivier was magnificent, but he was my age. I used to worry for your future.'

'I have no future now.'

'No! I will not allow you to believe that.' The pressure of Raoul's fingers increased. 'You restored my friend's sanity and his joy in life. His son needs a woman like you.'

'*Like* me, perhaps. But not *me*. Raoul, he is obsessed.'

'And you are frightened?' He looked at her with concern.

Georgia nodded.

'So you want to find him another woman, someone of his own age. It would not be good to return him to his mother.'

'He wouldn't go. And she . . .' Georgia's voice trailed away.

'She doesn't want him. I know that woman. She only took him away with her to hurt Olivier. So, if I can help in any way, I will.'

'I have to leave Fleur's. I need a girl to replace me.'

'That is as I thought. I have selected three, and they will perform in the club tonight. You can watch them without any difficulty. If you are sure.'

'Thank you. I would prefer Fleur's to close, but Dominic is keen to continue.'

'That may be more difficult than he imagines. Life is changing, Georgia, for all of us.'

She nodded, aware of the number of friends and clients who no longer had money for luxuries, and who feared the relentless rise of Hitler in Germany.

'And you, Georgia? What will you do?' Raoul looked concerned.

'Travel, perhaps. Find myself a new home. Maybe revisit England.'

'You still have family there?'

'Some remote cousins, no one important to me.' The

lie had become second nature to her now. But there was no one who would welcome her return; she was sure of that. Her disgrace had been spectacular. Young ladies, about to be presented at Court, are not supposed to run off with artists and live in Paris.

'So France is your home now.' Raoul's pleasure showed in his eyes. His voice was deceptively casual as he asked, 'Does Dominic know he has to run the business without you?'

Georgia shrugged. 'I only promised to help him until the end of the season. And if he fails, what would it matter? He could stay at Lusigny and run the estate.'

'But that's not what he wants to do.'

'No.' Georgia changed the subject. 'Now tell me about the girls you have found for me.'

'Three very different types. They all perform in my show. Celine, Mimosa and Caresse. They're young, clever and very beautiful.' Raoul kissed the tips of his fingers. 'If I were Dominic's age I would take all three.'

'If he chooses to do that . . .' Georgia was hesitant.

'But if he's like his father, he will not?'

'I suspect not.'

'An obsessive.'

The word hung in the air between them as they saw Dominic at the far end of the corridor, his dark, young face eager and proud. Quickly Raoul dropped an invitation card on the table, and whispered to Georgia. 'What about Theo Sands? He is back in Paris.'

'Theo? I never want to see him again.'

'What do you plan to do? Lock yourself away for the rest of your life?' He placed his hand over hers. 'Come with me to Theo's show. You have to see it, Georgia; he's having a wild success. And there are paintings from his time with you.'

She felt a cold chill hit the pit of her stomach. And then Dominic loomed over her, his face dark and sullen. 'Theo Sands has no place in our lives,' he said. He held out his hand. The starburst jewel winked up at them all.

He was uncomfortably close as his long fingers secured the clasp and slid fast the safety-catch. Georgia could feel his breath on her throat as the pin ran through the thin silk. His palm was pressing lightly on the curve of her breast and it seemed as if the dark length of his body shut out the daylight. She struggled for control, terrified that Raoul would see her reaction.

But his next words were cool and polite, dragging her back to reality. 'That was kind of you, Dominic. Perhaps you will join us in a glass of champagne?'

Dominic refused, ordering a White Lady cocktail which he gulped down, never taking his eyes from Georgia's face.

Raoul's voice broke through the sudden silence. 'I look forward to welcoming you to Le Grand Marquis this evening, Dominic.'

'Tonight?' Dominic leant forward, looking from one to the other. 'I thought Georgia and I had planned to have dinner together?'

'It was my idea. I would like to show off a little. Also I have a surprise present for you.'

Dominic raised one dark eyebrow as Raoul continued. 'You may take your pick of my finest girls to come to work with you at Fleur's. I can assure you this is an offer I do not make lightly.'

Dominic scowled. 'It appears, godfather,' he said insolently, 'that you intend to involve yourself in our business.'

'You are not pleased with my gift?'

'I have Georgia. Do you see any reason why I should require anyone else?'

Raoul's eyes flashed at Georgia, warning her to leave this to him. 'It is always wise to provide for the future,' he said smoothly.

'Don't you agree that she is still beautiful enough to excite men?'

Raoul's lips tightened. 'Georgia's beauty is not in

question, Dominic. But if it is her wish to retire you must respect that.'

'I respect her skill. I don't want to waste such a talent.'

'Without your father I am sure that her pleasure in her art has diminished.' Raoul rose to his feet and nodded at the waiter. 'We will eat now. And while we do so, Dominic, you can tell me your plans for Fleur's. It interests me, of course.'

Georgia settled into her chair in the beautiful Ritz restaurant with its painted ceilings and gilded decorations. Raoul's love of food was renowned and he refused to allow any serious conversation to diminish his pleasure in the rich flavours of his *timbale* of truffles in champagne. Deftly, he secured Dominic's agreement to join them at Le Grand Marquis and to look at his girls, if only out of a professional interest.

Georgia relaxed. It all seemed so much easier now. Why hadn't she come to Raoul for help before? For the first time in months she was enjoying her food. A sumptuous cut of rare châteaubriand was followed by a silver bowl of *fraises des bois* drenched in crème Chantilly. It was all delicious. The cherubs on the painted ceiling smiled down at her as she sipped a fine cognac and enjoyed Raoul's comforting presence.

He kissed the back of her hand. 'I look forward to entertaining you and my godson this evening. I will send my car.' He rose to his feet and nodded to Dominic before making a grand exit from the room, stopping at half a dozen tables to exchange a few brief words with friends.

'I resent Raoul's interference.' Dominic's black eyes glittered angrily as he hissed the words at Georgia.

'He was your father's friend, and he has offered his help. Do you believe Olivier would have approved of your insolence?'

Dominic caught her wrist. 'My father is dead, and I am now head of the family.'

'You asked for my help to set up Fleur's for the coming

season. You have no right to demand more of me than that,' Georgia said furiously. 'If you still want me to assist then you will come with me to Le Grand Marquis this evening, and you will behave more graciously than you have done now. Is that understood?'

Sullenly Dominic nodded. 'Am I to take it that you have decided not to return to Fleur's?'

She rose to her feet, dismissing him. 'There was never any question of my continuing longer,' she said.

Late in the evening, Raoul's chauffeur arrived to take them to the Rue de Pigalle. Georgia breathed a sigh of relief as Dominic joined her in the back of the luxurious Talbot saloon. Until this moment, she had feared he might refuse to come. They drove rapidly through the busy Parisian streets which seethed with party-goers at this time of night. Crowds spilled out of theatres, filling the restaurants and cafés, taking seats outside wherever possible to make the most of the cooler night air and to watch the world go by.

When they reached the Rue de Pigalle, Georgia was dazzled by vivid signs flashing over entrances to strip shows and night-clubs. Smartly dressed men and women flitted from one to the other. She felt a familiar thrill of anticipation as she saw the lavish black and silver entrance to Le Grand Marquis ahead of them. Surely Dominic would find a woman here to excite him?

The chauffeur left the car at the door and escorted them into the night-club. As they entered, Georgia saw a black, beaded curtain twitch as if someone had just disturbed it. Immediately a door opened at the end of the passage and Raoul appeared, immaculate in white tie and tails. He pressed his lips on the back of Georgia's hand before murmuring: 'It is a privilege for me to welcome you here.'

She shivered. The feel of his mouth on her skin sent a tremor of sexual excitement coursing through her. She was beginning to regard every man she met as a potential lover and, attractive as Raoul was, he had been too close to Olivier for her to feel comfortable with him in that role. Perhaps, like Dominic, she needed to actively look for a partner? Would that solve her problem?

She followed him to his private table. It was set apart from the main floor in a small alcove partly enclosed by two carved ebony screens. Georgia nodded to one or two acquaintances who had come to watch the show. Her presence here would not surprise anyone; Raoul often boasted that he filled five tables each night with guests from The Ritz Hotel.

Her dove-grey voile evening dress, discreet as it was, clung provocatively to her hips before dipping to her ankles. Her hair, fastened with a tortoiseshell comb studded with diamonds, was arranged in an elegant chignon. She felt glamorous and, after the seclusion of the past months, experienced a rush of excitement at being seen out in public again.

Raoul placed a flute of champagne on the black satin table-cloth in front of her, and proffered Turkish cigarettes from a wafer-thin silver case. Dominic affected indifference, gazing up at the ceiling, apparently intent on the curls of acrid smoke which drifted into a cloud above him.

Looking around her, Georgia was amused to recognise a beautiful, immensely tall girl, dressed only in a discreetly placed arrangement of snow-white ostrich feathers, who slipped through the black and silver curtains concealing the stage, languidly fitted a glossy jet cigarette holder between her perfect teeth, and draped her body provocatively over a black velvet chaise longue. Georgia knew that Lulu was one of the most famous transvestites in Paris, who was frequently to be seen in Le Grand Marquis. She turned to point her out to Dominic, but his over-bright eyes displayed a profound indifference and she held her tongue.

Almost imperceptibly, he leant forward in his chair just as a second champagne cocktail was placed in front of him. A few drops sprinkled the fine wool of his sleeve; he turned angrily to scold the waiter, saw instead a nervous young girl and bit back his words.

Georgia looked up in surprise. The girl's pale face whitened as she saw Dominic's displeasure. She was slim and fine-boned, with black hair brushed straight back over her shoulders and large eyes heavily outlined with kohl. Her brightly painted mouth was a shocking slash of scarlet on her white skin.

Georgia was puzzled by her, so different from the showgirls or the other, scantily clad, waitresses. She looked almost a child, wearing a crimson satin bolero, with a matching sash and baggy black trousers. Her hands shook slightly as she replenished Dominic's glass. He accepted the freshened drink ungraciously, and turned his back on the girl.

A faint flutter of applause greeted the slow slide of the curtains as they were drawn back by two long-legged dancers, whose slender naked bodies were painted with leaping silver flames. They stood, one on either side of the stage, their arms outstretched towards a gigantic, carved, black penis which dominated the space. From its monstrous peak swung a silver cage, studded with bright lights, inside which stood a blonde giant of a man, chained hand and foot to the bars. Lulu removed her cigarette holder, blew him a sultry kiss, and slid her hand invitingly along the inside curve of her thigh.

A tall, thin, black girl sauntered in, her slim feet encased in glossy patent leather high heels. Her dark hair was trimmed close to her scalp in a fashionable bob cut. She wore a shiny jet-black raincoat, tightly belted and dripping with moisture as if she had been out in a storm. The stage was deeply shadowed, illuminated only by occasional flashes of lightning. She walked towards the caged man, stood in front of him, flicked the ash from her cigarette over his bare, shaved chest, and turned away. She struck a pose, and opened the drenched coat to reveal her androgynous silhouette.

Georgia watched, fascinated, as the audience seemed to hold its breath. At Raoul's table the pale waitress silently refreshed their drinks and offered cigarettes as a second girl moved on to the stage. Red-haired and voluptuous, her creamy flesh poured out over a low-cut, silver lamé evening dress, which lifted up her high, full breasts, accentuated her narrow waist, and clung to the twin cheeks of her clearly rounded bottom. Georgia knew the secrets of a gown like that, the cutting away of lining over the breasts and buttocks, the almost imperceptible transparency of the fabric. She saw Dominic's blank expression. Could he really be so indifferent?

The girl stepped arrogantly towards the man whose muscles bulged as he fought to escape his bonds. With a professional interest, Georgia saw her bend her head over his stomach, brush his belly and jutting penis with her thick auburn curls, and move swiftly out of his reach as she slid the folds of silver lamé from her breasts. The girl threw the shimmering dress at her chained lover and lay naked on the floor beside his cage.

The spotlight now swung round to the centre of the stage, shining on to a third girl whose legs were draped round the black penis, straddling its glistening surface. She was blonde and petite, wearing delicate strands of crystal drops fastened to her nipples, and caught in a minute triangle over her pelvis. Her ash-blonde hair fell in a shimmering waterfall over her buttocks. Icy cool, she moved her hands over her honey-tanned skin, displaying silver-tipped fingers which reached out to stroke her slim hips before clasping the metal penis. Her blue eyes shone as she taunted the caged man.

Raoul whispered to Georgia. 'What do you think of Mimosa?' He sounded proud of the performance and sure of their response.

'She's sensational.' Georgia leant forward in her seat. This girl must attract Dominic. But his eyes were fixed on the ceiling; he blew a perfect smoke ring into the fume-filled air and drained his glass.

Georgia frowned. She had hoped one of these three would excite Dominic enough for him to take her as his partner. She raised an eyebrow, questioningly. He shrugged, stared at her, kissed one finger and drew it across the bias-cut voile stretched over her breasts. He gazed insolently into her eyes. 'No. None of them can take your place.'

'You have seen my three finest. But there are others to come,' Raoul assured them. On the stage Mimosa sat with her legs curled round the moulded penis, her honey skin gleaming in a pool of smoky limelight.

The clear note of a silver saxophone beat an insistent rhythm as, one by one, more girls came out from the wings, draped in shimmering sequinned strands of gold, rose, violet, emerald, topaz, black and white, with huge ostrich feather head-dresses framing their beautiful faces. They circled the glittering cage and lifted the bars to release the man.

Mimosa pushed past them, strands of ice-blue glass trickling down her back. She stood in the centre of the stage as the troupe dragged the man by his chains, and forced him to the floor in front of her. Sliding her lithe body over him, she stroked his bonded flesh with her silver-tipped fingers. Her tiny golden body rose and fell on top of him as the girls dipped their feathered heads, concealing the couple from the audience.

Georgia admired every detail of the show, but her attention was focused on Dominic's reaction. He sipped his cocktail with an air of profound indifference, his dark eyes hooded in a display of total disdain. If any of the dancers excited him, he was hiding it well.

Raoul looked around with an air of quiet satisfaction. 'Do they attract you, Dominic? Shall we call them to the table?'

The boy shrugged. 'They're very beautiful. It would do no harm to talk since we are here.'

Georgia felt dismayed by his casual attitude. She was impressed by the display of skill even if he wasn't. She knew any one of these girls could take her place tomorrow.

'Caresse, Mimosa and Celine, may I introduce my friends, Madame la Comtesse d'Essange and Monsieur le Comte.'

The girls were still in their costumes, although Mimosa had added two ice-blue shells which rested lightly on her pouting breasts, and her crystal strands were slightly more discreetly arranged.

'Ladies ...' Dominic rose languidly to his feet, and offered them chairs. Raoul signalled for champagne. The dark-haired waitress who had served them before appeared with a tray of glasses.

'You know why we are here?' Georgia asked the three dancers.

Mimosa wriggled delicately on the small silver-gilt chair, her back arching gracefully as she thrust her breasts upwards. 'You need a woman.' Her eyes were fixed on Dominic. Georgia watched carefully. The girl had character.

'Would you consider working for us?' she asked.

Mimosa's gaze slid over Dominic's lithe muscular body, elegantly defined by the sleek cut of his evening clothes. She rearranged the tiny shells on her beautiful breasts. 'That depends on what you want me to do,' she said, waiting expectantly for him to respond to her obvious charms.

'You need to check with my stepmother,' Dominic drawled. 'It's she who insists on leaving Fleur's.' He leant over towards Georgia, deliberately resting his hand on the dove-grey voile covering her thigh, before he glanced briefly back at Mimosa. 'Ask her to show you what she does,' he said. 'Ask her now.'

A glass shattered. Georgia looked up, startled, to see the young waitress, her pale complexion flushed to a deep rose, lose her grip on the silver tray. One by one the tall flutes of champagne twisted through the air and crashed on to the hard, polished parquet floor. Shaking, the girl dropped to her knees to pick up the jagged fragments. A swelling tear of blood stained the pad of one slim, white finger where a sliver of broken crystal had caught her skin.

'Natasha, what are you doing down there? Please get up immediately.' Raoul sounded more concerned than angry, but Georgia felt sorry for her; the girl was not to blame. The failure of the evening was entirely due to Dominic. He seemed half-drunk, and none of the dancers, not even the blonde beauty, had aroused his interest. They might as well return to the hotel before they disrupted the smooth running of Le Grand Marquis even further.

Turning to suggest this, she watched in astonishment as Dominic pushed back his chair and caught hold of the waitress's wrist. She felt ashamed at the embarrassment they were causing Raoul. Already several diners were watching the scene in open-mouthed amazement.

Caresse, Celine and Mimosa rose sulkily to their feet as Raoul dismissed them, signalling to a waiter to help Natasha. Dominic seemed determined to make an exhibition of himself as he towered over her, cradling her bleeding finger.

'Please release Natasha,' Raoul said coldly.

Dominic's hand held the girl fast. He looked surprised at his godfather's firm intervention. Then, as Raoul pulled out a chair for Natasha to sit with them, he slowly loosened his grip on her wrist, and settled her carefully on the padded, black satin cushion.

'Georgia, may I introduce Natasha?' The girl inclined her long slender neck. 'Natasha, you have heard me speak of my friend, Madame d'Essange, and my godson, Dominic.'

There was an almost imperceptible pause before the girl extended her undamaged hand. Dominic bent his head to the long slender fingers, and pressed his lips on to it. Again the girl's eyes flickered towards Raoul.

'Natasha is the daughter of one of my dearest friends,'

he continued smoothly, the warning in his soft voice quite clear. She was not a person to be treated lightly, even by a favoured godson. She was not on offer.

'Now perhaps we can return to the business in hand. You're not excited by any of my young ladies, I see.'

Dominic shrugged. 'They are beautiful. And talented. But . . .'

'But none of them thrills you?'

'No.'

Natasha sipped her champagne, her dark eyes studying Dominic intently. Georgia thought she sat as elegantly in her odd costume as if she were wearing *haute couture*. Her short jacket emphasised the slightness of her build and her delicate bones. And undoubtedly she had charm, despite the earlier disaster. But why had Raoul asked her to join them? Was it simply to avoid a further scene with Dominic?

Dominic's attention did not waver from Natasha. 'Do you dance?'

For the first time a faint smile curved the girl's lips as she glanced at Raoul. 'She can dance,' he said simply.

'So why did you not dance for us?'

'I do not choose to wear so little.' This time Natasha answered for herself. Her voice was low and husky, and her French was perfect, with the faintest trace of a Russian accent.

'And I do not allow her to perform on stage.' Raoul's voice was firm.

So she was his protégée. Georgia wondered if it was wise to continue the conversation, but she was too late to stop Dominic. 'Would you dance for us privately?' he asked.

Again, the girl checked with Raoul. Georgia saw him frown as she whispered urgently to him.

'If she would care to dance I see no harm.'

Natasha sat slightly higher in her seat. She nodded. 'If your guests would like that.' She stood up immediately. 'I will be ready for you in ten minutes.'

Dominic rose, and stood behind Georgia, ready to pull out her chair. 'Shall we go and wait for her?'

Raoul led them through a concealed door at the back of their alcove to an ugly, whitewashed passage behind the stage, smelling of sweat and greasepaint, and dust burning on limelight. At the far end was the rehearsal room, a large, windowless space, with bright, bare light bulbs that pricked their eyes after the shadowed gloom of the night-club.

A raised wooden stage jutted out from one wall, and Natasha entered through a door to the side of this, with a thin man who was carrying several sheets of music. She wore a short, white tunic, fastened round her waist with a narrow sash, and her face was bare of the make-up which had obscured her features before. In the bright light, Georgia could see that her dark-lashed eyes were a clear, deep violet.

Natasha stood completely still until they were seated, then nodded shyly to her pianist and waited for him to start playing. She swayed, her arms raised high above her head, moving her supple body in time to the music. Georgia saw Dominic lean forward in his chair, his eyes intent on the figure on the stage. Natasha's straight fall of dark hair swung in front of her in a wide, black streak, tantalisingly obscuring the outline of her youthful body.

Georgia wondered where the girl had learnt to dance. Presumably, she thought, there must have been some training in classical ballet, since many of her movements seemed to stem from that. But there was also a freedom to her style, an artless grace that was infinitely charming. Georgia found herself entranced by the virginal eroticism of the scene.

When the music stopped Natasha sank down in a deep curtsy. Dominic rose to his feet enthusiastically. He jumped on to the stage and lifted her up, whispering something in her ear. She stood back, her eyes searching his face. For a moment there was total silence in the room, then she nodded.

Dominic turned to face Georgia and Raoul. 'Natasha has agreed to see how we react to each other. If you will bear with us, we will continue the act, this time together.'

Raoul shrugged, glancing at Georgia. She kept her expression carefully nonchalant. 'Why not?' she said.

Raoul spoke up. 'This is acceptable to you, Natasha?'

'Perfectly.' The girl looked triumphant as she swayed gently beside Dominic, then he led her to the back of the stage, lowered the lights, and stood poised beside her. His powerful male body overshadowed his partner, as if she were a slender child on the stage, grown too tall for her strength; so fragile that it seemed as if a breath of air would knock her over. Then he lifted his arms, caressed Natasha's silky hair, and stroked it back over her shoulders, so that the sweet outline of her feminine shape demonstrated that she was indeed a full-grown woman.

A faint flush brightened her ashen face and her violet eyes glowed as she stood still, waiting for Dominic's lead. He slid one hand around her waist, holding his body so that the merest thread of light separated them.

Georgia saw Raoul lean forward in his chair. She felt the tension in the room as they watched the two figures move in perfect harmony. Dominic stroked Natasha's pale flesh, his dark, tanned hands enormous against her slender frame. He responded to every gesture of her dancer's body, shadowing her suppleness, demonstrating his desire and his control. He played with her, taunting her, arousing her, until she shivered at his touch and fell into his arms. Motionless, he held her until she raised her face to his, then he lowered his head and pressed his lips on hers.

Georgia felt the swell of her own aching breasts as Dominic held Natasha's limp body close to him. She saw Raoul shift uncomfortably in his seat, trying to hide his burgeoning erection from her. If Dominic and Natasha could arouse a man like Raoul, with all his experience, they would be a sensation at Fleur's. It was time to stop the performance. She had seen enough.

Dominic had a sure touch when it came to judging a woman's sexuality and, in this case, the ability to project that power to an audience. But Dominic's hands were continuing their relentless progress down the girl's body. Georgia could see the brilliant sheen on the girl's pale skin, the sweat glistening under the single light that shone on them both.

The music had stopped. The pianist rose to his feet as Dominic lowered Natasha's prone body to the floor. No one moved, watching as if mesmerised. Then Raoul strode towards the stage and jumped up. Dominic offered Natasha his hand and raised her up beside him.

Raoul clasped them both in his arms. 'Magnificent. Superb!' There was an expression on his face that Georgia could not fully understand. What was Natasha to him? She watched him hold out a robe, and help her into it. He moved her slightly away from Dominic. 'No doubt you will wish to shower and dress,' he said to them both. He turned to Georgia. 'I will talk with Natasha and learn her wishes. Will you forgive me if I leave you alone in my office for a short time? I will arrange for a cool drink to be brought for you.'

Georgia waited listlessly in the elegantly cluttered space where Raoul organised everything to do with his business. He was right. The display they had just seen was extraordinary. There was an air of unfulfilled passion and young love about it that she and Olivier had never achieved. Surely now, with this strangely exciting girl, Dominic would at last leave her alone. She sipped the sharp lemon drink with relief and struggled to ignore the fierce ache inside her. Wasn't this exactly what she had wanted?

Raoul returned alone. 'I think you may have found your replacement,' he said stiffly. 'I have spoken to Natasha and she insists she would like to work for you. Please Georgia, I beg of you, take care of her.'

'I'll talk to Dominic tomorrow. Where are they now?'

Raoul looked amused. 'He is taking her home, but we have no need to worry. She lives with her grandmother, who is quite capable of intimidating even my godson.'

'Are you happy that this has happened, Raoul? It wasn't what either of us expected.'

Raoul leant forward and took her hands in his. 'I am torn, Georgia. What more could I want than for her to be with the son of my greatest friend? And yet . . .'

'And yet you do not want her to work at Fleur's?' Georgia felt hurt. He obviously thought it was unsuitable for a lady.

He smiled into her eyes. 'It is only that she seems so young. But maybe it is I who am old. She likes the boy. More than that – he fascinates her. I watched them at the table. She couldn't take her eyes off him. This – from a girl who is so reserved I have had to ask if she would smile occasionally at the customers. Tonight she begged me to let her audition for you. I hadn't expected that.' He stared at the documents piled up on his desk. 'Who knows what will happen?'

He handed her a gold fountain pen and a sheet of heavy cream paper. 'I prepared this contract for one of the girls. Shall we sign it for Natasha?'

Georgia tried to concentrate. 'I have to read this through. Can you spare the time?'

Raoul smiled. 'All the time you want, Georgia. Breakfast, lunch, dinner, the night in my bed.'

Why not? Why not spend a night in the arms of an attractive man? Was she a fool to return alone to her empty hotel room? For a moment Georgia hesitated, then shook her head regretfully. She needed a stranger, not this old friend, not someone who had known Olivier. And especially not a man who was so disturbed by the thought of Natasha's transformation.

As he drew her attention to the details of the contract, his hand brushed against the inside of her elbow. She felt her flesh tingle. After the performance they had just witnessed, they were both aroused to the point where their need for sex was overwhelming. Any sex – with anyone.

Georgia placed her fingers firmly on the solid gold stem of Raoul's fountain pen. She signed her name with a flourish. Carefully she screwed the cap back on to the shaft and twisted the pen between her fingers, her eyes carefully fixed on the thick, grooved ridges of the design. She laid it down on the desk between them. 'I will do all I can to keep her safe for you.'

'Neither of us can do much,' he said. 'It is between the two of them now.' He bent his head and kissed the glossy twist of smooth hair in her chignon. 'You are right,' he said, helping her to her feet. 'We are friends and must remain so. It would give me great pleasure if on another occasion . . .' He let the words drop gracefully into the air between them as Georgia rose to leave.

On his desk, among a stack of stiff, white and gold invitations, she could see the card for Theo's exhibition. Fortunately, her time during the next week would be fully occupied with Natasha's preparations. And, starting tomorrow, there was a new team of young men to choose. She had every excuse not to visit the gallery.

Chapter Seven

Georgia knew she should be happy that Dominic had found someone to take her place. Instead, she was conscious only of an overwhelming loneliness. She must simply be tired, she thought, after yet another night spent lying awake on her own. The memory of Dominic holding Natasha in his arms had aroused her more than she had realised. She wondered if Raoul had felt similarly disturbed.

Of course not. He would have found someone else. Georgia knew that was what she should do. Paris was a great city, and if she had decided that the young men at Fleur's were out of bounds, and that she preferred not to complicate her life with Raoul, that still left thousands of possibilities. Today, after the fun of choosing new young men for the team, she would spend the evening looking for a man of her own.

She dressed quickly in a leotard and a pair of cool linen trousers and, as an afterthought, added a light jacket. Dominic should be waiting for her down in the lobby, ready to drive her to their appointment. Juan Sanchez, a Spaniard who had been one of Olivier's first employees, owned a gymnasium on the outskirts of the city, having bought it with money provided by a grateful client. He had found four young men for them to check out.

Juan's main interest was boxing, but not all the boys who came to him looking for a career in the sport were talented enough to win money prize-fighting. Georgia was interested in those who preferred to keep their beautiful bodies intact and earn their living in a different way. Juan had procured many members of their team in previous years and knew exactly what was required.

At ten o'clock precisely, Georgia left The Ritz with Dominic. He drove the Bugatti out of the Place Vendôme in sullen silence.

She tried to make conversation with him. 'Natasha's a beautiful girl.'

There was no response. She tried again.

'Was everything all right last night? Did you meet her grandmother?'

'I left Natasha at the door.' He appeared to have no interest at all.

'That wasn't very polite.'

'It was the way she wanted it. I think she had some persuading to do at home.'

Georgia was amused. It must be a new experience for Dominic to find a girl who was reluctant to introduce him to her family. Of course this was a different situation.

She spread out on her knees the photographs that Juan had sent her of the men they were about to see, and, when they stopped in the traffic, she picked up one to show to Dominic. She wanted him to know that she valued his opinion.

He waved it away. 'Tell me about your artist friend.' Dominic's voice was casual, but his face was tense as he asked the question.

Georgia paused. She did not want to talk about Theo. 'Forget him. We have work to do. Look at these. What do you think about him? And him?' She pointed, shuffling through the pile of pictures. 'We could take four, maybe six, from this gym. Juan is always reliable.'

Dominic produced a white and gold invitation from his inner pocket and flicked it against the steering wheel. 'Are you going to the gallery to see his exhibition?'

'Why are you so interested, Dominic?'

'Are you surprised? I see a portrait of my father's wife painted by a man who clearly regarded his work as something more than a job. That man worked on you as if every brushstroke was foreplay. He even put a bed in the picture.'

Georgia flushed. 'It was a perfectly sensible background,' she said shortly.

A magnificent four-poster had dominated one corner of Theo's studio, its crimson drapes providing colour and shape for many of his society portraits. It had added a tinge of raciness to the demure images of the young girls who had posed serenely for him, and whose mothers had found the discreet hint of sexuality a useful tool in luring prospective husbands.

During the season when Georgia had been a débutante, many girls from the best families had sat to have their portraits painted by Theo Sands, as she herself had done. The young American artist had made money from the work, money that he desperately needed to live on while his more avant-garde efforts failed to find any buyers.

'Theo Sands is a well-known artist,' she answered. 'I was lucky he was prepared to paint me.'

'You mean someone was able to offer him a lot of money. How much did my father pay for a portrait of his naked wife?'

Theo had painted it for her as a gift. Georgia's mother had been impressed by his reputation and had accompanied Georgia to the first three sessions, chaperoning her daughter carefully. Then an invitation had mysteriously come from a titled client of Theo's, and Georgia's mother had accepted eagerly, confident by then that

Theo was perfectly respectable and her daughter could be left with him.

Alone with the artist for the first time, Georgia had been shocked to find that Theo's method of working apparently required her to remove all her clothes.

She evaded Dominic's question, eager to change the subject. 'It was done some time before I met Olivier.'

'And did you keep on seeing your lover after you came to live with my father?'

'Theo was in America. We never saw each other again,' Georgia said shortly, snapping her briefcase shut on the photographs. 'Now, can we please concentrate on the work we have to do today, instead of delving into a past which doesn't concern you? You'll be running Fleur's on your own next year, and you have a lot to learn.'

'Is it really so difficult, Georgia dear?' Dominic pushed forward through a gap in the traffic. 'Surely all you do is pick the best-looking men and check out the size of their cocks?'

Georgia shot him a steady glance. If he was deliberately trying to antagonise her, he had chosen the wrong moment. She was prepared.

'You need to find men who enjoy their work. Men who like women,' she informed him.

She wondered if Dominic really enjoyed female company. Would he help a young girl as Olivier had helped her when Theo left her? There was no doubt about his pleasure in sex and everything to do with it, but the touch of cruelty which Olivier had kept strictly under control was more evident in his son.

'I thought all your friends liked to be dominated,' he said.

'Many of them do. That's why it's even more important that no one takes advantage of them. They're very vulnerable.'

'You think men aren't?' Dominic looked scornful.

'At Fleur's they need to keep emotionally detached. That's something you have to learn.' It would be easier to show him what she meant when they started to make their decisions about the young men they were about to see. And easier still, once Dominic was fully occupied with Natasha.

They endured a slow crawl through the narrow back streets of Paris to reach Juan's gym, heading east of the Bastille, past bustling markets and warehouses. Georgia directed Dominic to a small alley at the rear of a dank terrace of ramshackle houses. The club was situated on the ground floor of two buildings which Juan had managed to buy cheaply. The unpromising exterior hid a clean, well-equipped gym where Juan had trained several champions.

The main arena was in a spacious, airy room. Even so, there was a strong odour of healthy male sweat from the young men whose muscles bulged as they exercised with weights and punchbags. Juan led his guests to a row of comfortable seats with a good view of the action.

Dominic leant forward. 'Which ones are for us?'

Juan pointed to a huge man exercising on wooden wall bars. Deeply tanned, he flexed his muscles as he heaved himself up by his powerful arms, paused, holding the position, and lowered himself again. He was at least six foot five, with broad shoulders and a heavily muscled chest.

'That's Stefan, limbering up on the bars over there. And you see the boy using the punchbag in the corner? That's Philippe. Beautiful, aren't they?' Juan could not hide his pride at showing Georgia the magnificent examples of male youth he had selected for her. 'And those two, the ones sparring in the central ring now. What do you think of them?'

Georgia looked over at the raised boxing arena. Two young men, stripped down to narrow jock-straps, wrestled together, their bodies entwined, their skin already glistening with sweat from their exertions.

'They look wonderful.' She felt a surge of excitement as she studied the breadth of their chests, their slim, narrow hips and sharply defined muscles that had been honed to perfection.

'Shall we start with Pierre and Christophe?' Juan asked. 'I think you'll be pleased.'

'I'd like to watch them wrestle for a while before I check them out,' she said.

'Sure.' Juan leant back in his chair and gave a swift signal to the boys in the ring.

Pierre was the taller of the two, but Christophe was tough and wiry, and possessed an energy the bigger man lacked. He darted around the ring, displaying himself to advantage all the time, his lithe body showing full awareness of the group watching him. Georgia had a gut feeling that he would be good. He exuded an animal quality which was exciting even in this stark, white room. With training to enhance his natural sexuality, he could be sensational.

'Have you seen enough? Shall we look at the other two?' Juan asked. 'Are you ready for Stefan and Philippe?'

'Yes.'

The dark giant they had watched earlier exercising on the wall bars padded slowly across the room, his black eyes staring arrogantly at Georgia as he sprang lightly into the ring. He moved with the grace of a panther, despite his bulk. She felt excited. This man could thrill a room full of women on his own. She watched him slide his massive hands over Philippe's hips, forcing the boy to the floor, straddling his body as he overcame him easily.

At the far side of the room, a slim blonde girl sat cross-legged on the floor. 'Ask her if she'll wrestle with them,' Georgia murmured. 'I want to see how they react to a woman.'

Juan gave her a quick grin. 'How far do you want them to go?'

'Tell them to do whatever they're comfortable with. But I'll need them all to strip once they get going.'

The girl nodded as Juan spoke to her briefly, then she climbed up into the ring without a second glance at the watching visitors. She stood, arms at her side, waiting on the edge of the mat, as Stefan and Philippe wrestled with each other.

'Does she know what to do?' Georgia deliberately kept her voice low enough for Dominic not to hear. Last year she had joined the boys in the practice ring. Today she didn't dare risk it.

Juan nodded. 'She saw what you did last time you were here. But the boys haven't a clue. I've told them they're being tested for the *Folies Bergère*.'

'How old are they?'

'Three of them are eighteen, Stefan's a year older.'

'Do they have jobs?'

'Nothing they wouldn't mind giving up.' Juan grinned. 'I had the best time of my life at Fleur's.'

The boys were working harder now, their bodies gleaming with sweat under the bright lights. Georgia saw the girl Claire, watching intently, before she stepped in between them and tapped Stefan on the shoulder. He straightened up and leant against the ropes. Neatly she slipped out of her white cotton tunic, revealing a small, compact body with high, firm breasts. She smiled at him, slid her fingers quickly round his jockstrap and released it. He bent over, his breath coming in short gasps. As he stood up, his erection jutted out proudly. Georgia watched as Claire unstrapped the remaining man and prepared to wrestle.

Concentrating hard, Georgia assessed the bodies of the young men. This was becoming easier every year. Juan knew exactly what she needed, and it had become known that an opportunity for good-looking young men existed here. Her job was almost done for her.

Georgia was pleased that Dominic finally appeared to be watching carefully. Perhaps he really was keen to learn. He was certainly enjoying the performance. His healthy young body was reacting just as she had hoped, and his efforts to disguise his arousal merely drew attention to his condition. She waited for his erection to subside, giving him a cool look. He would have to learn to control that.

'What about the girl?' she asked Juan. 'We don't need her at the club, but she could come for the summer to keep the boys happy.'

'Not on offer, I'm afraid. She's married to my manager.' He laughed. 'I can't see him agreeing to let her go with you. But the boys are all yours if you want them.'

Georgia smiled at Juan. 'Thank you, I think they'll be perfect,' she said. 'May we check them out in your office?'

Juan beckoned to the group. All four boys looked up and walked across the bare floor towards them, swaggering a little as they saw Georgia assessing their bodies.

'Christophe, Stefan, Philippe, Pierre. Georgia, these are my very best young men.'

Georgia grinned. The boys might be beautiful, but she knew they would never make good boxers, or Juan wouldn't be showing them to her. These boys were better suited to the luxurious life she was able to offer. She stood in front of them, admiring them.

'Christophe.' She shook his hand, smiling, trying to put him at his ease. Gently she placed her hands on his shoulders, feeling the power of his muscles, assessing his sexuality and the attraction he would hold for her clients. She lowered her fingers, stroking his chest, satisfied that it was hard, firm and smooth-skinned, and that his belly was taut. She watched his reaction as she stroked his tight buttocks, and let her touch linger on the long stretch of his powerful thighs. He was very young, and his skin glowed with a rosy flush as she took his testicles in her hand and squeezed them gently. Georgia nodded approvingly. 'Would you like to work for us? I'm sure Juan can tell you it's not a bad job.'

Christophe beamed. 'I want to come. Am I good enough? Will you take me?'

'Yes. If you do well in your training. And I think you will.'

Expertly she checked out the other three. Juan had not let her down. All of them were perfect young male animals, all physically exciting to women, eager for the opportunity, and unable to hide their arousal.

How much easier it was for a woman to disguise her desire. Georgia felt her own body respond to the musky male scent which clung to her fingers, overwhelming the perfume she had sprayed over her skin earlier that morning. Her breasts were straining now against the lacy control of her light brassière, and she could feel its narrow straps biting into her shoulders. For the first time, Georgia realised that these men might become her lovers. After the summer they would no longer be out of bounds.

Fortunately the crisp linen jacket she had so carefully chosen to wear hid the eager thrust of her swollen nipples. Outwardly she was the cool and elegant Georgia d'Essange, maintaining an icy control as she assessed the beautiful male bodies she needed for her business. The ache she felt was internal; the sweet moistening of her thin silk pants was her secret, and tonight she would find a man to satisfy all her longings.

Dominic watched Georgia with mounting fury. How dare she stroke those sweating bodies so calmly, as if they meant nothing to her? Did she enjoy teasing men so much? Was that really all she wanted? He gritted his teeth as he saw her long, slim fingers cupping Christophe's testicles, caressing them, stroking the hard ridged length of the boy's penis.

He shifted uncomfortably in his chair. Georgia was right in front of him, and as she worked he could see the rounded cheeks of her buttocks outlined by her crisp linen slacks. When she bent to run her hands down the boy's thighs, her cheek brushed the stiffened shaft in front of her.

He had wanted to tear off the sheer silk lingerie which had thrilled him that night in her dressing-room, to slide his fingers beneath her lacy suspenders, and drive his aching cock into the deliciously creamy hole he had touched so briefly with the tips of his fingers.

He looked round for the girl. Claire was perched on the edge of a table, pouring herself a glass of water. Dressed once more in her short white tunic, she looked bored. No doubt she saw all these bodies every day.

Dominic rose to his feet and beckoned to her. Politely she followed him from the room and into a narrow passage. She looked pretty enough with her bright skin glowing, and the gleam of sweat on her body. She would do for the moment. Without giving her a chance to realise his intention, he pressed her up against the wall, slid his hands inside her loose gown, and stroked her hot, moist sex.

He felt her body go rigid against him, then a sharp stinging slap on his cheek knocked him back across the passage. Claire jerked her belt tight around her slim waist.

'If you weren't here with Georgia I'd have got you in the groin,' she hissed. 'Don't let there be a next time.' She strode off down the passage without a backward glance.

Furious, Dominic leant against the wall. He was used to women begging him to take them. His erection pulsed unbearably now, and he knew that at any moment he would lose control.

He looked down the corridor and saw several doors leading off it. Quickly he found a urinal and grabbed hold of his throbbing penis, letting a spray of semen spurt on to the red tiled floor.

He took a deep breath, and joined the others in Juan's office. Georgia had almost finished her examination and all four boys were still massively erect, displaying an extra tension when she touched them, their bodies reacting to every touch of her fingers.

Dominic was not prepared to let her leave Fleur's. No one else could ever be as good. He needed Georgia, and he would not give her up. He knew she would be magnificent with him. She could taunt other men as much as she wanted until, at the end of every performance, he would take her in front of them. He would show them all that he did not have to be controlled as they were. He would demonstrate his supremacy and make them understand that Georgia was his woman. If he could simply have her once, he was sure she would soon beg him to take her again and again.

As for Natasha, she wouldn't be a problem. He would find something to keep her occupied. She was just a child, and he could control her easily.

The assessment seemed to be over. Georgia had agreed to take the four boys for training, and she was ready to leave. Swiftly Dominic stepped beside her, taking care to behave like the dutiful stepson towards his father's widow. He made sure that no one else could see his hand slide up inside her jacket as he helped her into the car. His fingers brushed over the rigid bud of her nipple as he carefully ensured her comfort in the seat. Good, it was exactly as he had thought. Beneath that calm exterior, she was as excited as he was. When they arrived at the hotel, he would prove to her how much she needed him.

They drove in silence to The Ritz. She turned to face him outside the lift. 'We go our separate ways now, Dominic,' she said. 'Raoul has asked if you will take Natasha out for the evening. So go and enjoy yourself. Don't worry about me. I'll have a quiet meal alone.'

He forced himself to hide his anger. 'What are you doing until then?'

'I'll have a rest, and make notes on the four boys we saw this morning.' She pointed to the thick sheaf of large photographs in her hand, showing each boy filmed nude, front, back and sides. 'You would do well to do the same. After a few more days of this, you'll find it difficult to remember individuals.'

He moved forward, joining her in the tiny, gilded cage of the lift. He ignored the attendant, whose back was discreetly turned away from them. 'You haven't forgotten them yet,' he murmured as he pulled open the short jacket which covered her leotard, revealing the swollen peaks of her breasts. 'Look at you. You wanted them.'

'That would hardly be obvious to anyone else. Of course it's exciting. You're not exactly unaroused yourself.' Dominic saw her eyes swivel to the straining bulge in his trousers. 'Was it Claire you found so interesting?'

'She's a coarse little slut. You're the one I need to perform with the team. Why won't you stay on?'

He saw Georgia's tongue dart out and lick her full lower lip. So she might consider it! 'Are you trying to pretend you don't enjoy men?' he taunted.

He was hot and he was tired of waiting for her. The thrust of her breasts was driving him mad. As they reached the corridor outside her bedroom door, he bent his head and pressed his face between the soft, full mounds, feeling the blood surge through his body as she responded to him. His lips parted to suck one sharply jutting nipple through the thin silk. Before she could move, he transferred his mouth to the other swollen bud.

He could taste her through the fine fabric, and smell the scent of her flesh, mingling with the perfume she always wore. He felt her quiver in his arms, and knew that he could have her now. Satisfied, he stood back and stared at the damp silk, clinging to her dark peaks.

He pulled her towards him, forcing her to feel the full power of his erection as he thrust his hips against her. 'Think about it, Georgia. You know you want me. I'll take as long as you like, do anything you want.'

He was whining now, and he hated himself for it, but soon he would show her who was master. She would be the one begging for him after this. He swayed as he pressed himself against her, eagerly searching for the fastening of her trousers. He could smell her desire, and he longed to bury himself deep inside her hot and musky body.

She was melting against him, reacting exactly as he had imagined. This was the moment he had been waiting for. He heard her cry of anguish and then, as his fingers parted the crisp linen, he felt her pull away from him, knocking him off balance as she slammed the door shut and left him alone in the passage.

Georgia breathed deeply as she leant against her bedroom door, moaning as the wet fabric of her leotard teased the points of her aching breasts. She longed for Dominic's lips to close over them again; she knew that he was capable of satisfying the craving she felt.

Damn him! Did he always know her weakest moments? Even being in this public place had excited her, with the possibility that at any moment someone could walk past and see the two of them. She felt ashamed of her lust for display. Had all the performances at Fleur's turned her into an incorrigible exhibitionist?

She had denied him this time, but she could no longer control her need for a man. What had just happened made her decision easier to make. She had almost left it too late, but in a hotel of this size it would not be difficult to find a willing and discreet partner for the night. In the cocktail bar, after dinner, there were always men sitting alone.

She ordered a light lunch and a bottle of Vichy water to be brought to her room, and took a long bath while she waited for it to come. She twisted a thick, white towel around her head like a turban, and slowly rubbed scented oil into her skin, before tying a second towel in a knot over her breasts.

At a discreet tap on her door Georgia stiffened, anxious that Dominic might have decided to come back, but it was a young waiter who appeared, carrying a silver tray on his upturned hand. He was charming and, for a moment, she considered inviting him to stay, but she simply thanked him politely and locked her door again after he had gone.

In the chest of drawers by her bed, there were two boxes full of lingerie she had ordered from a small shop in the Faubourg Saint Honoré, which had supplied her for years. She wanted her clothes tonight to be new and fresh. She spread all the items out on the bed, and looked at them while she ate.

There were two dresses that she might wear. One was plain and elegant, and, although not obviously alluring, with the right undergarments, it displayed her body to full advantage. The other was so revealing that it was impossible to hide even the skimpiest brassière beneath its low-cut bodice. It was a dress for an evening alone with a lover. She had not yet decided.

When she had eaten, Georgia closed the curtains, lay down on the bed, and slept until it was time to prepare herself. She picked up one piece of lingerie after another, before she chose a tiny pair of flesh-toned knickers with matching suspenders. She put them on and decided that the sales assistant had been right. They were perfect for her figure. She rolled on her stockings and slipped her feet into a pair of high-heeled satin sandals, then she sat at the dressing-table, and brushed her hair down over her shoulders. She was struggling to control the excitement she felt at the thought that tonight she would take a lover. No, she corrected herself, a man just for sex, for one night only. She would make that very clear to him.

He would be only the third man to be part of her body in that way, and she felt horribly nervous. How it would surprise all the scores of young men who had performed with her over the years to know that she had so little real experience of men. Well, it was a challenge – and she had no choice. Unless she could satisfy the desire that racked her body, she would give in to Dominic as all her instincts drove her to do.

The two dresses hung on the cupboard door behind her. She examined her breasts in the mirror. They would look enticing in the lace brassière that was part of the set, and she longed for the feel of a man's hands unfastening the tricky hooks, but the fragile bare-backed gown appealed to her even more. As she reached up to take it off its hanger, she was startled by another knock on the door.

Perhaps the young waiter could help her with her decision. As he slipped his pass key into the lock, she turned round so that he could see her full on. If she excited him with only her knickers and suspenders, she would choose this dress.

But it was a maid who entered, and she demurely lowered her eyes as she collected the tray, murmuring that she would return later to turn down the bed. As the girl left the room, Georgia saw her look up and give a sidelong glance at her bare breasts before she disappeared out into the corridor.

The girl had flushed deeply, but it was with excitement, and not embarrassment. The decision was made. Georgia sat down again at the dressing-table and carefully applied a dark red colour to her lips.

Her silky lingerie emphasised her full curves, her slender waist and long legs. As she fastened the final stud of her suspenders, Georgia ran her hands over the tops of her stockings and smoothed down the sheer silk. Tonight, if all went as she planned, she would not be the one to remove her clothes.

She slipped into a wisp of draped crêpe de Chine, a delicate sliver of Patou's art, which hung from her bare shoulders by two wafer-thin shoe-string straps. It was cleverly bias-cut so that it clung to her body, emphasising her full breasts and the long line of her thighs as it flowed to her feet. She twirled in front of the mirror, as the light silk floated round her legs.

It had a matching short jacket, heavily beaded in shades of silver, grey and aquamarine, which shimmered at the back to a low point following the line of the dress, leaving an inch of bare flesh visible at the base of her spine. Outrageous as it was, it was the height of fashion, and perfect for dinner at The Ritz.

Georgia stopped at the top of the stairs. She wanted to go back, take the dress off, and put on something more discreet. Or order dinner to be sent up to her room. But no – that wouldn't do. She knew herself too well. Her resistance was at its limit. She had to find a man, or give in to Dominic. Georgia was under no illusions there. Each time he approached her, she was under greater threat.

Step by step she made her way down the grand staircase, holding on to the gilded iron balustrade. She must not hesitate; her plan was made, and all it needed was a little courage to see it through. It didn't matter that she had never done this before, as long as she looked in control. Surely, with all her experience, she could manage that. As she reached the bottom step, she was aware that the buzz of conversation in the lobby hushed.

The foyer was crowded with guests arriving for dinner, or meeting for drinks before an evening on the town. Calmly, Georgia acknowledged the greetings of a few casual acquaintances. There was no reason why anyone should imagine she was alone; it would be natural for them to assume that she was with someone. And, if they were surprised that she had so spectacularly discarded her mourning clothes, they would not blame her. It was time.

It was a sensational dress, which had cost Olivier a fortune, but he had intended it to be worn when he was with her, and it was a gown that demanded an escort. Georgia made up her mind. She would find a man before dinner, instead of later, in the bar, as she had planned. A meal together would give her an opportunity to make absolutely sure she wanted him in her bed, and she preferred not to eat alone.

She moved steadily through the throng, making her

way to the cocktail bar, where she would be at ease in familiar surroundings. It was a large, open room, light and airy, with glass doors which opened on to a stone-flagged courtyard so that the jasmine-scented night air wafted in. The atmosphere was relaxed, and it was not at all the sort of place where a woman would feel under pressure from male attention. Georgia knew that she had only to glance at the barman if anyone bothered her.

She ordered a bottle of champagne to be brought to her table, ensuring that its arrival was obvious to all the men. She started to enjoy herself as she sipped her first drink. Casually she looked around.

Georgia wasn't sure how to indicate that she was available, although she knew very well how to make it clear when she was not. Of course, there had been no problem with Olivier by her side, but, since he had died, she had spent all her time either working at Fleur's, or relaxing at Lusigny during the weekends.

She maintained an air of calm indifference, waiting until she saw someone who interested her. This ought to be simple, she thought; she was used to checking out men.

Her attention was caught by a tall, blonde young man coming into the bar. He walked well, his body loose and free like an animal in the peak of condition, and his clear blue eyes looked open and straightforward. He wore his hair long and, as he passed her, he tossed his head so that it flicked back from his face.

Georgia kept her glance casual. He was certainly attractive, and she would have no hesitation in testing him for work at Fleur's, but he was a little too young to be discreet. He was greeted familiarly by a passing waiter and responded in poor French with a strong English accent. Georgia looked away, dismissing him. She would never choose an Englishman. He might know her family.

A dark, olive-skinned man, of about her own age, stared back at her with an open invitation in his eyes.

He was attractive, but no, he reminded her too much of Olivier.

The third man was middle-aged, with crisp dark hair, greying at his temples. He sat quietly reading his newspaper, drinking a whisky and soda. Georgia drew in her breath. This was a man of the world. He might do.

She rose imperceptibly in her chair and caught his gaze, only to see a faint tinge of regret as his eyes slid over her body, before he looked away again at a beautiful young girl who rushed in, flung her arms round his neck, and lifted her face for a kiss. He obviously had other plans for this evening.

Georgia felt embarrassed. She had indicated her availability to the older man. He had been so discreet that she was now unsure if he had understood her unspoken message, or even if he had found her desirable. She had deliberately avoided sending any signals to the young Englishman, or the smouldering Latin, who had preened himself since her initial lingering assessment. She had never had to play this game before. She had thought it might be fun. Now the champagne chilled her as the bubbles trickled down the back of her throat.

'May I join you?' A soft voice murmured the words behind her, and she felt a warm hand cover her shoulder. 'I see that your friend is not with you this evening. I, too, am alone, and I would welcome your company.' He stood waiting for her invitation.

Georgia waved a hand at the empty seat beside her, hoping that anyone watching her would assume that she had been waiting for this guest. 'Please sit down. My friend, as you call him, is my stepson. He has far more exciting ways to spend his time than dining with me.'

'Few men could imagine a finer way to spend an evening than with you.' He refilled Georgia's glass and, at her request, poured one for himself. 'I am Jean Pascal. I am honoured to meet you, Madame d'Essange. Forgive me. I took the liberty of asking your name.'

He spoke slowly, his eyes gazing full into hers, while

he held out his hand. Georgia looked at him. For the first time in her life, she was considering a man for sex. Not being chosen. Not teasing. Coolly she checked him out. Thick, dark blonde hair, worn a little long; gentle, hazel eyes; the first fine traces of laughter lines in a deeply tanned skin; and a habit of twisting one corner of his mouth higher than the other when he smiled, which he did often as he talked to her. His beautifully cut suit probably flattered his body; she wondered what he would look like naked. Nothing like the young men she had chosen this morning, she was sure. And yet, she thought, she would rather have him in her bed tonight.

'My stepson and I are staying in Paris while we attend to some business. Tonight he is dining with a young lady.'

Not by a flicker of an eyelid did he display surprise that she had not made another appointment for this evening. 'I, too, am here on business,' he told her.

But Jean had found time to visit the theatre, the racecourse and the exhibitions. His conversation, light and amusing, refreshed her, easing her tension, as he treated her as a friend, with only an occasional glint in his warm, brown eyes giving any hint of a deeper interest. It was simple for her to agree to his suggestion that they dine together, and his tall, handsome figure made her realise how good it felt to be with an attractive man again.

Georgia followed him as he quietly led the way into the gilded restaurant, and discreetly secured an excellent table from the *maître d'hôtel*. Jean stood behind her chair until she was seated. His hands, touching her bare shoulders as he slipped off her beaded bolero, hesitated only a fraction too long, and if she detected a faint tremor it was hard to tell if the reaction was his, or her own. What did he expect from her this evening? She wondered if she needed to make her intentions clearer.

She saw Jean's eyes lingering on her *décolletage*, but he quickly recovered himself and looked away. She had never worn this dress before; it wasn't at all suitable for dinner parties at Fleur's when she preferred to let the clients shine. Tonight she was offering her body honestly, and felt good to know that she did not have to hold back. She looked straight into his warm tawny eyes. Had he understood her? She was unused to this, and unskilled.

Georgia's toes wriggled in the cool satin straps of her sandals, as she sipped her champagne and studied the menu. What should she choose? All the dishes listed on the gold-tasselled menu sounded delicious, and after her light lunch she was hungry, but she must take care not to eat too heavily.

Jean chose the same dishes as she did. She enjoyed each mouthwatering flavour all the more as she saw his own pleasure in the delicacies. A crayfish mousseline quivered under her fork as she took her first melting mouthful, relishing the food. As Jean's fingers stroked the chilled stem of his champagne flute, she shivered, imagining his hands cupping her breasts later in the evening. She looked up to meet his eyes as he raised his glass. 'To our friendship,' he murmured. She saw his cuff draw slightly back, revealing strong, lean wrists, and she longed to run her hand over his slightly rough, tanned skin.

Foie gras, poached in champagne, was followed by a White Lady sorbet. Jean made her laugh as the icy froth cascaded down the inside of her throat. His light, amusing conversation held her attention as her sharp knife sliced the meat from the tiny bones of quails, nestling on a bed of creamed morels, and airy cushions of crisp *Pomme de Terres Soufflées* melted on her tongue.

Jean was a perfect companion. How wonderful it was to enjoy an evening free of all worries. She bit cheerfully into a slice of peach sprinkled with Armagnac and smiled up at him. Yes, he was charming. She would take him to bed. Was that what he expected? Or was dinner with her all he had in mind?

Surprised by a sharp sense of disappointment, she allowed the scented fruit to fall back on her plate. Suddenly, her dress felt inadequate, too light, too skimpy, and too blatantly provocative. Why had she done this? Surely she could find a man without picking up a total stranger in a bar?

Jean took the fork from her hand and laid it gently on her plate. He refilled her glass, and then his own. 'There are many things I would like to do with you, Georgia,' he said softly.

'Oh?'

'Yes.' He raised his glass. 'We could go to a night-club, see a show, dance, even walk along the river.' He hesitated and she took a sip of champagne, feeling the bubbles fizz under her nose. Why had he stopped talking? What was he going to say? Goodbye?

'But most of all, I would like to make love to you.' His voice was casual. 'Are you shocked?'

'No. I'm not shocked.' Relief flooded through her.

'I thought you might walk out of the room. You're too much of a lady to slap my face in here.'

Georgia smiled at him. 'We could walk out together.'

'So that you can slap my face outside?' Jean's touch was more positive now as he slipped her jacket over her shoulders.

She stood still for a moment, feeling his arms around her. 'So that I can give you my answer.'

She was aware of the interested glances around them as they walked out of the restaurant together. In the foyer, Georgia slipped a note with her room number into Jean's palm and discreetly said good-night, leaving him to join her soon. When she reached her bedroom, she saw him at the far end of the long corridor. He took her key from her shaking hand and opened the door. The maid had tidied away her clothes and turned down the bed. Her night-dress was laid out neatly over the white sheet.

Suddenly she felt even more uncertain. What was he

expecting? What would he do right now if she stripped him as expertly as she knew how? Her hands hung by her side; her fingers played with the beaded panels of her dress.

Jean moved closer to her; she could feel the heat of his body against hers as he asked: 'Are you nervous?'

Georgia smiled. How Dominic would laugh if he heard the question. And yet how perceptive Jean was. This was a new experience for her. 'A little. I hadn't expected . . .' her voice trailed off.

She felt his hands resting lightly on her shoulders as he slid her jacket to the floor. His fingers stroked her bare back, and once more she felt exposed in the flimsy dress. She didn't want to make the first move.

He looked into her eyes. 'You are the most beautiful woman I have ever seen,' he said quietly. 'And I want you more than I would have believed possible. May I take you to bed?'

'Just for tonight?'

'If that's the way you want it.' He let her go and stepped back.

He was waiting for her, allowing her time to think without pressure. It was a novel experience. She watched as he took off his jacket and laid it on the back of a chair. His hand touched her bare shoulder and stole beneath the slender band, dropping it slightly to one side. She slid her finger inside the knot of his tie, and loosened it so that it fell down over his white silk shirt, and she undid the mother-of-pearl stud at his throat.

He lifted his hands to her shoulders, and lowered the tiny shoe-string straps down over her arms. The sheer crêpe de Chine rested precariously on the swell of her breasts.

When she had undone two more of his buttons, she eased her hands inside his shirt. She wanted to see him now, to feel his skin close to hers. He felt warm and smooth, and she let her dress slip as she moved closer to him, so that she could feel him pressing against her.

Georgia gazed at Jean. Naked, he seemed vulnerable, less sure of himself. Perhaps it was simply because she was used to seeing men who were trained to flaunt their bodies and use them to excite women. She moved towards him and held out her arms. She would have to be careful not to frighten him; gentle loving would be a new experience for her. At the moment, any loving at all would be a new experience.

Jean raised his head and looked at her. She moved into his arms and allowed him to hold her, enjoying the comforting warmth of his body against hers, and the way his hands gently stroked her skin. Hands which trembled in his eagerness. Georgia lifted her face and kissed him softly on the lips, surprised at the sweetness of the contact, the sensitive response of his mouth, the steady swell of desire which flickered through her as Jean's tongue explored her mouth.

Jean's large hands cupped her buttocks, pressing her against him, and Georgia could feel the thrust of his engorged penis pushing comfortingly between her thighs. She led him to the bed, wondering what he would do to her if she lay back and allowed him total freedom of her body. How strange it felt to realise that it was not her place now to tantalise and tease, to arouse a man only so that he could give pleasure to another woman, while she was left tense and frustrated. After seven months of that, she longed for him to take her.

Jean looked hungrily into her eyes. She felt his need as strongly as her own, raised her arms over his heavily muscled shoulders and drew him down on top of her. She felt the weight of his thighs part her legs, the stiff smoothness of his penis seeking out the damp heat of her eager sex. She had felt so many men touch her there; now she needed to feel him thrusting deep inside her.

She arched her back and rose to meet him, each nerve-ending longing for him. There was no holding back as his long, slim penis climbed higher and higher. Georgia lifted her pelvis towards him as he drove his entire length into her, sucking his swollen flesh into her aching core, shuddering as wave after wave of release darted through her limbs.

She felt Jean's shock at the immediacy of her orgasm, felt his arms envelope her as he steadied his full strength inside her body. Then she smiled up at him, stroking the firm line of his chin, and gently raised her hips again encouraging him to join her pleasure, thrilling as he thrust harder, leading him on and on until her next climax made her cry out, and crush her lips against his chest until with one final thrust, she felt him come inside her.

He held her to him quietly, stroking her moist skin, his lips brushing against her throat, murmuring her name. She felt the soft residue of his manhood stir comfortingly inside her. Warm and relaxed, she let her head fall on his shoulder, and she slept.

The first glimmer of early morning light glinted through part open curtains. Georgia stirred, rolled on her side and felt Jean's warm body next to her. He lay comfortably asleep, his elegant head still noble in repose, his firm body agreeable to look at. Georgia traced his chest hair to below his stomach with her finger, amused at the sleepy smile her action aroused. It would be good to spend the day with him. As it was . . .

She increased the pressure of her finger, lowered her head and brushed his lips with her mouth. The curve of pleasure on his lips deepened; he stretched his body in an animal awakening and reached out for her, holding her to him. Georgia sank into his arms, responding immediately to the strength and protection of a man's arms. She curled herself around him, pressing her body into his. She laughed at his instant erection, curving her fingers round his swollen manhood. 'I want you, too,' she murmured. 'But . . .'

'But you have a busy day. And a young man who will

check you out? I understand.' He pulled her to him. 'Don't worry. I need you so much it will be quick.'

Their sleepy bodies moulded into each other with the relaxed pleasure of familiarity. Georgia's clitoris, swollen from the night before, responded immediately to his entry; she felt her muscles tighten around him as he deepened his thrust, and gave herself up to the sensations flooding through her.

'Jean, Jean,' she murmured, twisting her fingers through his thick, blonde hair. She was coming with a slow, blissful orgasm which swept over her like the waves of the sea. Jean groaned, lifting her legs as he drove deeper, gasping as he lost control and his need became more urgent.

He pumped faster and faster, taking her beyond her pale pleasure into a realm of ecstasy. She lifted her hips, sucking him deeper into her, hearing his groan of pleasure with a thrill she had forgotten. As she felt the throb of her climax wash over him, and his instant release, she moaned sweetly. There was such pleasure, so much a man and a woman could give each other. She burrowed her face into his shoulder and felt a tear of relief wet her cheek.

'Thank you,' she murmured. 'Thank you.' Her body felt silky smooth and relaxed. She stretched and slid her legs over the side of the bed. She stood for a moment, breathing in the fresh morning air, before she walked briskly into the bathroom and ran the bath.

In ten minutes, after a final embrace, he had walked along the hotel corridor and out of her life. Jean was a charming man. She wondered who would be next.

Chapter Eight

*A*fter Jean had left, Georgia flung open her bedroom windows and leant out over the balcony. Below her, in the courtyard, she could see waiters preparing tables for those guests who preferred to take breakfast outside, and, yes, there was Jean, walking out with a newspaper tucked under his arm.

She waved and, for a moment, considered inviting him back. But there was too much to do today, and she preferred to take things gently. She hummed the tune from Le Grand Marquis under her breath and danced around the room. She felt alive again. For the first time in months her body glowed with sexual satisfaction. Thank God for men!

There would be no more problems with Dominic; already her mind was filled with the prospect of whether she might find another man for tonight. It was a pity that she couldn't try out any of the new team members yet, but until they were trained, and she was no longer involved with Fleur's, it was out of the question. She was beginning to understand why her clients found the club so useful.

Today she could relax. They had made an excellent start, finding four new members of the team. And

Dominic had chosen a woman for himself. Even if Natasha was not experienced, she had shown real talent.

Dominic had picked up on Raoul's choice of Schiaparelli for Natasha. They had an appointment booked, and were due there at any moment. Schiaparelli had moved from the Rue de la Paix in the winter, opening here in the Place Vendôme on New Year's Day. Out of loyalty to Chanel, Georgia had not yet set foot inside the magnificent new premises, although she longed to see it all. Now she had the perfect excuse.

She should hurry, but first she had to decide what to wear. There was the visit to Schiaparelli, followed by lunch at Fouquet's, which was currently the most fashionable place in Paris for lunch. After that, there was Theo's exhibition.

She had agreed to visit the gallery this afternoon in a vain attempt to silence Dominic. What would it matter to her after all? It would only take an hour of her time. Theo wouldn't be there – it was not the opening day. She needed to let Dominic know that Theo Sands meant nothing at all to her now, and hadn't done for years. And if she did not see the show for herself, and it became known that she had once been Theo's favourite model, her absence would be more damning than a casual visit with her stepson and Natasha. Yes, Natasha's presence made it all much simpler. They would go immediately after lunch.

But before that, there was Schiaparelli, and Georgia was already late. She panicked as she wondered what to wear. A trunk full of clothes had seemed enough for a week in Paris, even for her, but now she wished she kept a larger wardrobe at Fleur's. Her mind had been on auditions at the gym, the evening at Le Grand Marquis, and obviously, in the back of her mind, one sexy dress. And that had worked!

But – for this morning? The racks of garments hanging in the hotel wardrobe seemed boring and unappealing. Impatiently Georgia searched through the staid blue, black and cream colours of the suits and dresses she had chosen to bring to Paris. She owed it to Madame Chanel to look her very best this morning. Schiaparelli was Chanel's main rival and Georgia could not let her friend down.

She rejected one outfit after aother, and threw them on to the bed. None of them would do. Georgia picked up the telephone and asked for a private number she seldom used.

She waited for the explosion. 'You demand the impossible. Schiaparelli? How can I fit you out with anything I have for my models? You have a *poitrine*!' There was a muttered conversation at the other end of the line. 'Wait, there is something.'

In twenty minutes a box was delivered to her door. Mme Chanel delivered it personally with the gleam of war in her eyes. There were a few stitches required, because Georgia had lost weight. Coco was pleased.

Georgia had wanted something young and feminine, to reflect her mood, something extravagantly luxurious for lunch at Fouquet's. She slipped on Chanel's scarlet chiffon dress with a short, white piqué jacket, and perched a gossamer-light, osprey-feathered hat over one eye. It was an outfit unlike anything she had ever worn before, and the floating skirt outlined the long length of her thighs seemingly by accident, while the tiny bolero jacket gave her an air of youthful *joie de vivre*.

She glanced at her watch; she was already late. Dominic and Natasha would have been at Schiaparelli's for some time. But Dominic had his father's exquisite taste. Neither of them needed her, except as a matter of courtesy, although of course, she was interested. And this was the perfect excuse to visit the new salon without seriously offending either Chanel or Patou.

She gave one final twirl in front of the mirror, put on her gloves, and took a deep breath to calm her down before she made her way downstairs.

She heard a faint but unmistakable murmur of admir-

ation as she crossed the lobby. Parisian women appreci-
ated style and elegance, and their glances showed their
approval as much as the warmth in the eyes of the male
guests.

'Madame.' A slim figure crossed the hall towards her.

Georgia frowned. 'Natasha? I thought you would be
with Dominic. Have you already chosen your wardrobe?' It seemed unlikely. Natasha's frock, though neat
and tidy, was hardly *couture*, and it certainly would not
do for lunch. There must have been some delay.

Natasha shook her head. 'I understood that Dominic
would meet me here. But I have been waiting since ten
o'clock and he has not come.'

'Ten! You've been here for over an hour?'

'Perhaps I should have gone alone to Madame Schiaparelli, but I did not wish to do so.'

'Of course not.' Georgia was shocked by Dominic's
rudeness. For Natasha to enter alone, without an escort,
and with no means of demonstrating her ability to pay
for the clothes, would have been unthinkable. She tried
to disguise her anger at Dominic's behaviour as she
reassured Natasha.

'We will go there now. Perhaps there has been a
misunderstanding, and he thought you would meet at
the salon. But that was foolish of him.' She patted
Natasha's hand. 'We'll choose together. Sometimes it's
easier to present a man with a *fait accompli*. You will
have your own ideas and Dominic will simply have to
accept your choice.'

Natasha appeared so desolate that Georgia began to
doubt whether she would cope with lunch in a fashionable restaurant. The confidence she had displayed when
she danced was missing now, and she looked once more
like the sad, awkward waitress who had dropped the
tray of drinks. It seemed that her evening with Dominic
had not been a success.

Well, she would try to make up for that. New clothes
could do a lot for a woman, and Georgia was excited at

the thought of buying them for Natasha. Schiaparelli's designs were outrageous, but fun. And – in certain lights – the girl was beautiful.

She took Natasha's arm and led her out of the hotel through the revolving glass doors. Outside, the sun bounced off the pavements and the square was full of people eager to finish their business before the full heat of the day.

Schiaparelli's mansion was intimidating, but Georgia was eagerly greeted by the *vendeuse* at the door who led them up to the first floor salon. Natasha held herself well; she was obviously determined to carry this off. But, as they entered, Natasha's eyes fixed immediately on a group at the far end of the room.

Georgia followed her gaze. Five or six women fluttered around a man lounging in a gilt armchair. Dominic stretched out indolently, surrounded by several *vendeuses* carrying armfuls of clothes. Two mannequins leant over him, parading their elegant figures in semitransparent novelties of brightly coloured turquoise, amber and topaz. He rose languidly to his feet, bent to kiss Georgia's hand and nodded briefly to Natasha.

Georgia had no wish to create a scene, certainly not on her first visit to the salon, but his behaviour exasperated her. This was Natasha's day and everything possible should be done to help her enjoy it.

She remembered her first fitting with Patou. She had been thrilled to accept Olivier's advice, had known that his choice was right; and that she would have had no idea what to wear without him. She had adored the outfits he had selected in wonderful, clinging fabrics, cut on the bias to emphasise her voluptuous curves and full breasts. They were a joy after the stiff brocades and heavy velvets that Theo had draped around her, or the demure organza ballgowns chosen by her mother. Would Dominic do as much for Natasha, or had he lost interest in her?

He indicated a pile of clothes thrown casually over a

sofa beside him. 'I've chosen these,' he announced, scarcely bothering to greet her. 'Try them on.'

Natasha stiffened, but dutifully accepted one of the garments handed to her by an eager *vendeuse*. She held it up in front of her and studied the effect in a large, gilt mirror. She handed it back to the *vendeuse* and tried another. One after the other, she checked each item in the mirror.

'No. I will not wear those.' Natasha's voice was soft, but determined. She slid a shocking pink jacket off her shoulders, and handed it regretfully to an assistant. 'I wear clothes in white, black, or violet,' she said calmly. 'Only those colours.' The assistant looked across at Dominic, who rose angrily to his feet.

Georgia put out her arm and restrained him. 'Let her find something she likes, Dominic. Wait and see.'

The *vendeuse* returned soon, rather flustered, followed by a woman with distinctive short black hair. Elsa Schiaparelli had come out of her office to see for herself. She stood back, gazed at Natasha, and issued some rapid instructions. In a few moments the two mannequins were parading around the room in clothes of every shade from lilac to deepest purple.

The couturier nodded at Natasha. 'Take these and try them on. If they do not please you, we will find something else.' She smiled at Georgia. 'So, Madame d'Essange – you are here at last.'

'I am here for Natasha, of course, not for myself.'

'I understand.' Elsa took a gown from her assistant. 'But perhaps you might consider trying something like this, while you are waiting? Just a little something for the summer?'

She held up a pair of beach pyjamas in apricot satin, wide-legged, with the top embroidered with deep russet sea-horses, and amber buttons shaped like baby starfish.

'Or this?' She showed a caftan in shimmering sapphire blue. 'Would you try them on to please me?' she teased.

In less than an hour, Georgia had spent a fortune and

had completely forgotten the original purpose for the visit. Full of guilt, she smoothed down the floating panels of her Chanel outfit, and returned to where Dominic was waiting in the salon.

Natasha appeared hesitantly at his side. Georgia stared at her. She looked magnificent. The outfit, chosen by Madame herself from her ready-to-wear collection, was pure white, trimmed with coils of black braid. High-necked, yet sufficiently revealing to inflame the dullest male mind, it was so chic that it would gain the respect of every woman at Fouquet's.

Dominic stretched his long legs out in front of him and glanced at Georgia. 'Satisfied?'

'She looks very beautiful.'

'And innocent? How innocent do you think she looks?'

Georgia drew in her breath. What was Dominic getting at? What had he done to the girl? But however hard she searched Natasha's face, Georgia could see nothing except a natural flush of excitement on her pale cheeks. She checked her watch. 'We must leave now, Madame,' she said, as she extended her hand to the most powerful couturier in Paris.

Madame Schiaparelli looked her in the eye. 'You would not consider cutting your hair?' she said. 'Or do you keep it still because it pleased your husband? What about Mademoiselle?' She shrugged as Georgia shook her head. 'A pity, but perhaps another time. So, Madame, you will come again. Your friends will see you wearing my clothes. And so will Madame Chanel. That will be a pleasure. Natasha's winter clothes will be ready in three weeks for her first fitting. She will come back to Paris then? Enjoy your summer, Mesdames, Monsieur.'

Madame Schiaparelli reached out and opened a drawer. 'I have a gift for Mademoiselle. She will do good things for my clothes. One day I will feel privileged to have dressed her.' She held out a tiny, beaded, cocktail hat. 'Keep this for her until she cuts her hair.'

'Her hair is beautiful.' Georgia was hardly going to add that it was a very necessary accessory for her act.

'I am sure she will make a sensation. But the hat will be better when she cuts her hair.'

Marc waited in the Place Vendôme to drive them the short distance to the Champs Élysées. As he held open the door for her, Georgia saw him smile appreciatively as he looked at Natasha and held out his hand to help her in. The girl had won him over and that was no mean feat. She almost relaxed.

At Fouquet's Georgia looked at Natasha, who waited for Dominic to take her hand, and stood back as he led the girl into the midst of the most fashionable society. Georgia watched the gossips stare, then carefully avert their eyes and bend to whisper. She was ready to encourage Natasha, but her smile was unnecessary. The girl was fully in command of the situation, her hand resting lightly on Dominic's arm, her great violet eyes coolly summing up the scene ahead of her.

Fouquet's was a world of its own, full of smoke and gossip, with soft golden lighting as if the sun was not blazing on the streets outside. It was bustling with customers at every table, and Georgia nodded to several familiar faces as they walked in. It was, as always, the place to see and to be seen. Heads turned as they followed the *maître d'hôtel* to their table, and Georgia acknowledged the greeting of some acquaintances, all discreetly assessing Natasha.

The outfit was perfect. Her pale skin and the glossy black hair which fell in a straight column down her back, complemented the pure lines of the black and white dress and shoes. Without the heavy make-up she had worn at Le Grand Marquis, her face looked delicate and vulnerable.

Georgia shook her head in amazement as she thought of the girl who had danced so wantonly at the night-club, seducing Dominic as they performed together.

They had been in total harmony with each other, but it had been more than that. It had been the magic of pure physical attraction. Whatever it was, that power had been as elemental as a spring gushing from the earth. Was she simply an actress? Or was Raoul right? Was the child in love with Dominic? Could it happen so suddenly?

With a shudder of remembered passion, Georgia thought of the moment she had first seen Theo, and then immediately she chastised herself for thinking of him, and not Olivier. But with Olivier it had been different. At first, he had simply been a refuge. She had felt nothing for him, or for anyone at that time, her body and her mind numbed by Theo's desertion. Olivier had taken her out of that dark despair and she would always be grateful, but there had never been with him that first overpowering shock of recognition, that had enabled Theo to change her entire life.

Not that it had mattered to him. Georgia pulled herself together. She had to stop thinking of Theo. She was here to launch Natasha into society, and to allow her to be seen. More importantly, she was here to see if the girl was presentable, and if she could cope with the spoilt women whose respect she had to gain, if she was to assist Dominic to run Fleur's.

But he seemed more interested in learning how Georgia had spent the previous night. 'Did you eat alone in your room?' he pressed her.

'No, Dominic, I met up with an acquaintance and we dined together.' There was no point in trying to hide the fact that she had been with a man; Dominic was quite capable of checking with the hotel staff. But a small white lie would help. 'A friend of your father's,' she continued smoothly.

She turned to Natasha. 'Don't look round now, but one of our best clients has just arrived.'

The Comtesse de Grives would not acknowledge Georgia's presence in such a public place, and certainly not when she was accompanied by her husband. The Comtesse's taste at Fleur's was for considerably younger men, for whom her appetite was apparently insatiable.

But the Comte stopped at their table and bent low to kiss Georgia's hand. 'Madame d'Essange. I was sorry to learn of Olivier's death. He and I were friends in our youth.'

Yes, they had attended his funeral, Georgia remembered, but now the old man's eyes were fixed on Natasha. 'May I introduce Mademoiselle Lanier?'

The Comte's eyes gleamed, and he wobbled, clutching the silver handle of his ebony cane for support, as he murmured, 'Charming.'

'And this is Olivier's son.' Georgia introduced Dominic before the Comte's obvious interest in Natasha antagonised her client. That would not help their business.

Two more of her clients were here for lunch, both of them with their husbands. Georgia had chosen a table in the centre of the room and, now that they were comfortably settled, she took time to survey the room. The mirrored walls ensured that everyone could be clearly seen, without the effort of turning round.

A couple of slender mannequins from Molyneux sat on a banquette, so closely entwined that it was difficult to tell which one possessed the long legs, elegantly crossed beneath the table-cloth. They nibbled tiny morsels from each other's plates and stared into the mirrors. At one time, Georgia had employed them both for Yolande, but their bony bodies had failed to give satisfaction.

One client, who kept her own room at Fleur's, was dining alone with her husband. Her upstairs room was full of her choice of equipment, and the plaited, shell-pink, leather restraints that were specially made for her, were not a matter for discussion here. Not by a flicker of an eyelid did Georgia acknowledge Nadine's presence. There were some secrets that her clients relied on her never to reveal. But Dominic's eyes sparkled as he caught sight of the couple, and Georgia hurriedly drew his attention back to the menu.

Maxine was a different matter. She had always been a problem for Georgia, since there was no reason for her to be discreet about the club. She was an American heiress who changed her husbands every other year. The current one, an impoverished Italian prince, was with her now although he looked as if he would soon be on his way out. Maxine's eyes were fixed on Dominic. Georgia knew that it wouldn't be long before she came over to their table.

She was right. Maxine leant over them, displaying a totally unsuitable *décolletage* for this time of day. She held out her hand for Dominic to kiss and left it draped over his shoulder.

'Georgia darling,' she breathed. 'Won't you introduce me to your charming companions?'

The previous year Maxine had taken two young men from Fleur's on holiday with her. It now seemed that her mind was on a more permanent replacement. Across the room, Georgia saw the prince drain his glass of champagne, refill it rapidly and stare furiously at his wife's back.

Maxine was obviously taken with Dominic. 'We may meet again soon,' she murmured. 'I'm thinking of taking a villa on the Riviera, near yours. Perhaps we shall see each other.'

'But you know we are there to work,' Georgia protested.

Maxine's bosom rose and fell eagerly at the thought. She might well be an inconvenient neighbour, Georgia realised, hoping that Maxine would change her mind and spend her summer elsewhere. She was relieved when the prince abruptly left his seat and stalked out of the restaurant, swiftly followed by an indignant Maxine. Their marriage did not seem to be quite at an end yet.

Dominic was looking bored. He toyed with his *tarte*

aux framboises and ostentatiously checked the time on his watch. He took the invitation out of his inside pocket. 'You must be excited at the prospect of seeing your friend's latest work,' he said, laying the card on the white table-cloth. 'I find it strange that you've neglected to follow his progress up to now. He appears to be very successful.'

'So I believe.'

'Are you expecting any more of your portraits to be on show?'

Georgia fitted a black Sobranie cigarette into her jet holder. 'It's hardly likely, Dominic. I haven't seen Theo Sands for fifteen years.'

But she was worried. She had sat for Theo hundreds of times while she lived with him, and she had usually been naked, or at best scantily draped.

What had happened to all those paintings? She hoped that if they had been sold, they would be safely in America, and that none of the visitors to the show would be aware of them. Above all, she hoped that none would be on display that afternoon.

Dominic pushed back his chair and stood up. 'We won't delay any further,' he said. 'I'm sure you're eager to renew your acquaintance.'

No. He was wrong. Theo would not be there. If there had been the slightest danger of that, she would not have agreed to go. Theo hated being seen in public; he preferred to spend all his time in the studio. How many times had he told her that it was the gallery owner's job to sell his work? She was worrying unnecessarily; this would soon be over.

It was an easy walk to the Rue Fliquet. The season in Paris had not quite ended and there seemed to be some excitement in the street. She was dismayed to see such a crowd. She didn't know this smart gallery, having kept well away from the art world since she left Theo. He had always sold his work through a small local shop, but the owner had died while he was away. Michel had been a friend, someone else whom Theo had let down.

Dominic propelled her towards the door. 'I think we should go in, don't you?'

Georgia shot him a cool look. She had no intention of letting him know just how much she cared. 'Why not?' she said, struggling to keep her voice calm.

The gallery was modern and glossy. As soon as they entered, a smooth young man offered them martini cocktails and wrote their names in a large, leather book.

There were only four paintings in the studiously bare, first room. She recognised them all. There was a still life of a plate of oysters on a rough pine table, and a couple of small, detailed paintings, which she hated, of a square in Boston where Theo had grown up. The last was of a young girl, draped in a jade-green shawl lying on a four-poster bed. The model's face was hidden, but Georgia still owned that shawl, and kept it locked in her bedroom cupboard.

She glanced at Dominic, but there was no reason for him to recognise her in the painting, and she was certainly not going to enlighten him. Georgia ate the olive out of her martini and walked up three steps to the second room.

Here the walls were covered by huge blocks of searing colour; scarlet-streaked brushstrokes swept across massive, black and maroon canvases, dominating the central space. In an adjoining alcove, hundreds of tiny frames reinforced the theme. She hated them, hated the arid control of form, and she did not understand them at all. Nothing was drawn from life; there was nothing here but a brilliant, hideous, outpouring of emotion.

They spoke to her of anger, pain and misery. She put her hands to her head to shut out the sight of them, and then she caught sight of the single word 'Georgia' etched on a brass plaque beneath each work, with the date, 1923, the year he had gone to New York. She felt a wave of fury flood through her. How dare he? After all he did to her, how dare he expose her name like this?

Ahead of her, an austere, wrought-iron staircase curved to an upper floor. Georgia moved like a zombie towards it, aware that already faces were staring at her, checking the brass nameplates and realising there was a link.

Steadily, she climbed the stairs. Dominic stood at the top. She wondered if he had known what she would find here. He was smiling and holding out his hands to her, but he said nothing. As if in a trance, she let him take her by the arm and walk her round the upper gallery.

Through the metal railings, she could see a crowd of people staring at the paintings below. Up here, the colours were different, a blaze of light and sunshine, cool blue-greens reflecting splashes of pure white.

As she sipped her martini, she felt faint and the room seemed to swirl around her in a cocoon of cool sapphire. She stared at a series of disjointed heads, shoulders and eyes. She felt alone, and out of place. She wondered who the model was; there was beauty even in the fashionably distorted features. Georgia felt jealousy flood through her as the images swam in front of her eyes.

So this was how his style had evolved. She had known that Theo had talent, but she had not known how far it would go. She felt in awe of these paintings, so different from the society commissions that he had churned out to earn his living. And a world away from the portrait she had hung on her wall for so many years. Had that, too, been drudgery for him? Had he hated everything he did then? Had he painted her simply to please, or to seduce her? Theo had painted from life, always from life. Who had inspired him to do this?

She had done what Dominic had asked of her. She had come to this place and now she wanted to leave. She moved towards the stairs, but Dominic was by her side, refilling her glass and gesturing towards the paintings.

'I think we should make a purchase, don't you?

Patronise the arts? For old times' sake?' He pushed her forward, digging his fingers into her flesh, hurting her. The martini fuddled her brain. She must not let him know how she felt.

She stared at the paintings on the walls. 'Yes, of course, Dominic.' She would do anything to get out of here. There was one plain, aquamarine canvas, drifting with clouds of colour, restful and soothing. She pointed it out. 'Why don't we take that?'

'What about this one? Are you sure you wouldn't prefer this?' Dominic placed his fingers on the dark brown nipple of a disembodied breast, lapped by small, blue tongues.

Georgia shuddered. She pointed to her first choice. 'We'll take that one.'

The gallery owner was at her side, his expression intent. She did not want to give him her card, with her address. 'Would you please have it delivered to The Ritz?' she asked.

'Of course, Madame.' He flicked his fingers at an assistant to take the painting from the wall. 'Madame, Monsieur Sands will be in this afternoon. Would you not care to meet him?'

Georgia felt drained. 'Unfortunately I have another appointment. Tell him – ' she hesitated. 'Tell him I admire his work. Would you please arrange the details of the purchase with my stepson?'

She moved towards the iron staircase, desperate to escape into the fresh air and have a few moments alone to recover. At the top of the stairs, she looked down. The room below was even more crowded than before.

She was aware of Theo's presence before she actually saw him. There was a murmur in the room, an excited buzz of recognition as his name was breathed from person to person. She saw the flare of interest in Dominic's eyes, too, as he walked towards her, and she stiffened, shifting back against the wall, so that she could not be seen. Somewhere at the back of her mind was the hope that Theo would not see her, that if she remained in exactly this spot, without moving, she could stay unnoticed, and not have to look at him or acknowledge him in any way.

What a fool she was to have come here. Now he would think that he still mattered to her, that she was interested in his work and had forgiven him. Never. She would never forget the way he had left her.

She saw Theo look up to where she was standing. He made his way through a crowd which parted for him respectfully. The women's eyes lingered on his now famous features as longingly as they had once gazed at the beautiful, male body which had been his only asset when Georgia had loved him. Why had he come back to torment her? She saw his eyes fixed on her as he climbed up the wrought-iron treads towards her, and then she turned away.

Dominic raised his hand and caught her elbow just as she felt that other touch on her rigid shoulder. It was the merest brush of his fingers on her skin, but she had no doubt that it was him. The gallery was completely silent now and she felt a cold rage force her to turn to acknowledge him. She would not let him humiliate her in public.

He was so close that she could see only the gleam of a sparkling white shirt in front of her dazzled eyes. Theo! Why was he here? He hated galleries, hated selling his work. Even in the old days he had hardly bothered. Why should he do so now?

She held out her bare hand, letting him see the exquisite sapphires that weighted her fingers. Theo ignored the proffered hand, and she had to raise her head uncomfortably to look at his face as he bent to kiss her. For a moment she stared up at the open, tanned face, the warm amber eyes, the long, tawny hair, curling over his collar, then she was caught up in a bear hug and swept off the ground in a fierce embrace that was startlingly familiar.

The oily spirit tipped out of her glass before he let her go. 'Theo.' She nodded coolly, praying that her cheeks did not burn as fiercely as she feared, praying above all that he would not say her name in this crowd which would make an immediate connection between the series of paintings downstairs and her presence here.

He took her hand and held it lightly. 'Madame d'Essange,' he said softly. 'It is a pleasure to see you here. What do you think of my work?' He took the dripping glass from her fingers and signalled for a waiter to replace it.

Around them the gossips pretended to talk of other things, and the tension in the room lightened as Theo led her away to his latest group of paintings. 'My style has changed,' he said, 'now that I no longer have the same inspiration.'

Georgia struggled for words, anything to give her time to end this intolerable situation, to allow her to leave gracefully without creating a scene. 'You're very successful,' she said shortly.

'I have been for a long time.' He seemed to dismiss all thought of his admiring patrons as he held her hand. 'I heard about your husband. I'm so sorry.'

At the mention of Olivier, Georgia drew back. How dare Theo talk of him? She stood rigid in front of him. 'Thank you,' she said coolly.

His clear brown eyes looked up at the ceiling. 'Either you've changed, or you haven't forgiven me, Georgia. Which is it?'

He had always been direct. She refused to allow him the satisfaction of an argument. 'We have nothing to say to each other. Please excuse me. I am with friends.'

'You are with Olivier's son, and,' Theo bowed and took Natasha's hand, 'with the most beautiful young woman I have seen in Paris. May I paint you sometime, Mademoiselle? Would you allow it?'

Natasha inclined her head. 'You are very kind, Monsieur.'

'No. You would be kind to sit for me.' He stepped back. 'There is something there I'd like to understand. A mystery. And passion. Yes it would be a privilege. Who must I ask? Is it your decision?' He laughed with her. 'Or this gentleman's? Monsieur d'Essange, is it you I must ask? For permission to paint this enchanting child?' He saw Natasha frown. 'A child only in my imagination. If I permitted myself to regard you as a woman, who knows how far we might go, and then it would never be allowed, would it?'

Georgia moved towards the iron staircase. 'I am afraid that we have to leave now. We are already late.'

She saw Theo look at her and stiffen at the frost in her expression. 'I hope we may meet again in less formal circumstances,' he said. 'Thank you for buying the picture, Georgia. I am delighted by your choice. It was painted for you, you know, after your eyes. The colour of the Californian sky. Remember?'

Somehow she found her way outside, and found Marc waiting with the car. Safe in its dark interior, she watched Dominic standing outside in the street, leaning against the plate-glass window of the gallery and smoking a cigarette.

Where was Natasha? What could she be doing to take so long? Georgia's clothes felt sticky and uncomfortable, and she longed to be able to go back to the hotel to change. The naked body of the young model rose in her mind: dark, young flesh with sharply defined nipples, virginal yet debauched. No wonder Theo's painting had become a wild success. Even without her own memories of the artist, his pictures were blatantly sensual.

'What took you so long?' she snapped at Dominic as he finally entered the cab, his dark hair flopping appealingly over his forehead. She felt his body tense beside her as he placed his hand on hers, sending a trickle of desire pumping through her.

'We are both waiting for Natasha. She seems very taken with your friend.'

They watched Natasha walk out of the gallery, the glass doors held wide open for her. Marc hurried to let her into the car. She pulled down the small spare seat in the back of the car, as she apologised for her delay.

'I'm so sorry. I was merely ensuring that the painting would arrive safely. I thought you would like to have it at the villa this summer; the colours are so suitable, don't you think? So I have given Monsieur Sands that address. He says it will be no trouble to return it to Lusigny at the end of the season.'

Georgia felt a cold chill as she understood what Natasha had done. Dominic turned towards her as Marc drove off.

'You look tired, Georgia,' he said. 'We'll look after you this evening.' He squeezed her hand comfortingly and gave her that wry, charming smile that reminded her so forcibly of his father.

She wound down the window and allowed a breath of air into the stifling interior of the cab. 'How thoughtful, Dominic. As always.'

Chapter Nine

*L*ate in the afternoon, the downtown area of Marseilles was hot and steamy, smelling of sweat and rotting fish. Narrow streets leading to the harbour front swarmed with sailors who had come ashore to drink and buy themselves a woman for the night.

Georgia was relieved to be out of Paris. Their leisurely drive down to the south had been successful and relaxing, and, although Marseilles was unpleasant in the summer, they would not be here long. So far they had done well in their search for a new team. Stefan, Christophe, Pierre and Philippe had already been sent to their villa at Cap d'Antibes, and would be joined there by the others they had picked out during the past week. They had only two more to find.

Georgia was glad that Marc was able to accompany them. This was his home town, and his tall, powerful body discouraged unwelcome attention. Every year she had come to Marseilles with Olivier on their way to the villa. Together they had checked out the harbour bars for fresh talent, looking for men with raw, untamed energy, who would provide a contrast to the beautiful boys they had already selected. It had proved to be a successful formula.

Dominic looked uncomfortably out of place. His easy grace seemed to desert him as they pushed past the rough crowds, and he gave a snort of disapproval when Marc led them through a shabby, green-painted door, and down a narrow staircase into a dark, smoky bar.

'Marc!' A tall man, unshaven, with a ballooning belly and a crumpled cigarette dangling from his mouth, hurried forward and embraced him. 'I have kept a table for you.' He shook Georgia's hand respectfully. 'Madame, a pleasure as always. You are still caring for my friend here? He looks well.'

The man's eyes rested admiringly on Georgia before he shifted his gaze to Natasha. 'Mademoiselle.' He smiled at her, and then at Dominic. 'So you are the son of Monsieur Olivier. I am pleased to meet you,' he said, pumping Dominic's hand up and down. 'Your father was a great man, a great lover. And you – he would be proud of you. Here . . .' he swept some plates and glasses on to a tray. 'Please – sit down.'

The four of them perched on bare wooden chairs. The bar was packed with sailors, eager to forget their hard lives in a haze of alcohol. They looked rough and dirty.

Georgia knew that this would be the most difficult part of their selection. Olivier had taught her that the addition of one or two rough sailors or fishermen gave an edge to their act. Even after training they kept a raw, male magnetism that thrilled their clients. They needed Marc's local knowledge to help them to avoid any real villains.

Tomorrow night, if all went well, they would drive to the villa where they could settle down to the serious work of training their new team. In the meantime, however, there were two more to choose.

The proprietor came over to them, placed a couple of *pichets* of red Bordeaux on the table with some tumblers, and sat down beside Marc. 'There are a few you could look at,' he said. 'And many you should not go near. See that man over there? The one by the stairs? He killed his girl last week. The police have no evidence, but he won't be around for long.' He shrugged. 'She had a couple of brothers.'

Georgia watched Dominic look around the bar in disgust. She understood how he felt. She, too, had been horrified on her first visit here. She grinned at Marc, remembering the ruffian he had been then. Who would have expected him to become such a good friend? She hoped that Dominic would think about that and realise that this part of their work was worthwhile.

Natasha looked striking in a straight, black cotton skirt, slit high on her thigh. A low-necked, violet jumper stretched over her breasts which, though small, were well rounded with high, pointed nipples. Her hair shone in a straight streak down her back and her eyes, as at the night-club, were outlined with a thick line of kohl. She had been so discreetly dressed and so demure since they had left Paris that Georgia was surprised to see her like this, but she felt pleased that the girl had made an effort to fit in here. In the short time they had been together, Natasha had begun working with the men they had already chosen, and had learned a few of Georgia's routines.

Georgia pointed out the men recommended by Marc's friend. 'What do you think?' she asked.

Natasha seemed unsure. 'Can we talk to them?'

Georgia shook her head. 'Watch them first. Take a careful look, and then decide whether you think you could work with them or not. Marc can explain to them what we want.'

'Maybe Natasha has the right idea. Maybe she should talk to them.' Dominic grimaced as he tasted the rough red wine. 'This looks like her sort of place.'

Georgia looked at him sharply. He had been less trouble than she had expected during their trip down here. This was the final stage, and she hoped that he would not make their task any more difficult.

'Let me see what I can do.' Marc stood up and crossed

over to the bar. He spoke briefly to the proprietor, then took a jug of wine over to a corner table and offered a drink to a young man sitting there alone.

'What do you think?' asked Georgia, discreetly watching Marc's companion.

Dominic shrugged. 'He'll do,' he said, without enthusiasm.

Georgia saw Natasha glance at a dark-haired man slumped over a drink at the bar. He was powerfully built and looked young enough, but his swarthy face had a badly healed scar that ran from his jaw to the corner of his eye.

He seemed to interest Natasha. 'That one is exciting,' she said. 'What about him?'

'He's hideous. You'll never make anything of him,' Dominic sneered.

Natasha looked up at him. 'I thought we needed a contrast to your perfect good looks,' she said quietly.

'So you choose a monster?' Dominic bit his lip. 'That's going too far.' He gestured towards a young sailor sitting with a girl in a corner of the room. 'What about that one?'

Natasha shook her head, and scraped back her chair. She walked slowly over to the bar, and arranged herself seductively on a high, pine stool. 'A Pernod, please,' she ordered. Marc looked away from his companion and gave Georgia a warning glance.

Dominic scowled at Natasha's slim back. 'What the hell are we doing here? We've chosen ten already.' He glanced round the room. 'These men are scum.'

Georgia looked at him steadily. Dominic was making no effort to take this seriously. 'Marc came from here,' she said quietly.

'So what? He's nothing special.'

'How can you say that? Besides, we need the contrast.'

'I don't want her here.' Dominic's eyes rested on Natasha's provocative pose.

'She needs to see the men. She has to perform with them.'

'Later. She doesn't know what to do yet,' Dominic said petulantly. 'And look at her. She's behaving like a tart.'

And Georgia had to admit that Natasha seemed to know what she was doing when she curled her slim legs round the rough, wooden bar stool. One black leather shoe slipped off her foot and clattered to the floor. The girl balanced delicately on the edge of her seat stroking beads of moisture from the chilled surface of her glass of cloudy Pernod. She raised one knee provocatively and stared at the scarred man.

Georgia watched uneasily. Natasha was taking a risk by invading his territory. Without a word, the girl gestured to the barman who brought her another tall thin glass. The smoke in the bar thickened. Most of the tables were now taken, and several of the girls who had entered alone had found men to buy them drinks. One or two left after agreeing a price for their services. Many directed angry glances at the beautiful girl sitting at the bar.

Natasha sipped her second glass of Pernod. Her foot arched down to the floor. She shifted her fallen shoe, but failed to replace it on her foot. She stared hard at the dark man. Slowly he stood up and walked over to her, bent to pick up her shoe and pushed it on to her foot. He sat down on the stool next to her. She signalled for a drink to be brought to him, and when he put his hand in his pocket for money, she smiled, stroked the rough skin on the back of his hand, pushed away the coins and whispered in his ear. He stood up, knocking over his stool.

Natasha's eyes never left the young man's face. Georgia shivered. That scar dominated his face. Without it, he would have been good-looking. She looked questioningly at Marc's friend.

He shrugged. 'He's never been in any trouble here, but he must have upset someone to look like that.'

112

Natasha slid elegantly off her stool, slipped her hand through the sailor's arm and led him over to their table. 'Luc would like to audition for us,' she said. 'I'll go back with him to our hotel. We need one more man. That one will do.' She gestured casually across the room to the man sitting with Marc. 'You and Dominic can bring him to me. Then we'll work with both of them tonight.' She turned her back on them and walked up the stairs with Luc.

Dominic rose furiously to his feet. 'I'm going to stop her. What the hell does she think she's doing?'

Georgia held him back. 'Leave her. Let her find out for herself. She has to be allowed some freedom. And besides,' she said pointing to the doorway, 'Marc will go with her and make sure she comes to no harm.'

Dominic sat down, his face sullen, his eyes angry. 'Why don't you and I go straight to the villa tonight? Natasha can stay in Marseilles with Marc if she likes.'

'We all stay.' What was Dominic trying to do? Georgia felt hot and sticky in the airless bar. She, too, hated Marseilles and longed for the Riviera. The thought of their villa had kept her going throughout this long, hot summer. But they could not leave until their work was done.

'We need twelve men, Dominic. And we're almost there.' She drained her glass, wishing it was cold champagne. The rough wine hit the back of her throat, and the thick smoke hurt her eyes. 'Now, let's talk to Marc's young man and see if we can persuade him to come and audition tonight.'

Natasha allowed Marc to lead them through the dark streets to their hotel. She knew that she was probably not yet ready to perform, and that this evening she would be tested to her limit. Dominic had made it clear that he thought she wasn't as good as Georgia, and tonight he had had a strange look in his eyes, as if he wanted her to fail. Well, she would show him.

She glanced at Luc, nervous now of the massive frame that towered over her. Had she made a terrible mistake? Of all the men in that filthy bar, he had been the only one to look at her with a degree of warmth in his eyes. He hadn't leered or scowled at her. Now though, in the dim yellow lamplight, he looked dark and menacing.

Two men they had chosen the day before were waiting at the hotel. They looked presentable, but their eyes were wary and they seemed unsure of themselves. Marc sent them to their room to prepare for the audition.

'You need to go and get ready, too,' Marc advised her when they had gone. 'I'll explain to Luc what we're doing, and sort him out a bit.' He clapped the young man on the shoulders. 'It's the good life for you now, my friend. I wish I could start all over again, myself.'

Luc's shoulders tensed, then he took a deep breath and stared at Natasha. 'Let her come with us,' he said suddenly. 'Let her decide how I'm going to look.'

Marc opened his mouth as if to refuse, but Natasha stopped him. 'Please Marc. It's all right. Maybe he has a point.' And, she thought, perhaps it would help her to do well in the performance if Luc was on her side.

In the stark white hotel bathroom, Luc seemed even more out of place, with his straggly, thick hair, his big, rough hands and torn fingernails. And nothing had prepared her for the sight of Luc's naked body as he stripped off his shirt, exposing a muscular, tanned chest. She watched, fascinated, as his fingers tugged at the heavy, metal buckle at his waist. He held her gaze as if he dared her to lower her eyes, as if he knew that she had never seen a fully naked man.

The palms of her hands were damp with sweat, and she clenched her fists to hide her panic, thankful that her dark eyes hid her emotions. The Pernod she had drunk in the bar was doing nothing to calm her nerves. She kept telling herself that if she could only keep cool, and pretend that she had done this before, then she would be all right. She kept her eyes firmly on his face as his pants dropped to the floor and he stood aggressively naked in front of her.

She was supposed to be checking him out! Trying to appear calm, she stared at his chest, at the thickly matted hair, narrowing to a dark, furred line over his taut belly, and down lower until she was forced to look directly at his penis, at that long, thick organ hanging between his thighs. It stirred slightly as she held her gaze. Quickly she nodded to Marc as if she was satisfied, and hoped that Luc would submerge his body in the hot soapsuds awaiting him before he swelled any further.

She took a deep breath and choked back a burst of laughter. What was happening to her? This wasn't funny. But so far, she was coping all right. She wondered if it would be any easier to try to control Luc now that she had seen him naked, but she had a growing fear that it would not.

By the time he was washed, with a towel safely tied around his waist, and sitting in a chair waiting for Marc to cut his damp hair, Natasha felt more in control. 'Leave it long,' she insisted. 'Don't try to make him look like the others.'

'If that's what you want.' Marc checked the time. 'You go and change now. You need to start in ten minutes.'

They had booked a large room in which to stage the audition and Natasha went there as soon as she was ready. She wore a skin-tight white top and leggings, as Georgia had advised, but she felt quite naked. When she had looked at herself in the mirror in her bedroom, she had seen how the outfit clung to her slender body, outlining her high, pointed breasts, and the curve of her rounded buttocks.

Silently she repeated to herself Georgia's other instructions. Keep looking into their eyes to let them know you are in control. Never be cruel. Excite them, tease them, but never go too far. If one or two want to come, let them, the clients love it. But not too many, and never the ones who are booked for after a performance. Above all, remember – if you lose control you are at risk.

It had been so easy to dance for Dominic at Le Grand Marquis and, when he had joined her on the stage, she had responded instinctively to every movement of his body. She was sure he had felt the same thrill.

That night she would have done anything he wanted. She had never seen such a beautiful man, or felt anything like the surge of excitement he had instilled in her. She had scarcely listened to Raoul's words when he counselled her not to accept the job. From the first moment she saw Dominic in the night-club, she had longed to touch him, to be close to him. If she could perform well tonight, she hoped that he would want her too.

She saw Georgia and Dominic come in and sit on a couple of armchairs in the corner of the room. Natasha felt their eyes on her, but she didn't look at them. She waited, standing quite still, until the door opened again and Marc brought in the four men, simply dressed in black cotton shirts and slacks.

Marc had achieved a great improvement in Luc's appearance already but, compared to the other three, he still looked unkempt. His hair remained long and wild, and his chin was shadowed with dark stubble.

As they had been instructed, they stood in a semi-circle in front of her. She thought they were as nervous as she was, still not aware quite why they were there, or what they were expected to do, but eager to earn the money they had been promised.

As they watched, she padded over to them. She stopped in front of the first man, and ran her hands over his body, feeling a surge of pleasure as she felt him respond to her light touch. She raised her arms and waited. Not one of them moved. Her dancer's body twisted between the men, taunting them, sliding in and out of their group.

Natasha knew that Dominic and Georgia were testing her as much as the men. She had to make a success of this. More than anything else in the world she wanted Dominic to be proud of her.

She pretended that there was no light fabric covering her, and that she was naked in front of these men. Each time she raised her arms above her head, she watched their gaze fasten on her breasts. She could feel her nipples jutting out stiffly as Georgia had shown her.

She thrust her hip-bones forward, drawing attention to the pronounced mound of her pubis, with its faint shadow of dark curls visible through the thin silk leggings. She turned quickly on one foot, letting them catch a glimpse of her high, taut buttocks, and the clearly defined division between them.

She saw Dominic lean forward in his chair, and she thrilled at his attention. Quickly she caught the men's eyes again, maintaining control, as she struggled to remember what she must do next. All four men were already aroused. Natasha could see the hard outlines of their swollen penises stretching their tight, black trousers.

She knew that the men were almost naked when Georgia performed with them, and that some of them touched her with total abandon. She wondered how it would be when she came to do that, and how Dominic would feel when he saw her.

Natasha had seen how it excited him to watch Georgia, and she was determined to do anything that Georgia did, anything at all that would arouse Dominic. But she could not risk taking her eyes off the men now to see how he was reacting.

Luc stared at her insolently, his black eyes glittering. The memory of his nakedness seared through her brain as she moved towards him, keeping her eyes fixed on his. She reached up, and put her arms around his neck, moulding her body against him as Georgia had taught her, then she slid her right leg up and around the back of his thigh, pressing her crotch on his heavily muscled flesh. It was a delicious sensation.

She could feel his hands pulling her hard against him, and felt the swift surge of his penis rise against her hips. She wondered what it would be like to have a man inside her. Would Dominic respond like this? Would he desire her as Luc did now? She slid her leg higher over his buttocks, pushing him firmly down on to his knees, and pressed his head against her breasts, feeling his hot breath on her skin as she caressed his deeply scarred cheek.

She wanted to strip off her tight suit and free her body, but Georgia had warned her not to do anything like that at this stage. That would have to wait until they were safely at the villa, and she had more experience. It was too dangerous just yet.

Her breasts ached. She wanted to feel Dominic's lips sucking on them, and his hands stroking her thighs. Sliding down on to her knees, she straddled Luc's chest, lowering her body until she could feel the thick ridge of his strained cock between her legs. She rubbed herself on him, feeling the heat of his body throbbing against her.

She heard Luc groan as she writhed on top of him. For one moment she felt him draw back, then his huge penis sprang free from the black cloth, and his hands grasped her buttocks, tearing the thin silk from between her legs, as he reared up beneath her. She felt the swollen tip of his penis pushing against her soft inner lips, heard him gasp as she froze, unable to pull away.

She felt strong hands grip her shoulders, dragging her off. She threw back her hair and stared triumphantly into Dominic's eyes.

'I can tell you're going to enjoy the work,' he sneered, as he pulled her to her feet. 'Now go and change. We're leaving tonight.'

'Tonight?' she questioned eagerly. Did he really want her to be with him?

'Get rid of that man,' Dominic snarled at Marc. 'He's an animal.'

Natasha was puzzled. Had she lost Luc his job? Wasn't his performance exactly what they had asked for?

She was relieved when Georgia defended him. 'Don't be too hasty. He could be just what we want. Did you see what he did to the others? They're scared of him. There's an electricity between him and Natasha and she can learn to control it.'

She turned to Natasha, looking worried. 'Are you all right? It isn't easy. I shouldn't have let you do this, when the boys aren't trained at all.'

Natasha felt conscious of her torn clothing, and remembered the anger in Dominic's eyes; now he looked cold and indifferent again. She wanted him to feel jealous, but it seemed that he didn't care at all. She hoped things would be different once they were at the villa. Then there would be time for her to learn how to excite him.

Luc raised himself on one elbow. Natasha could see a slow smile soften his scarred mouth as he looked up at Dominic, and then he sprang lightly to his feet and stood, arrogantly erect, beside them.

Natasha heard Georgia whispering to Marc. 'Find them all some girls before you take them to the villa. They need to calm down a bit after this.'

So Marc would provide them all with women for the night, she thought. Was that how it was with all men? Could any woman satisfy them once they were aroused?

As she covered herself with a towel, she wondered what Georgia really thought of her performance, but the older woman had turned away to follow Dominic out of the room, and it was Marc who spoke to her. 'Go and change quickly, Natasha. He won't wait long.'

Georgia waited outside in the hotel's small garden. She loved these warm, balmy nights. She felt aroused by Natasha's skill, understanding how exciting her own performances must have been for her clients.

The promise that the girl had shown in Paris had been

fully realised. Something seemed to happen to her on a stage, so that the demure young girl was taken over by a wild, free spirit. And Natasha had been right about Luc.

Georgia had been amazed by Natasha's action in the bar earlier in the evening, but could not fault her choice. Luc was a natural, and the contrast between his tall, swarthy hulk and Natasha's slender black and white colouring was dramatic. But it had been a mistake to let the girl practise with untried men. Georgia knew that it was her own reluctance to perform in front of Dominic that had made her agree to Natasha's suggestion. It would be a pity if they had to let Luc go, although she was sure that Dominic would insist on it.

Maybe she hadn't explained things properly to Natasha. She would have to go more carefully. With training, Natasha could learn to keep her body under control. So long as Dominic accepted the situation, they would be a great success. He had been sulking ever since they had left Paris, and now Natasha looked exhausted. So much had changed in her life in the last week.

At least they would have a few days' rest if they drove to the villa tonight; they could all relax far better there. Maybe Dominic was right to decide to leave now. It was not worth arguing about. In a way, Georgia sympathised. She, too, had had enough of hot, smelly Marseilles, with its seedy bars and airless streets.

It had been hard work putting together a team, but they had succeeded in finding twelve men who should do. They might as well go home. And if Dominic wanted to keep Natasha away from Luc for a while, he was making a wise decision.

In the meantime, Marc could look after the boys in Marseilles for a few days, kit them out with clothes and tame them down a bit before they joined up at the villa. Maybe she should stay behind with them. It would be good for Natasha and Dominic to have some time alone. And the coast road was so romantic.

But Dominic refused her suggestion immediately. He jangled the car keys in front of her face. 'We all go together. You hate Marseilles. Of course you come with us now.'

It was three o'clock in the morning when the large car purred out of the lock-up garage where they had stored it for safe-keeping. The streets were dark and badly lit. Occasionally they passed a couple entwined in a back alley or doorway. Apart from them, and a few drunken brawlers on street corners, there was utter silence. Natasha slept, stretched out on the back seat. Dominic had insisted that Georgia join him in the front.

Georgia was sleepy, too. She envied Natasha her ability to drift off as soon as she closed her eyes. And yet she wanted to see the road; it was so full of memories for her. Even in the dark, she could see an occasional glimpse of the Mediterranean with its still surface illuminated by the faint light of the new moon.

'So what did you think of her performance?' Dominic's voice was curt.

Georgia glanced at the back seat. Natasha's eyes were firmly closed. 'She moves beautifully. Her body is graceful. And she's exciting.'

'She's exciting all right.'

Georgia waited for Dominic to say something about Luc. But he didn't.

'Do you think you made the right decision, Dominic?' she asked quietly. 'Are you happy with her?'

'Happy? That hardly matters. She's here to work. And she seems to have picked it up quickly. She'll do. I want to see her with you.'

'I'll show her the rest of the act, of course.' Georgia wanted to coach Natasha alone, not with Dominic looking on.

'No. I want to see the two of you together,' he said casually. 'I want her to copy exactly what you do.'

'She has her own style. I thought that's why you chose her.'

'She needs training.' He ran his fingers lightly over Georgia's thigh. 'She's out of control. I want to see you tame her.'

'Surely that's up to you?' Gently she lifted his hand off her leg. 'If you had worked with her tonight, she wouldn't have been at risk from Luc.'

'It was Natasha who encouraged him. You can show her what to do with him. He wouldn't dare go so far with you, would he?'

Georgia wondered about that. She had watched with increasing anxiety as Luc had reared up over the girl, as he had covered her with his body and torn the fabric from between her legs. If Dominic hadn't stopped them, he would have had her. And Georgia had struggled to control her own hot ache as she watched.

'We agreed that Natasha would train her own team,' she said. 'We shouldn't confuse them.'

'I thought that too. But now I'm sure she needs to see you work with Luc. Unless you don't believe you can control him either?' His voice was light, but she saw his eyes dart towards her. 'Did he arouse you? How did you feel when you watched them?'

Georgia felt a swift surge of desire as she relived that moment. 'He showed promise,' she said, hoping that Dominic would soon change the subject.

'We'll keep Luc on one condition,' he murmured, as he caressed her knee. 'I want to see you perform with him.'

Georgia was hot and tired, and her pants felt damp and sticky. When Dominic's hand stroked her leg for the second time, she shifted uncomfortably beneath the pressure, feeling the heat rise between her thighs. She wanted to push him away, but instead she felt her back arching instinctively towards him.

Dominic pulled off the road and stopped the car. She felt him move closer and bend over her so that his lips brushed against hers. How did he always know when she was most vulnerable? His tongue flickered inside her mouth, inflaming her already feverish desire.

She was sure he knew exactly how she felt as he expertly unfastened her buttons and slid his fingers inside her blouse. She wanted him to squeeze harder, but his feather-light touch tantalised her without relieving her aching nipples. Her breasts were bare now in the moonlight, and she felt his lips close round them as his hand pressed down between her thighs, gently snaking deep into her eager sex until he found her swollen bud and stroked it.

She came immediately, and he laughed. 'Next time it'll be this.' He took her hand and laid it over his throbbing penis. 'Think about it.'

Georgia fought for breath. Her whole body was shaken by the strength of her orgasm. As she sank back on to the soft leather seat, she felt his cheek warm against her breasts, his long hair silky on her skin. She wanted to lie there and feel him holding her like this, but there was a faint movement from the back of the car.

It was a shock to remember that they were not alone. She sat up quickly and fastened the buttons on her blouse, but when she looked round, Natasha's eyes were still closed. Georgia felt ashamed at how little she had done to stop Dominic doing whatever he wanted. She had been as eager as he was.

As Dominic drove along the coast road, Georgia breathed in the cooler night air, scented with rosemary and jasmine and the dominating salt odour from the Mediterranean. He was driving too fast, but the road was deserted and Georgia did not want to risk a confrontation with him by complaining.

How triumphant she and Olivier had always felt together at this stage when the hard work of choosing the team was behind them and they could look forward to the summer. Often they had stopped on the way home, pulled off this road on to a secluded beach, swum in the sea and made love until dawn.

Occasional flashes of moonlit sea lifted her spirits, and the scent of eucalyptus as they neared Cap d'Antibes reassured her with the reminder of previous happy summers. They were only one mile from the villa now. Sand and pine needles covered the narrow dirt track as they dipped down towards the coast and saw in front of them the high, blue-washed walls of the Villa d'Essor.

Georgia stepped stiffly out of the car. Her skirt still felt moist around her legs; she hoped it would not look too obvious. They had telephoned their housekeeper, Mathilde, to expect them and she might well have waited up.

Dominic dumped their cases unceremoniously in the hall. She felt him close to her. Please don't let him touch her now, she prayed.

Georgia moved away from him as Mathilde emerged from the shadows. The old lady had looked after the villa for years and hated not to welcome their arrival. 'Everything is ready, Madame,' she said.

'Thank you. We're very tired.'

'And the young lady?' Mathilde had expressed a keen interest in meeting Dominic's new friend.

'Asleep in the car. Dominic will bring her in. You shouldn't have waited up for us, Mathilde, but it was kind of you. Go to bed now.' She called out to Dominic. 'Look after Natasha. I'll see you both when you wake up.' She had to keep out of his way; she could not be near him any longer. She knew now that she wanted him too much.

Natasha lay on the back seat, listening to the voices. She wiped a tear from her cheek with the hem of her dress and uncurled her legs. She didn't want to go into this house which belonged to Georgia, as everything belonged to her, including Dominic.

She had heard everything. She felt chilled by the thought that he was only using her to get Georgia to perform for him. It was Georgia he wanted. Nothing she could do would excite him; he hadn't even been jealous of Luc. Poor Luc. She felt dirty and ashamed; he had been honest with her, and she had tried to use him.

Exhausted, she clambered out of the car and saw Dominic standing in the doorway of a pale stone house which glowed in the moonlight. She supposed that it was beautiful, but to her it looked cold and unfriendly. She wanted to leave here and go home to Paris; Dominic would never love her. She held on tightly to the car door, swaying with exhaustion.

With a cry of annoyance, Dominic strode towards her. Roughly he picked her up and carried her into the house. As she struggled in his arms, she saw around her a wooden staircase and a spacious hall. She felt Dominic's hands holding her tightly and felt his chest beating; breathed in his strong, heady, male odour, closed her eyes and buried her face in his chest.

She heard him kick open a door, before he threw her down on the bed. He stood over her while he pulled his shirt over his head and tugged his trousers down over his slim hips. She stared. He was fully erect and moving purposefully towards her.

She tried to sit up, to move away. This wasn't what she wanted. Not now. Not like this. She felt his hands on her legs, forcing them apart. She heard the tear of silk as he tore off her pants, then he pushed up her dress and buried his face between her thighs. She felt his lips sucking at her sex and then she pushed him away, beating her fist on his chest and clawing at his face.

He moved back. 'What the hell are you doing? You've been begging for this all night. I had to pull you off that man. What is it? You only want a street boy? Aren't I rough enough for you?' His face was contorted with anger as he spoke. 'Well go to hell. You're not the only woman here.'

'You think I would have sex with you like this?' she said, trying to cover her nakedness with the skirt of her dress.

'That's why you're here.'

'I thought I was employed to perform, to arouse the ladies who watch, just like your stepmother does.'

Dominic caught her wrist. 'Don't speak of her like that.'

'Why not? Because it's her you want to make love to? Do you think I would take you in my bed when you ache for another woman?' Natasha snatched her hand away and pressed her fingers on the stiff column of his erection. 'That's not because of me. Go and take her. You both need it.'

'Bitch. Whore. Who will you use to satisfy yourself? Luc? Is that why you made a play for him?'

Natasha turned her back. 'Get out of my room or I call Georgia.'

Naked, he strode from the room and slammed the door. Natasha lay huddled on the bed, tears drenching her cheeks. He would go straight to Georgia, she was sure of it. But she didn't want it to be like this. Not the first time. What would he say if he knew she was a virgin? Throw her out in disgust?

Chapter Ten

Georgia woke early to see a shaft of sunlight filtering
through the slats of the shutters on her bedroom
window. The polished floorboards felt warm under her
feet as she pushed the shutters wide open, took in a deep
breath of the salty, pine-scented air and stretched luxur-
iously in the warm breeze. The garden, shaded by silvery
olive trees, was deserted except for Mathilde's cat, asleep
on a sunny flagstone on the terrace. Beyond the garden,
below a steep cliff, lay the sea, endlessly blue and
perfectly calm.

Later, Marc would exercise the team on the beach. In
only ten days he had worked wonders. His coaching,
together with sun and healthy exercise, had turned
rough young men into confident, assured performers.

If only she had been able to do the same with Natasha.

Georgia slipped on a pair of comfortable slacks and a
loose top. She held an old pair of tan leather sandals in
one hand as she shut her bedroom door and padded
silently down the stairs. She could hear Mathilde's voice
from the kitchen, humming to herself as she prepared
breakfast. Mathilde was always up early and for a
moment Georgia considered stopping for a cup of coffee.

But she needed a walk alone to clear her mind. There

was a lot to think about and some decisions had to be taken soon. It wasn't working out here. Certainly, things were easier for her. She could swim, sit in the sun, eat Mathilde's delicious food and pretend that all was going well. But she was here to do a job, and unless Natasha improved her performance, it would be impossible for Georgia to leave and plan her own future.

She crossed the garden, slipping on her sandals to protect her feet from the coarse grass and rough sand. Picking a couple of ripe, warm figs from the tree at the corner of the wall, she set off down the steep path to the beach. The track was precarious; a thin layer of sand covered sharp stones, some of which broke loose under her feet.

At the bottom, there was a long, sandy beach, bordered on each side by high rocks. It was completely private. She sank her toes into the gritty, firm sand, enjoying the way it stretched the muscles of her feet as she walked fast along the shoreline.

She had to do something. The team was working well on its own, but the rehearsals with Natasha were a disaster. It was impossible to believe that the girl who had danced so powerfully at Le Grand Marquis was now incapable of stimulating any interest at all in a group of healthy young men.

What had gone wrong? The girl had looked so good until they reached here. She had taken an active part in choosing the rest of the team, and the only concern that Georgia had felt up to now was over the risk that Natasha had taken in Marseilles.

She let the seawater wash over her feet as she remembered how close they had come to disaster that evening. She had over-ruled Dominic when he wanted to get rid of Luc, and maybe that had been a mistake. Perhaps if Luc went away, Natasha would feel free to loosen up and Dominic might sulk less.

From the far end of the beach Georgia could hear bursts of male laughter. Marc was exercising the team already. Keeping out of sight, she clambered up the cliff path and stopped half-way. She found a patch of shade beneath a stunted pine growing out of the rock, and sat down to watch the rehearsal. Afterwards, she would talk to Marc, and take her decision then.

Below her, on the sand, the boys were standing in the familiar circle, hands on hips, stripped to light shorts. Georgia leant over, shading her eyes, trying to pick out Luc from the others, finding it difficult from here to see sufficiently clearly to recognise the boys as individuals. But Natasha was visible enough, sitting hunched up under a huge, black and white beach umbrella.

This year Georgia sunbathed freely, permitting a faint tan to tinge the alabaster tone of her normal colouring. There was no longer any need for her to maintain a perfect pale complexion so that she could shock an audience with the contrast between her creamy flesh and a dark, male tan. Now it was Natasha who had to cherish her ashen loveliness.

Georgia shivered despite the heat. She envied Natasha her new beginning. And her new love, even if Dominic showed no sign of returning it. She wondered if Dominic would learn to love Natasha as she obviously loved him. There was always one who loved more. As Olivier had loved her. As she had loved Theo. Nothing had ever made her feel as alive as she had done with him, not even Olivier's devotion and the passion he awoke in her.

Natasha had moved inside the circle now and was pacing around in front of the men. Her body looked stiff and uncomfortable, hindered by a long, violet robe, which flapped awkwardly around her ankles. Georgia realised that the sun was already hot enough to burn the girl's delicate skin.

She was reluctant to interrupt them but she would have no choice if this went on much longer. Natasha looked exhausted already. It must have been a strain for her to come here, and take on a new way of life with virtual strangers. Georgia felt guilty, knowing that she should have been more thoughtful. And where was Dominic? Surely he could have been here to give some support?

She felt the increasing strength of the sun burning on her arms as soon as she left the shade and started off down the path. Before she reached the bottom she waved to Marc, who immediately came over to her.

'How's it going?' she asked, knowing the answer, but wanting to hear it from him.

'Not well, there's no spark at all.' He scuffed his bare foot in the sand. 'It's too early to say, but we may have to think again.'

'Try working inside this afternoon. Natasha's better out of the sun. She may find it easier if she's not wrapped up like an Egyptian mummy.'

Marc nodded. 'Fine. We'll have a go.' He hesitated. 'I'm concerned about Luc. He's making her nervous.'

'Dominic wasn't happy with him from the start. Maybe we should change him.' She looked round at the group. 'Why isn't he here?'

'I haven't seen him this morning.'

Georgia frowned. Marc was too discreet to say that Dominic hadn't been there for practice the day before either. 'I'll have a word with him,' she said, 'and make sure he comes this afternoon.'

'We need you there, too, Georgia. There are decisions to be made, and you're the only one who can do it.'

She patted Marc's shoulder. 'I'll take Natasha up with me now. Shall we meet in the barn after lunch?'

Georgia beckoned to Natasha who had been watching her while she talked to Marc. She waited for the girl to walk slowly across the sand before she questioned her. 'Do you know where Dominic is?'

'He went riding in the wood,' Natasha answered sullenly. She looked up at Georgia. 'What do you want me to do?'

'Why don't you come up with me and relax out of the sun for a while? You could do with a break.' She slipped

130

her arm through Natasha's, and led her up the path. 'Let's drink something long and cool before lunch.'

'Thank you, but I'd prefer to go to my room. You're right. The sun is very hot.' Natasha pulled away and clambered ahead up the rocky slope. Georgia saw her long robe billow around her as she pushed open the gate at the top and disappeared over on to the terrace.

Before Georgia could follow her, Mathilde bustled out with a pot of steaming coffee and a bowl of fruit. 'So you are here! Late for breakfast. Dominic was looking for you.'

'I was watching the practice. I thought he would be there.'

'He missed you. He went to your room to look for you. I think he wanted to come with you to check out the team.'

Georgia sipped her coffee. Mathilde was making her feel that she was to blame. But Dominic followed her around, inventing one excuse after another to spend time alone with her away from the villa. She was only doing this for him, and while they were here she wanted to work. Was Mathilde right? Was it her fault that things weren't working out?

She would do as Marc had asked. She would go to the rehearsal that afternoon and she would do all she could to help both Dominic and Natasha. So long as they both turned up.

Natasha walked fast over the stony garden path. Looking behind her to see if Georgia was watching, she quickened her pace, crossed the rough, pebbled drive and ran out past the carved stone pillars guarding the entrance to the villa. She made her way up the lane, and took a path she knew into the woods, running until she was out of sight of the track and the house.

Here, the foliage of pine and evergreen oaks was so dense that only a few stray shafts of sunlight pierced the canopy of leaves. It was cool and quiet, and she felt safe.

131

She flung herself down on a patch of thick, mossy turf and lay motionless, too drained to do anything but rest there, too miserable even to cry. She had thought she could do this, had wanted so badly to give Dominic anything he asked of her, but since that first night he had hardly spoken to her. She had failed. Why had he brought her here simply to hurt her? He didn't want another woman. He had Georgia.

She had been determined to show him how good she could be. If he wanted a woman to perform in his club, she would show him she was the best there was. He had chosen her, so she must have pleased him somehow. But since the evening at Le Grand Marquis he had paid her no attention at all; until the bar in Marseilles he had ignored her completely.

The practice this afternoon would be her last chance, she decided. If Georgia didn't throw her out, she would leave anyway. Natasha crushed a clump of moss between her fingers. She hated the barn with its strange, painted walls and cold, shuttered darkness. But if Dominic was there, she would try. Her dancing had impressed him at the night-club, so perhaps, if she worked really hard, she could interest him again.

She rolled over on to her back, feeling the springy forest floor under her shoulder blades. It was deliciously cool, here in the shade of the trees, and she stretched out blissfully. She lifted up the annoyingly long folds of her dress and tied up the excess fabric in a knot on her hip.

As her fingers trailed over her cool thighs, stroking her skin, she wondered how it would feel to have Dominic touch her there. Her hand explored further. She was thinner than Georgia, smaller altogether, and lacking her presence and voluptuous body. If that was what Dominic wanted, she knew she had no chance. And her efforts to arouse Dominic had ended in disaster.

Dominic had wanted sex with her and she had refused. But that night, after what she had heard, she had felt too hurt to let him touch her. She would dance with him this afternoon, and she would do all she could to make him desire her again. This time she would not turn away.

The thought of him excited her; her fingers trembled now as she imagined Dominic performing with her. She curled up tighter on the ground, pushing her hand clumsily through the soft triangle of hair at the base of her belly, feeling cautiously for the sensitive lips that ached for satisfaction. Secretly, she probed deeper inside her softly padded cleft, carefully at first, then more strongly as she felt her body respond. Would she ever be able to give this much pleasure to Dominic?

She stared up through the trees, seeing the sun glint through the leaves. It dazzled her and she closed her eyes, letting the new, warm feelings wash over her.

Luc's voice startled her, and she quickly pulled her dress down over her bare legs. 'So, while you are here you comfort yourself?' he said.

Natasha's hand dropped guiltily to her side.

'Luc! Why are you here?'

'The same as you. I feel alone.'

He stretched out his hand and stroked her thigh. 'Why not let me help you?' His hand felt hot and rough on her skin. She jerked back. He still frightened her.

'Don't you like feeling a man's hand on your body?' he asked. 'You seemed to enjoy it in Marseilles. You didn't hold back then.'

'That was different. We were working.'

'Working! Is that what you call it?' The scorn in his voice shamed her. He lifted his hand towards her again, and she tensed, prepared to run away, but he didn't touch her. He simply stared at his fingers and muttered. 'You wanted me then. It was real.'

He stretched out on the mossy earth and closed his eyes. 'It isn't you he desires, you know.'

She felt the sick pain curl through her stomach again. 'What do you mean?'

'He's crazy about her. Georgia.'

'You're wrong. He brought me down here. He chose me.'

'Like you chose me.' Luc rolled over on one elbow and looked at her. 'I don't understand any of it. They offer me money, more than I earn on the ship in a year. They buy me clothes and give me a good bed, a room to myself. What are they after?'

'They have a club in Paris which makes a lot of money for them.'

'Is that where you'll work?'

Natasha nodded. She tried to look away, but Luc's eyes held her.

'You want him. That's why you're doing this. You know what you are? A bitch. A tease.' He leant over her and pushed her dress further up her thighs. She felt the heat of his body next to her as his fingers tightened on her skin.

She felt hot, and scared. She tried to calm him down. 'It's just a job. And a good one. Do you want to stay on the boats for ever? You like to live rough?'

'What do you know about that?'

'I've been hungry.'

'So now you've found a rich boy to keep you. Only he's not satisfied, is he?' Luc's hand rode up her leg, stroking her. 'And he's driving you mad.' She felt crushed by the weight of his body as he rolled over on top of her. 'I can give him cause to feel jealous, and I can make you happy.'

She hesitated. Luc's fingers felt so delicious that she didn't want to stop. If she let him go on, if she had some experience, then she might attract Dominic.

She stiffened. It wasn't fair to treat Luc like that. She had done it once and Dominic had been excited, but it hadn't worked.

Luc gripped her hard. 'What's the matter, Natasha?' he urged. 'Do you only like it when he's watching you? Do I have to wait until he's there this afternoon?'

She felt his fingers pushing into her again, and tried to

134

ignore the hot surge of desire flooding up inside her. She buried her face in his chest. 'Please Luc, don't. I love him, I want him so badly. And . . .'

'And you're a virgin.' Luc flung himself back on the turf. 'Do you think I don't know? That it's not obvious to everyone but that fool?' He scowled. 'Go and have him then. And when he's tried to satisfy you with the dregs his stepmother doesn't want, come and beg me to show you what a real man is like.'

He jumped to his feet and kicked at the rotting branches at his feet, showering her bare legs with torn clumps of moss. 'Just don't leave it too late.'

Georgia was furious. Natasha had disappeared. There had been no sign of her at lunch, and afterwards Dominic had driven off at speed without saying a word to anyone about where he was going. Now it was time for their practice session and they were both still missing.

She walked angrily towards the large barn they used for rehearsals. It was a typical building of the area, of sun-bleached, blue-washed, local stone with a tiled roof. Inside, it had been transformed. Olivier had ordered the high walls to be painted with pure white lilies on a dense, burgundy-coloured background, their massive, green stems writhing and curling down to the base of the bare, dried-mud floor. Grotesque flower trumpets, twenty foot high, shone in opalescent white on the red-brown wash of the walls, sending their stamens cascading over the ceiling, through and over the ancient black-ened beams.

The barn was perfect for training the boys in the sort of heady atmosphere where they would eventually work, although Olivier had preferred to use it for private sessions with Georgia. Practice that usually turned into love-making on the rich Persian carpet that covered the centre of the room.

Today the windows were firmly shuttered against the strong Provençal light, and only two massive candles, held on tall, wrought-iron columns, illuminated the arena.

The room appeared empty, but a strong beat of music pulsed through the air. As Georgia pushed the barn door further open, and her eyes became accustomed to the semi-darkness, she saw Dominic sitting high up in the long gallery that ran the length of one wall. He wore the plain, black cotton shirt and loose trousers that all the team used for rehearsals.

Georgia felt a surge of relief. Now, if only Natasha would turn up, the afternoon might be a success. She sat down beside Dominic on a narrow bench, and waited. She could smell fresh lilies. She thought that her senses were playing tricks on her, until she saw great baskets of the flowers placed in each corner of the room. Had Dominic put them there? Was that where he had been? At the flower market? She wanted to thank him, but before she could do so, Marc led the team into the centre of the room, and held the heavy wooden door open as Natasha slipped in behind them.

Dressed in a plain white tunic, she looked totally incapable of coping with these huge young men. Georgia shifted uncomfortably on the bench, wondering why she had ever permitted Dominic to bring the girl here. Natasha remained outside the circle. She was staring around her at the big, old room, and she looked alone and frightened.

Georgia tried to catch Marc's eye, but he was concentrating on the team. She sat down again and leant against the wall. It was only fair to give Natasha her last chance. Marc had every right to feel pleased with his team; the boys were magnificent.

Suddenly Natasha seemed to gather strength. She began her performance confidently. Georgia was impressed by the way that she now seemed more in control of the men, even Luc, although he still looked as if at any moment he would overpower her. Don't choose him, Georgia prayed, willing Natasha to turn away from him. Don't make him a favourite. But she had to admit that the emotion between them made the act even more exhilarating.

The darkness was intense, with little light coming from the two flaming candles. Once again, Georgia felt that she was intruding, becoming a voyeur; it was strange for her not to be the centre of attention. Natasha was managing to fill the room with her presence, and her fragile hold on the men was electrifying. Georgia watched intently, prepared at any moment to call a halt if the girl was in danger.

Georgia slid forward on the slippery wooden bench. Natasha was moving into her rhythm now, steadily taunting each man until the tension in the room reached fever pitch. She had chosen two of her three men.

Marc leant against the wall; he was smiling. Then Georgia saw him lean forward anxiously, and she followed his gaze. Natasha had stopped in front of Luc; her fingers trailed over his broad chest. She took one more step towards him so that their bodies were almost touching. Swiftly, silently, on bare feet, Marc paced round the outside of the circle. Georgia hoped that he would stop Natasha. She must not choose Luc again.

She felt Dominic's thigh pressing against her as he sat uncomfortably close on the bench. He slipped his arm around her shoulders in what could be interpreted as a friendly gesture, if anyone had been able to look up and see them in the darkness of the high gallery. Only Georgia could feel the pressure of his finger against the curve of her breast. Damn him. If she moved away now, it would be obvious to everyone what he was trying to do.

Natasha's ghost-pale figure undulated to the insistent beat of the music, like a wan, fragile version of the monstrous lilies on the wall. Her head was bowed, level with Luc's chest. For a moment she lost her rhythm, then she stepped forward.

Dominic shifted in his seat. 'You see, Georgia? She's

doing well. Watch her.' He shouted out loud, his voice echoing through the barn.

Natasha lowered her arms. They fell by her side as she moved back from Luc, and circled the group again. She looked up at Dominic, then turned away, her steps faltering. Natasha stood motionless now, fixed in the centre of the room beside the two prone figures of the boys she had already chosen. Her small figure seemed like a petal, fallen from one of the lilies.

Dominic rose to his feet. He climbed slowly down the narrow staircase. His eyes scornfully raked the room before resting on Natasha's frozen body. Arrogantly he leant against one wall, his body covering one thick green stem, his eyes fixed on her pale figure. He held out his hand and pulled her towards him. She moved listlessly in front of him.

Georgia wondered why they couldn't reproduce the magic they had achieved on the stage in Paris; there was not a trace of that excitement left in their movements together. Dominic loomed menacingly over the girl; he looked rough, almost brutal, and yet there was none of the passion that Luc demonstrated.

She leant over the gallery rail and called out. 'What the hell is wrong with you two? You were so good. Why can't you do it again?'

'Come and show her how,' Dominic taunted from the centre of the room.

He thrust Natasha aside and started to climb back up the staircase. Georgia felt trapped. She was sitting at the far end of the long gallery. There was no way she could get out without pushing past Dominic, and he was blocking the way. He held out his hand.

'Now, Georgia,' he insisted. 'Natasha needs your help. Come and show her how it's done.'

Perhaps she could do something. If she could persuade Dominic to try the solo dance with Natasha as he had done in Paris, it might give Natasha the confidence she needed. And if she had to do it first, that was a small price to pay.

She had not prepared herself to work this afternoon. She was wearing a faded, cotton dress, which still gave her pleasure, although its vibrant, topaz colour had washed out long ago. It tied loosely at the front, and was cool and comfortable, but it was totally unsuitable for a rehearsal.

She slipped out of her espadrilles at the foot of the stairs, and stepped on to the rug. She had never practised with any of these men and, although she had watched them with Natasha, she knew nothing of their response to her, or how she would feel about them. There were always one or two men every year whom she treated with special caution.

It would be best to limit her work to showing Natasha a couple of movements that she had found effective in arousing her audience. She could do that quickly, and then return to a safe distance.

She walked into the centre of the room. 'Look, Natasha,' she said. 'Sometimes it's easier if you start like this.'

She moved slowly round the circle, looking into each man's eyes, reaching up to run her fingers down the base of their throats, and down over their chests, assessing their reactions as she gently ran her long fingernails over their small, stiffened nipples.

Luc pulled back imperceptibly as she touched him, but he could not hide his response. Swiftly Georgia placed her hand over his swollen penis and held him firmly. She looked up into his eyes to warn him, and met an unflinching, arrogant gaze. He raised his arms to her neck, thrust his huge, seaman's hands inside her cotton top, and ran his fingers over her breasts.

Georgia shivered as she felt him touch her. With half her mind she knew that this was exactly the way the performance should go, that her initial reaction to Luc was right, he was exciting. Her other response was more basic; she didn't care how an audience might feel, all she wanted was for him to hold her. He was refusing to be controlled, and she loved it.

But now she had to restrain him. Icily calm, she stepped back, and released her hold on his throbbing penis. Instantly, he let her go, and took his place in the circle. Her breasts were fully exposed now, and she sensed the heightened tension as she moved on to the next man. Again, she raised her arms to his throat, stroking his smooth skin. She looked up into his eyes, and saw Dominic.

No one moved on the floor of the barn. Marc stood outside the circle, behind Luc. They were all watching her. Dominic moved a step forward, and pulled her bare breasts hard against his chest. She stopped dead, and took a deep breath.

Dominic's shirt was tucked into his black trousers. He tore it off, threw it to one side, and stood in front of her, naked to the waist, his lean hips solid and still.

Now her body refused to obey her brain's commands. It felt so sweet to move in such harmony with another human being, that she could not, would not move away. She lost all track of time, feeling her juices flowing and her muscles expanding, ready to accept a man.

Abruptly she drew back. Where was Natasha? Why couldn't she do this with Dominic? Why couldn't she claim him for her own? Georgia did not want this torment.

'Enough, Dominic. Enough.' She pushed him away from her.

Dominic put his hands on her shoulders. He wrapped one thigh round her body, forcing her down on to him; his fingers cupped her buttocks, crushing her against him. She fought for control, looked round for Marc to help her. What was Dominic trying to do? Take her in front of the whole team?

But the room was empty. She had not seen them go, but the door was now shut tight and she was alone with

Dominic. A pattern of green stems flashed in front of her eyes. Fresh lilies, fallen from an upturned basket, scented the air.

She wanted to give in, to let Dominic take her. She felt the thick stem of his manhood pressing against her, as the heat rose between her thighs.

The door swung open, and she saw Luc outlined against the light. For a moment he stood still, and Georgia felt his gaze burn through her contemptuously. 'Natasha's gone,' he said. 'I thought you should know.'

For a moment longer, he stared at them arrogantly, then he turned and walked across the yard in the blazing sunshine. Dominic's fingers never ceased their pressure, but Georgia pulled away. She closed her eyes. 'We have to look for Natasha. You can't let her leave here like this.'

'Forget her. She's always going off into the woods. She was there today, with Luc.'

'With Luc? How do you know?'

'I saw them. Natasha isn't the young innocent you imagine. She seems to know exactly how to behave with a man.'

The beat of the music pulsed through the air. The gramophone would stop soon, and she couldn't bear to move to turn it off.

She had been mad to agree to practise with Dominic, and a fool to ignore all the warnings her body had given her. She wanted him. What point was there in denying it? Her body ached for sex; she was on fire.

She felt his hands grasp her shoulders again. She arched her back as his hands slid over her, cupping her breasts; she felt sweet honey moistening her sex. His fingers slipped down inside her thighs, pulling her legs apart. She moaned, and then cried out, as the full length of his hard penis thrust deep inside her.

'Oh God,' she moaned. She moved with him, longing for him to lose control too. She felt his body tense, then with a wild cry he drove harder and harder into her, like

141

an animal taking its mate. It had been so long, so long. As she heard his shout of release, she called out 'Olivier.'

Georgia felt Dominic draw back at the sound of his father's name. Slowly, his fingers released their hold on her breasts and slid down her belly until his thumbs dug into the swell of her hips.

She shivered in his arms, but he held her fast. The pressure of his hands increased, twisting her until she faced him, her breasts an inch from his chest, so close that she could feel the heat of his skin on her outstretched nipples. His still engorged cock stood out proudly, brushing her damp mound as his breath rose and fell.

'Look at me.' His voice was harsh.

Georgia felt too weak to lift her heavy lids and look into his eyes.

'Look at me,' he said, more softly now. 'Look at me, Georgia.'

Reluctantly she opened her eyes, raising her head until she saw straight into his bronze depths. His gaze never wavered as the whole, hard length of his body reared over her, with the head of his penis touching her quivering sex, stroking but not entering. His thumbs pressed over her hip-bones, moulding her flesh against his.

As he knelt over her, she longed to feel him inside her again, but the smooth, swollen head of his penis pressed on her vulva without entering. She felt the sweat gathering between her breasts as his fingers played with her rigid nipples, taking them between his soft pads until she moaned in ecstasy.

His face was shadowed in the darkness, as he lowered his head and took each aching nipple between his hot, firm lips. She felt his tongue rasping against her swollen ridges as he sucked on the stiffened buds, first gently, then more insistently. She writhed beneath him, seeking to enclose him, to feel that pulsing, throbbing probe enter deep inside her as she had felt him before.

He raised his head and gazed into her eyes, holding her arms spread-eagled at her sides. She lay, transfixed, beneath him, feeling the weight of his body lower on to her, and the swollen head of his penis steadily, insistently, pushing deep into her quivering hole.

Deeper and deeper he came until he filled her totally, and still he pressed in. She gasped as his entry seemed unending, then felt her hips rise to take him still further. For one long moment, he lay unmoving inside her, letting her feel the throbbing force that had entered her, then he drew back, only to drive down hard into her once more. She cried out, powerless beneath his pounding rhythm, her hips moulded against his, her thighs parted wide as he thrust again and again, until she shuddered beneath him in a wild pulse of black energy.

His lips never left hers; his body never ceased the insistent thrust which forced her further and further into an unending swirl of sensation. His body was her master now as he pumped into her, until she no longer knew when one wave of pleasure melted into another.

Later, much later, she lay in his arms, his hands clasped tightly around her, holding her to him. She saw his long lashes outlined against the sweet curve of his cheek, and brushed back the thick fall of his dark hair, feeling the cool, smooth strands pass through her fingers.

Her body throbbed from his passionate love-making, and yet she longed for him again. Her body seemed out of her control, as her hips quivered against his with an almost imperceptible rhythm that seemed answered by his semi-conscious flesh. For hours they lay half-asleep, half-awake, clinging to each other on the floor of the barn.

His body seemed an extension of hers, part of her, to use freely, at will. Her face was buried in his warm young chest and his thighs were wrapped around her, enclosing her. She breathed in the sweet smell of a virile, young male, and the odour of sated sex that scented their entwined bodies.

She was scarcely conscious when, sometime during the night, he picked her up and carried her across the dark courtyard, up the stairs and into her bed.

Chapter Eleven

Georgia woke alone in the bed. Half-asleep, she rolled over on to her side, and reached out her hand for Dominic, dimly searching for the presence which had formed part of her existence since the previous night. She would have thought it had been a dream except for the persistent throbbing inside her, the sweet ache of fulfilment.

The door opened and she saw Dominic, a black silk dressing-gown hanging from his shoulders, outlined against the light beaming in through the doorway. He padded across the room and placed a tray on the bedside table. Georgia smelled the mingled fragrance of strong coffee, hot bread and sun-warmed fruit.

He sat beside her, trailing the tips of his fingers over her naked breasts as he bent to kiss her. He laughed as she reached up for him, and he caught her hands in his, pressing them to his lips.

What a fool she had been to wait so long. This was the man she was made for; the partner who could satisfy her as no other. As he leant over her she felt that she was drowning, aware of his body close to hers, fulfilling a need she had denied for too long.

'Taste this. It's delicious.' Dominic pressed a thick slice

144

of fresh peach between her lips. When a trickle of juice slid down her chin, he bent over her and parted her lips, licking the drops from her skin.

'Coffee?' he asked. 'Or champagne?'

Georgia stretched out her hand for a cup of coffee. 'This is what I need right now.' She stroked the back of his hand lightly. He was so beautiful. How foolish she had been to try to resist him.

'Natasha has left us,' he said smoothly, rising and walking over to the window.

'Left? Where has she gone?'

'Marc took her to Antibes last night. He thought she was going to catch the train, and he wanted to wait and see her safely aboard, but she told him she was meeting someone first.'

'I didn't know she had friends here.'

'Natasha seems capable of surprising us all, occasionally.' Dominic came over and sat beside Georgia on the bed.

'What about Marc? Has he told anyone about Natasha?'

Dominic looked unconcerned as he leant over her. 'Marc has said nothing. The team is practising as usual. I've told the boys that you're having a day off, and after that you will be rehearsing with them. They know it wasn't working out with her.' He stroked the long curve of her spine, calming her. His dressing-gown fell open, exposing his smooth young chest. Gently, he took the coffee cup from her hand and set it down on the bedside table.

'You're the one who interests me,' he said, as he drew back the sheet and ran the tip of one finger along the line of her hip-bone, over her belly and down between her thighs.

The sun was high when they finished making love. Guiltily, Georgia realised that they had completely ignored Marc and the team. What must they be thinking? She sat up in bed, wrapping the sheet around her. She could hear Mathilde out in the garden, clanking dishes noisily as she laid the table for lunch.

Lunch! Georgia felt a chill of alarm at the thought of lunch on the terrace with Marc, Mathilde and the team. They would all know that Dominic had spent the night in her room. One look at her would tell them everything. And she wasn't ready for that yet.

'I can't go down.' She felt sick with panic.

'Why ever not? They have to find out sometime. Why do you want to keep it a secret?' Dominic looked unconcerned as he lay back on the pillow, his eyes half-closed. It wouldn't matter to him, of course. She was the one who would feel ashamed.

'Just for a day or two, Dominic, until I get used to the idea,' she pleaded.

'Is it so hard to accept that I'm your lover?' He opened his eyes and stared at her coldly.

She reached out for him and wrapped her arms around his neck. 'I still can't believe it. I've been very stupid, haven't I?'

'You think so?' He kissed the soft skin on the inside of her wrist. 'I asked Mathilde to prepare a picnic basket for us. We can drive along the coast and spend some time on our own.'

She felt an overwhelming sense of relief. 'That would be perfect.'

He pulled on a pair of cotton slacks and a loose shirt that he had brought with him. 'I'll go and pack up the car,' he said.

She lay back on the bed for a moment after he left the room. He did understand, after all. It would be so much easier for her, later on. She chose a cool, cotton shift in her favourite aquamarine, and picked out a new swim-suit to take with her.

Georgia felt an intruder in her own house as she descended the staircase. Thank heavens Dominic had gone on ahead. She began to believe that she had worried unnecessarily. Perhaps everyone thought that Dominic

146

had brought up her breakfast, and no more than that. There was no reason for them to know that he had spent the night in her bed. And maybe the glow in her cheeks came from weeks of sunshine and rest, not from the attentions of a wonderful young lover.

No one was in sight. The stairs and hall were deserted and there was no sound from the kitchen. Briskly she crossed the hall. The heavy pine front door was wide open, and she could see Dominic outside in the sun, leaning against the car.

He drove fast along the coast road, and Georgia was exhilarated by the speed, the wind blowing through her hair, and the sight of Dominic's long, tanned fingers on the steering wheel. To their right, the sea was a continuous, blue crescent beyond the ribbon of sand, their view broken only by the trunks of palm trees as they flashed past.

Dominic pulled into a lay-by off the main road. He led her up to a secluded spot on the cliff top and spread out a rug. Mathilde had filled the basket with food and wine, but Georgia had the feeling, as she took out cold chicken, a baguette and some fruit, that it had not been done with love. Was she imagining that less care had been taken than normal, and that Mathilde was annoyed with her? She could not say so to Dominic; he would think that she was paranoid, and she felt too relaxed to worry much about it now as she lay in the sun with him.

There was a bottle of chilled Chablis in Mathilde's basket, and Dominic poured her a glass as she stared out at the sea. He sat beside her, his fingers resting lightly on her bare knees. She felt as if her body existed only for him. Up here, on the cliff top, only the two of them mattered.

She looked at his bronzed face, at the smooth dark column of his throat rising from his open-necked white shirt, and reached out to stroke his powerfully muscled arms, bare to the line of his rolled-up sleeves. His skin was so young and smooth, the flesh firm to her touch.

147

He rolled over on his side towards her and lifted her thin, blue shift over her head. She lay quietly beneath him as he slipped off her lace pants and threw them on the sandy grass. She watched him strip out of his white shirt and light cotton trousers, freeing his beautiful body of all restrictions until he lay naked beside her.

He smelled of the fresh grass and pine needles that were crushed beneath him, as he stroked the soft, inner flesh of her thighs, gently kneading her sex lips between his thumb and forefinger until she stirred slightly and lifted her hips so that his fingers slipped further inside her. She saw the first sheen of sweat glisten on his skin as he sought the warm bud of her clitoris and felt it swell at his touch.

A deep languor spread all through her body as the rhythm of his fingers quickened and he raised himself over her. She waited as if in a trance for the head of his penis to find the rich source of pleasure he had prepared, writhing beneath him as his smooth warm tip parted her eager lips and entered her.

For a moment he lay over her, completely still, except for the pulsing heat of his manhood. Then she felt the full force of his throbbing erection leap up inside her as he crushed her into the ground. He held her wrists wide apart as he thrust into her with all the powerful strength of his lean hips. She felt drugged by her joy, conscious only of the urgent needs of her flesh and Dominic's hot breath on her lips as he called out her name and shuddered at his climax.

She stroked his dark hair, its auburn lights glinting in the glare of the sun, as he lay spent beside her, his arm thrown heavily over her breasts. There was a desperation, an urgency in his love-making that overwhelmed her. She had been cruel to deny him for so long. He needed her as much as she needed him.

Later in the day, in one of the villages, they found a small café for a light supper, and lingered at their table, reluctant to end the evening. The courtyard was in darkness when they returned, except for a crack of light showing under the barn door.

'Should we see what they're doing?' she asked.

Dominic put his arms around her and led her towards the house. 'I want to take you to bed,' he murmured. 'We can check them out another time.'

A week flashed by, a week full of sun and love and laughter. Dominic seemed to have endless excuses for Georgia to miss rehearsals, and she was far too happy in his company to care. So what if Marc and Mathilde openly showed their disapproval? Georgia felt content to spend each day alone with Dominic.

And where was Natasha? A note had arrived, stating briefly that she was well, with friends, and they were not to worry – she would take the opportunity to have her fitting with Schiaparelli.

Georgia expected to hear from Raoul. Was he so angry with her that he would say nothing? She had lost a friend. If she had accepted Dominic at the beginning, Raoul would have understood. But now, because she had encouraged Natasha, and then hurt her, he would never forgive her.

Each morning they ate alone on her bedroom terrace, and most days they drove out along the coast and found a peaceful bay where they could lie in the sun. Georgia hadn't worn anything other than a swimsuit or a sundress for a week. Her skin was really tanned, her hair dry and out of condition, and her feet rough and scratched. A quick shower before breakfast that particular morning hadn't helped. She needed a day in a beauty salon.

Georgia pushed away her coffee and stared down at her bare toenails.

'What's the matter?' Dominic bit into a fig and followed her gaze.

'My feet are a mess.'

'Your feet are perfect.' Dominic picked them up and

149

laid them in his lap. They were still damp from her shower and she saw a few drops of water trickle over his bare thighs. As always, when he touched her, she experienced a rush of desire for him.

She wanted to feel beautiful for him. 'I need to go to Antibes,' she told him. 'Just for a few hours on my own. Would you mind?'

'Of course I'd mind. There's no need.' He held out his arms and waited for her to come to him.

'Now,' he said. 'Lie down on the bed and tell me what to do.'

His hands stroked her skin. 'You've become a sun-worshipper,' he murmured, 'and your tan is lovely.'

He poured drops of soothing oil over her breasts and smoothed it in, circling round and over her shoulders and down, over her ribs to her belly. She wanted him to stop working and make love to her again, but he was taking his task seriously, kneading her flesh between his strong fingers until every inch of her body felt soft and sleek.

He took her hand in his and gently spread her fingers wide as he opened a new jar of topaz varnish and started to paint each nail with long, sweeping strokes. While the first layer dried, he took her toes and coloured each tip with a bright, shiny coat.

The arch of her foot pressed against his hard, flat stomach as he worked, bending over her in total concentration until each nail was perfect. Then he laid her back on the bed.

'You have to let them dry now,' he murmured, as he took first one breast and then the other into his hands, stroking them as if he knew exactly how his touch had excited her. She could feel him breathing in her perfume as he teased her nipples into rigid peaks, his skin cool and smooth against her scented flesh.

'Don't move,' he said, as he covered her with his body, the tip of his penis sliding into her eager sex, his dark eyes burning into hers as he waited for her response.

Steadily he rode on top of her, holding her down as he stared into her eyes, watching every movement of her body as he pleasured her.

He pushed her back as she rose instinctively against him. 'Lie still,' he ordered. 'Let me do this.'

She felt his hair falling over her throat as he bent again to suckle on her swollen nipples, biting them gently between his teeth as his tongue rasped on her sensitive flesh. The pressure increased as she trembled beneath him, her hips locked against his as he climbed higher inside her. His powerful penis filled her as he thrust deeper and deeper into her sex, while his teeth nibbled on her breasts until she cried out in pain.

And yet she didn't want him to stop. She loved his need for her, and the way he cried out as he drove into her. Her nipples ached where he had taken them between his teeth, and she gasped when he bit on them once more. And then he pulled back and knelt over her, his penis trailing over her vulva as he stared deep into her eyes. She writhed beneath him, her thighs parting instinctively to take him into her again.

She saw him smile as his hips lowered once more, and he thrust into her. Nothing could stop her coming now. She felt a wild joy as she realised how much he wanted her. She climaxed as she felt him come, rising with him as her own orgasm washed over her. He said her name over and over again as he buried his face between her breasts, and she put her arms around him and stroked him as he drifted into sleep.

It seemed hours later when Georgia woke to see Dominic across the room, checking through the racks of clothes in her cupboard. 'What are you doing?' she called out sleepily.

'Choosing something for you to wear for lunch.' He held out the apricot pyjamas she had bought in Paris. 'These will be perfect,' he said. 'We are going to Antibes for lunch, my darling. I want to show you off.'

'The Meurice?' Georgia felt a cold chill at the thought of Antibes' smartest restaurant.

She felt his lips softly touch her forehead as he murmured. 'You always look wonderful. You will be the most beautiful woman there.'

She let Dominic brush her hair into a cloud of black curls as she sat on the balcony in a pool of sunlight. When he was satisfied, he kissed the top of her head. Her hair felt warm and fluffy, and he was right – she did feel beautiful. But she was still nervous about the hotel.

She had learnt to ignore Marc and Mathilde's pointed looks, and the bewildered glances from the team, but a fashionable restaurant was quite another thing, especially The Meurice. It was bound to be full of people who knew her. Why couldn't they simply go on as they had done this last week? Wasn't being alone with her enough for him any more?

Dominic slipped the bright, satiny blouse over her shoulders, caressing the back of her neck as he fastened the starfish buttons. 'So, we are ready,' he laughed, 'and you look magnificent.' He took her by the arm and led her down to the car.

Antibes was swarming with summer visitors and the streets were crowded. As they neared the hotel, Georgia saw a slim figure slip past a corner, a streak of violet and cream, snaking through the crowd, no more than a splash of colour against the sun-faded walls. Georgia twisted round to see more clearly. Somehow the figure reminded her of Natasha, but she could not be sure. When she looked again, there was no sign of the girl. She must be mistaken. Natasha was in Paris.

The conversation hushed as they entered the foyer, but she soon realised it wasn't her they were admiring; all the women's eyes were fastened on Dominic. They sat in the terrace restaurant, poised on a rocky cliff top looking out over the bay. She felt more alive than she had done for months, delighted to realise how good she felt to be with him, and what fun it was to see the other women's envy.

To her horror she recognised Maxine. Georgia had forgotten her threat to come to the Riviera. Normally they would have met before this at one of the countless social events that took place during the summer, but this had not been a normal year. Maxine leant forward in her chair, looking interested; Sergio seemed less pleased to see them, especially when Maxine left him and walked across the room towards them.

Georgia watched indignantly as she trailed her fingers round the back of Dominic's neck. 'We meet again, darling. I'm surprised we haven't bumped into each other before. You must have been busy.'

This was exactly what Georgia had feared.

Dominic removed Maxine's cerise-painted nails from the back of his neck. 'We've found it delightful to be on our own,' he murmured. 'Now, will you excuse us if we continue with our meal?'

Maxine looked hard at him, then turned away and moved back to her husband. Georgia felt concerned. 'Darling, she's a client. You shouldn't have been so rude.' And yet she had loved his arrogant response. It was time that Maxine was put in her place.

Dominic was studying the menu. 'Will you allow me to order for you?'

Georgia was used to having her food chosen; it was something that had always given Olivier pleasure. Dominic was like his father in so many ways.

He chose well. A terrine of tiny fish in aspic quivered on the plate in front of her. Dominic leant forward, speared one silver sliver with his fork, and offered it to her.

'They should be delicious,' he informed her. 'I hope you like them.'

The grilled lobster that followed, steaming hot and dripping with butter, was cooked to perfection, but Dominic seemed to lose interest by the time the *pêches*

Melba appeared. He finished it quickly with little sign of enjoyment.

'Quick,' he said. 'Let's go.'

Georgia licked the last scoop of ice-cream off her spoon. 'What do you have in mind?'

'A beach. There's a place I haven't taken you yet. First we'll lie in the sun, then swim, and when we can wait no longer, I shall make love to you in the water. I want you now.'

She wanted him, too. If he had stretched out his hand then, she would have lain down on the floor and let him do anything he liked. Thank God he was prepared to wait.

She went quickly to the Ladies room, while he paid the bill. Checking in the mirror, she brushed her hair and revived her lipstick. Georgia decided that perhaps Dominic's compliments were not as far out as she had thought. She did look good. Maxine had every reason to feel envious. Quickly replacing her make-up in her bag, she went out to the main staircase to look for Dominic.

Maxine was with him, talking with great animation. To her relief, Georgia saw that he was looking bored and impatient. It was a joy to see the spark return to his eyes when he caught sight of her. He brushed Maxine away rudely and took Georgia's arm.

'What did Maxine want?' she asked.

'She was telling me more about the party she wants us to go to. I said we'd think about it.' He changed the subject. 'I told you that you would be the most beautiful woman here. I was very proud.'

She could not prevent a rosy flush of pleasure spreading to her cheeks, as he led her down the hotel steps and out to the car.

The Bugatti purred along the coast road, until Dominic turned off down a narrow dirt track. Georgia's heart sank. Not here, she thought, please not here. She opened her mouth to speak to him, to suggest some other place. Any other place.

But he turned to her enthusiastically.

'Do you know this beach?' he asked. 'I've been here before so many times. Always alone. I knew it was where I wanted to bring you.' His fingers lingered on the open neck of her blouse. 'You know how long I wanted you?' His head bent over her exposed breasts. 'And now we're together. This is what you want, isn't it?'

She tried to calm her doubts She couldn't explain to him how she felt about this place.

'Yes.' She put her arms around his neck. 'Yes, darling, it's what I want.'

At the foot of the path he jumped down on to the sandy beach and held out his hand to help her follow him. She had taken off her smart kid shoes and stood barefoot now. The apricot satin of her trousers flapped round her ankles, matching the bright varnish on her painted nails.

She hesitated, and saw him frown as his hands dropped to his side.

'It's him, isn't it? You're thinking of my father. Is that how it's been all the time?'

'No.' She wanted to reassure him and stepped awkwardly off the rock on to the hot sand, catching the fine fabric under her heel. 'It's simply this place, Dominic, just this one place.'

He had been so kind to her, so gentle. Surely he would understand? It had been such a wonderful day until now. But he was impatient. He caught her arm and pulled her towards him, tearing the extravagant suit slightly as he tried to lift it over her shoulders. She drew back abruptly, feeling exposed, here on the beach. It was as if the thought of her fine clothes being ruined, that he had the power to do that, excited him. Was he already so bored with her that he had to play games?

He wouldn't listen to her. He walked fast across the sand to the shoreline and stared out at the sea with his back turned against her. She ran after him and put her arms around his waist but he shook her off.

Every year since they had first found this place, it had become a ritual for Olivier to bring her here after lunch at The Meurice. How strange that Dominic should have had the same thought. Surely he could understand that she wanted to keep one place special? She started to feel angry towards him, and then he turned round and she saw his face. His eyes were cold and creased with pain. He still didn't trust her and he was wrong. She loved him so much. She had to prove it to him.

Her fingers fumbled with her buttons as she pulled her blouse off over her head, then dropped the trousers on to the sand. She was naked beneath the suit as he liked her to be. She stepped in front of him, lifted her arms to his throat and undid each button on his shirt. He stood, unmoving, staring past her far out to the horizon.

'Dominic, listen to me. It's you I want. Only you.' She was frightened. He looked as if he couldn't see her, although her actions had aroused him. As she lowered his trousers, his penis sprang out fully erect and yet he made no move towards her. His arms hung loosely at his side with the fists clenched into rigid, white-knuckled balls.

'This bay reminds you of him, doesn't it? Will you always think of him, wherever we are? Has my father been in your thoughts each time we made love?'

'No, no Dominic.' He was wrong. That had all changed for her. He was the one who filled her days and her nights. She reached out for him and kissed his bare chest. He looked so beautiful, standing naked on the edge of the sand with the sea lapping over his bare feet. She wanted to show him how much she loved him.

She dropped to her knees in the shallow water in front of him, and buried her face in the dark nest of soft curls at his groin. The heady scent of a virile young male intoxicated her as she pressed her cheek against the

156

strength of his manhood. Her tongue darted out to lick the ridged stem of his penis, flickering over the flesh which had taken over her body and dominated her mind. She felt it stir at her touch and opened her lips to take him fully into her mouth. The smooth swollen head of his powerful cock tasted sweet and exciting as her tongue rolled around his engorged shaft, revelling in his urgent, uncontrolled response to her increasing desire.

Her fingers curved around the hard, smooth contours of his buttocks as she took him deeper into her mouth, sucking more fiercely as she felt him push into her. She stroked the palms of her hands over his back, sliding her nails gently into the cleft between his cheeks, feeling him tense at her touch. His hard, muscled thighs pressed against her rigid nipples as her tongue flickered over the sensitive tip of his powerful organ. Her lips worked faster over the silky smooth head in a rhythm which was echoed by her own need, the hot ache which burned inside her. She longed to feel his strength satisfy the lust which rose fiercely in her sex but he was coming too strongly now to hold back. His warm hands gripped her shoulders as he groaned in ecstasy and a surge of sweet, salty semen flooded over her.

She closed her eyes as he put his arms around her and lay on the sand beside her. All the tension had left him. Did he finally trust her now? She felt the comfort of his strong arms holding her as the sun beat down on the two of them, but the day had been spoilt for her, and she felt sad and alone as he slept.

'Dominic.' He didn't move.

She let a handful of sand trickle over his flat stomach, tracing circles with the tip of one painted nail. He was as appealing as a child asleep in the sun. In these last few weeks he had erased almost all her sad memories. The coast, the woods, the town, everywhere that had been tinged with sadness now reminded her of Dominic. And now even here, this private beach that she had thought known only to Olivier and her, had become his. She would have come here with no other man.

'Dominic.' She raised her voice, bit gently on one dark brown nipple. She moved her head lower and pushed out the tip of her tongue to touch the end of his penis. Perhaps if he made love to her now, the dark thoughts which filled her would ease. She slid one leg over his thigh, raising herself to her knees and knelt poised over his stirring penis, waiting for him to take her again.

He opened his eyes sleepily and stared up at her. He reached out for his shirt. 'We're late. We should be going.' He picked up her crumpled suit and threw it over to her. 'I'll buy you another one,' he said, kissing the top of her head and pulling her to her feet. He took both her hands in his, twirled her round fast on the sand, throwing back his head and laughing out loud with pleasure before he took her in his arms and carried her over the sand, up the rocky path to the car.

'Did you enjoy the day?' Dominic asked her as they drove back to the villa.

Georgia forced a smile. 'Of course I did,' she assured him. She had loved her lunch at The Meurice, revelling in the envious stares from the other women in the restaurant. But, overshadowing that, the afternoon on the beach had unsettled her. Could they ever be free of Olivier's shadow? She stroked the back of Dominic's neck, letting the sensitive pads of her fingers absorb the warmth of his skin, the slightly gritty, sandy, saltiness of his hair.

Her memories were harming their relationship. She should feel thrilled that this beautiful young man loved and wanted her. It was understandable that he should need reassurance. Maybe she could persuade Mathilde to give them dinner on the balcony, just the two of them. Mathilde didn't approve of their affair, but she liked them out of the way, so she might be persuaded.

'So you are looking forward to tonight?' he asked.

He was even thinking the same thoughts. 'Oh yes, just the two of us.'

'Two?' Dominic slammed his foot down hard on the accelerator. 'Two? What do you mean?'

'I thought we'd eat upstairs.'

'Georgia, have you forgotten? Maxine invited us to her party.'

'A party? Tonight?'

'Of course tonight. She mentioned it when she came to our table to say hello.'

Georgia hadn't really been listening to the conversation. She had been concentrating on Maxine's arm resting on Dominic's shoulder and the predatory gleam in her eye. And Maxine had never been a friend of hers. But the invitation had only been given today; there was no obligation to attend. 'We don't have to go,' she wailed.

'Of course we don't. But I want to, don't you? I want to be seen as the man escorting the most beautiful woman on the Riviera. And I know just the dress you will wear.'

He was driving far too fast down the narrow track towards the villa, raising a cloud of dust behind the car. So, instead of an evening at home, she would have to spend at least the next two hours getting ready, and then most of the night at a party she didn't want to go to.

Dominic screeched to a halt, leapt out of the car and opened her door. He looked fresh and excited, and she felt mean at the thought of dampening his enthusiasm. Of course he would enjoy a party. It would be spectacular; Maxine's soirées always were, and this summer must have seemed quiet for him. How could she be so thoughtless? 'Of course we'll go,' she told him.

She hoped Dominic would choose a new gown she had ordered from Chanel. It flattered her face and her figure, and she thought it was exactly what she needed for tonight.

His decision, after her shower, shocked her; the Patou

crêpe de Chine she had worn at The Ritz was far too revealing. The low-cut bodice dipped deeply between her breasts, over-emphasising their size and shape; the skirt was slim and straight, with high slits down the front and back. She wanted to wear something elegant and discreet for her first social occasion with Dominic, not this frivolous froth. And it reminded her too forcibly of her night with Jean.

But Dominic adored it. 'It's gorgeous. There won't be another woman at the party in anything like it.'

'That's the problem,' she moaned. Why couldn't he understand? It was too blatantly sexual.

Dominic gently lifted the towel from her body. He turned her round to face the mirror, holding the dress up in front of her. 'There,' he said. 'It's perfect for you. Will you wear it for me?' He looked so eager. And she had promised him he could choose.

She had always loved sexy clothes, but this was so outrageous, the way that it emphasised the size of her breasts and left little to the imagination. She would love to wear it for dinner in Paris with Dominic, alone, but for one of Maxine's parties it made her uncomfortable.

Her hair had suffered from the sea and the sun. And at least half the guests would be flying in from Paris for the night, looking chic and sophisticated. She would have to try to capture her flyaway curls into some sort of smooth chignon. It wasn't going to be easy.

And her skin. She liked her tan; it made her look healthy, but after a day in the sun it was too vivid and not at all fashionable. Although a few women came back bronzed after the summer, copying Coco Chanel, most Parisiennes maintained a lily-white complexion.

Later, when she was dressed and almost ready to go, she felt his hands run over her bare shoulder blades as he watched her standing in front of the mirror. 'Do you really think this will do, Dominic?'

'No, not quite.'

She felt an overwhelming relief, quickly dispelled by

his next action. He slid the dress up over her thighs and slid his fingers inside the waistband of her knickers, sliding them off together with her stockings and suspenders.

'I want you naked underneath, waiting for me.' He crushed the flimsy scraps of lace in one hand and threw them on to the chair. Without stockings, her feet felt strange in her delicate, satin sandals, and the dress seemed even more unsuitable for a formal evening.

Dominic had no such fears. 'You look sensational, darling.'

That was not how she felt when they arrived at the party. Lights from Maxine's villa shone for half a mile down the coast. Cars coming from all directions blocked the road near the gateway, where two flaming torches, nine feet high, blazed into the night sky.

In the past, Marc would have driven them here, but he had made no move to offer his services that evening. They parked as near as they could, and Dominic took her arm as he led Georgia up the palm-lined avenue to the enchanting, pale pink mansion. The beaded crêpe de Chine slid over her naked buttocks, affecting the way she felt, the way she walked. Dominic slipped her bolero jacket off her shoulders, swinging it from one hand, as they walked into the brightly lit entrance.

She felt that everyone was staring at her. Carefully, she rehearsed the words she had prepared to introduce Dominic. 'My stepson, Dominic d'Essange, Olivier's son.' If it wasn't so obvious that they were lovers, she would have been thrilled to have such a handsome escort, and grateful for his company. She took a deep breath, careful not to disturb the fragile equilibrium of her bodice, and prepared to face society.

Dominic was attracting the same level of attention that had thrilled her at lunch, and the women were openly envying her now.

Maxine swooped down on them. 'Darlings, I'm so glad you could come. How fascinating you look, Georgia. Do come with me. There are people I want you to meet.' She took them both by the arm.

What else had Maxine whispered to Dominic at The Meurice? Did she intend to try to seduce him tonight? Maxine looked ravishing, but then she had probably prepared herself for this evening for months. 'My dear, you should have come over earlier,' she told Georgia. 'My hairdresser flew down from Paris. He could have done something with your hair.'

Maxine led them both towards one of the swimming pools where a small statue stood at the edge of the water, surrounded by tiers of shallow coupes, steadily filling with wine which foamed from the nymph's breasts. 'Champagne?' she offered, filling a glass from each spouting nipple.

More flaming torches surrounded three tiered pools, reflecting their light in the water, where pale pink petals drifted on the surface, having fallen from over-hanging bushes of bougainvillaea which twisted between the balustrades of a curved staircase leading up out of the top pool to the villa.

Georgia saw Maxine's eyes fixed on Dominic, watching his reaction to the extravagant display. 'My husband is dying to take you in to dinner, Georgia, darling,' she murmured. 'Will you allow him to show you what he has arranged?'

Georgia looked up to see the prince by her side, and felt his hand slide around her waist as he took her up the steps. Sergio led her through the main conservatory, blazing with brightly-lit chandeliers, to a secluded corner where there was a chaise longue surrounded by oleanders. Lush flowering plants filled the room, and everywhere the air was perfumed with the scent of gardenias.

'Stay here,' he whispered, 'and I will bring you something to eat.'

From her seat on the chaise longue, Georgia could see part of the dining-hall. Lobsters, langoustines, prawns and shrimp rose in coral spirals from a table

162

consisting of a single massive block of ice, inside which were imprisoned thousands of vermilion, full-blown rose blooms.

In the centre of the room four dusky Algerian girls lay naked beside a flesh-pink column of frozen sorbet, each on a bed of fruit. One was half-buried under a mound of grapes, bunches of which dangled from her lips. Another offered strawberries; the third squeezed ripe nectarines between her thighs, and lay back so that the fruit could be sucked out of her warm sex. The fourth girl was peeling peaches with a sharp knife and covering her breasts with the glistening slices. As the guests bit into the succulent morsels, the girls encouraged them to delve deeper into every crevice, crushing more fragile fruit beneath the weight of their bodies as the juice was sucked off them.

The girls looked so delicious lying there, that Georgia longed to lie down beside them so that she, too, could feel eager lips, sucking the sweet liquid from her. Instead, she forced herself to pay attention to what Sergio was saying. 'Come and dance with me. I want to feel you close,' he murmured.

From the top of the steps, Georgia could see the gardens laid out in front of her. Three separate marquees, each with its own orchestra and themed decor, pulsated with crowds of dancers. Water, dyed the colour of dark sapphires, cascaded down the central portion of the great staircase, filling the tiered swimming-pools. In the top one, swans circled majestically; below them, a string quartet drifted on a floating platform; the lowest pool, level with the gardens, was filled with rose blooms which covered the surface in a myriad shades.

She looked around for Dominic. She saw him on the cypress-lined path leading to the water. Maxine was behind him, looking cross. Georgia breathed a sigh of relief. She wanted to dance with him, to spend the evening in his arms. She wasn't sure if he had seen her and she tried to catch his attention, but the prince caught her arm and diverted her.

She heard a splash. A girl in a silver sequinned dress like a mermaid's tail, toppled slowly backward into the lower pool and floated among the petals. Her long, blonde hair drifted around her as she lay, immobile, on the surface of the water, then her legs dipped under the heavy weight of her trailing skirt and pulled her steadily down. At the edge of the pool, Georgia saw Dominic strip off his jacket before he plunged in after the girl.

She reached the bottom of the steps just in time to see him staggering out of the pool with the girl in his arms. She saw Maxine move anxiously towards them, then glance up at her before she signalled to a servant to help them.

As Dominic and the girl walked back to the house, Maxine stepped towards Georgia.

'Quite the dashing young hero, isn't he, darling?' Maxine murmured in her ear. 'I've offered them my bedroom so that they can dry out. Were you and Sergio on your way to dance? I'm sure Dominic won't be too long.'

Maxine walked with them to the largest marquee, which was lined with sea-green silk and supported by massive, open, conch shells, inside which were piles of shiny pink cushions. In here a Cuban band, the musicians all dressed as shipwrecked sailors, kept up the insistent rhythm of the rumba.

'Sergio will look after you until Dominic is free,' Maxine told Georgia. 'Won't you, darling?' she said, turning to her husband.

She held both their arms firmly in hers as she walked towards the figure of a naked girl carved out of ice. A steady stream of vodka gushed out from between the transparent, frozen thighs, and Maxine held two crystal tumblers between the legs to catch the chilled spirit. She laughed, stroking the delicately carved labia, then whispered in Georgia's ear. 'I wanted a penis, but they said it would melt too fast.' She handed one glass to Georgia and the other to her husband. 'Enjoy yourselves,' she urged, as she whirled away and disappeared into the crowd.

Sergio sipped. 'Do you like vodka?' he asked. He filled a silver spoon with caviare from a mound chilling in the ice statue's upturned hands, and offered it to Georgia. She tasted the salty, fishy eggs bursting on her tongue in an explosion of flavour, as she followed it with a shot of vodka.

Sergio put his arms around her waist, and held her close as he moved in time to the pulsing rhythm of the band. 'You are angry,' he said. 'Is it with me?'

'No,' she reassured him. None of this was his fault.

'Then with my wife,' he persisted. 'She loves to play games, doesn't she?'

Georgia looked up to see warm, brown eyes smiling into hers. He knew exactly how she felt! But Dominic hadn't been forced to rescue the girl. He had been all too eager.

The prince's arms held her close as they danced. The wild beat of the music pounded through her ears, and the heaving bodies around them all seemed to be overwhelmed by the powerful, sexual movements of the dance. She could feel the vodka going straight to her head as Sergio held her close. One hand cupped her left buttock and he pulled her hard against him as they circled the dance floor, locked together.

The feeling was not unpleasant. She loved dancing and the vigour of his body pressed against her was exciting. Her nipples swelled as they rubbed against the sequins of her dress, a fact that the prince obviously attributed to his own efforts.

She tried to look round for Dominic but her head was spinning, and Sergio's lips were gently caressing her throat in the most exciting way. She could feel the warmth of his hand on her naked back, a warm, dry, well-manicured hand. He must have taken advantage of

Maxine's team of beauticians in the afternoon. Georgia could imagine him lying back being pampered by efficient young girls. His smoothly rounded nails traced the outline of her spine, lingering on each bone until she was tingling with delight and she felt her body melting into his.

The music changed to a tango and Sergio smiled down at her. His hand moved away from her spine. She felt him find the slit in the skirt of her dress, as one finger slid inside, parting the beaded silk and cupping the bare cheek of her bottom. As he pressed against her she felt his erection through their light clothes; it was impossible to move further apart or his condition would be obvious. She could not resist sliding her hips forward so that she could feel the length of his penis against her mound. She had heard about Sergio; there had been rumours, of course, from his previous wives and girlfriends who spoke of him with affection and awe.

His hand still rested on her bare buttock beneath the loose panel of her skirt, but he held back as they tangoed over the smoothly polished wood floor of the marquee. As they danced, it was she who pressed against him. His hand on her bare skin was driving her mad. She swallowed hard – she wanted Sergio – and he knew it.

He manoeuvred her into one corner of the room, next to the open mouth of one of the massive conch shells. She knew she shouldn't let this go any further; she wanted to be with Dominic, but she loved the feeling of Sergio's fingers sliding up and down her bare back as his body throbbed in time to the music. He murmured his appreciation at her nakedness as, with hardly a break in his rhythm, he unbuttoned the front of his trousers, and took out his huge penis. She felt its pulsing heat through the thin silk and looked down. The rumours had all been true. If anything, he was bigger than she had heard. His enormous size shocked her. Was this the reason why Maxine had lavished so many millions of dollars on him for the last two years? It fascinated her; she reached out to touch it.

Sergio caught her admiring his startling equipment and laughed. 'Don't let it frighten you. It exists to give pleasure, and we can both enjoy that.' He guided her into the shiny core of one of the shells and laid her down on a mound of feather cushions inside the glossy, pink interior of the conch.

'Let me take your mind off Dominic,' he murmured, as she ran her fingers over his swollen, throbbing manhood. From the dance floor Georgia knew that it must look as if he were merely kissing her as his gigantic organ rested for a moment between her thighs, then he lifted her bare breasts free of their flimsy covering and took them into his mouth as the first few inches of his magnificent penis eased inside her sex. Slowly and carefully he pressed deeper inside her as his tongue fluttered over her rigid nipples. The steady beat of the guitars drummed in her ears and her blood pulsed through her veins as Sergio continued his steady progress, still in perfect rhythm to the pulsing beat of the tango.

Through the open mouth of the shell she saw Dominic emerging from another grotto across the dance floor with the girl from the pool. She was replacing the strap of her dress on her shoulder and laughing.

Georgia gave a small moan of pain which the prince took to be her response to his driving passion. He steadied himself, anxious not to hurt her and kissed her gently on her lips to reassure her. Her breasts pressed on his starched shirt front and the platinum and diamond studs on his chest bit into her skin as he gently climbed deeper into her sex.

She gasped as the massive head of his penis reached the hot bud of her clitoris and the first waves of her orgasm swept through her. He held back, letting her suck him deeper and deeper inside her, to penetrate her innermost depths. And still she knew that she had not yet taken all of the monstrous length inside her.

She sank down on the cushions in the hidden centre of the shell, pulling him back with her as she vibrated with pleasure. Her body moved with a rhythm of its own as she urged him on, letting him know how good it felt to absorb his incredible manhood.

He eased the last few inches high up against the neck of her womb, and she came again with a wild abandoned spasm. He must have known then that he had not hurt her and he began to ride faster up and down, gasping as his iron control weakened and he acknowledged his own passion. He covered her mouth with his as he came massively at the end, stifling both their cries, his slackened manhood still huge and throbbing inside her.

Sergio lifted himself carefully, so that their bare flesh could not be seen by the crowd circling the dance floor, and bent to kiss the moist curls of hair between her legs.

'You are a magnificent woman,' he said huskily, as he reluctantly replaced the delicate crêpe de Chine over her thighs and raised her narrow straps on to her shoulders. She trembled beneath him as she lay on the mound of cushions, her eyes half-closed in the dim light as he gently wound a few loose strands of her hair back into the diamond clasp.

Then he kissed the still exposed swell of her breasts and carefully smoothed her dress into perfect order.

'My wife will be looking for me soon,' he muttered, as he briskly buttoned up the front of his trousers and took her arm in his.

Georgia felt lethargic as he led her back to the main dance floor. The prince looked very sure of his sexual prowess as she drooped slightly in his arms.

'Forgive me, Sergio,' she murmured. 'I must tidy myself up a little.' He nodded, and held her hand as he led her back across the lawns to the glittering mansion. At the foot of the grand staircase, he released her and fled, obviously intent on further conquests before Maxine returned to claim him.

Georgia walked in a daze to the far end of the garden and looked out over the bay as the sun rose on the horizon. She had not seen Dominic since she saw him leaving the shell in the marquee. She assumed he was dancing now with one of the young girls who had surrounded him earlier. She imagined him making love on the soft bed of cushions inside the shell, and wondered if he had seen her with Sergio. How had she allowed him to arouse her so rapidly? She had thought that Dominic was the only man she wanted.

She must find him and go home. Her thighs felt uncomfortably sticky, and her dress was stained and crumpled. Around her, in the soft morning light, young girls looking as fresh as daisies drifted over the lawns.

Viennese waltzes were being played by the orchestra at this side of the house. The waltz was a dance she loved, and she had always associated the music with the happiest moments of her life. Now she felt as if the violins were wringing the last dregs of misery from her soul.

She was not going to search the dance floors for Dominic. There was a chance that he might have left the keys in the car so that the servants could move it, if necessary. She would go and see. She could at least try to save herself the humiliation of begging a lift home, making it even more obvious that Dominic had deserted her.

By the fountains, waiters were busy pouring more champagne for breakfast, with coffee for those few, less hardy souls who had decided that, for them, the party was coming to an end. In the steadily increasing light, Georgia felt dishevelled and tawdry. She hurried out through the main gates and walked along the rows of parked cars.

Chauffeurs looked up as she passed, surprised to see a woman, alone, out here. She ignored them and continued to search for their car. It couldn't be much further. She was sure that they had left it near here. Across the road, under a palm tree, she thought she spotted it. Please God, let the keys be inside, she prayed. She couldn't face walking all the way back again, with the men all staring at her over-exposed breasts and crumpled dress. Her hand shook as she tried the door. It was open. But she must be mistaken, there was someone inside. Perhaps this wasn't their car.

And then he stirred and smiled up at her. Dominic! She had misjudged him. He must have been here all the time, exhausted, and she had jumped to the conclusion that he was with another woman. She had never felt so ashamed.

She slid in beside him. 'Take me home,' she murmured.

Georgia dozed on the way back. She decided that she would spend the day in bed. She was exhausted, so tired that vivid dreams disturbed her. She could see Dominic dancing; Dominic in the swimming pool, surrounded by girls; Dominic having sex in the car without her. Why hadn't they both left earlier, together? He must have realised that she would want to be with him. Then she told herself off for worrying again. She was simply overtired.

'Did you enjoy the party, Dominic?' she asked, immediately wishing that she had chosen to say nothing. 'I looked everywhere for you.'

'It's hardly the thing to spend the whole evening with one's partner,' he stated blandly.

She felt sick.

'And you seemed to have your own entourage,' he continued smoothly. 'But I'm pleased that you wanted me.'

Dominic looked fresh enough to start again. They drove home in silence. Mathilde would make them a late breakfast, and then they could sleep all day. After that, they must get back to serious work again. Marc was still training the team, but Dominic had to play his part.

Georgia was surprised to see a dark red Hispano-Suiza parked outside the villa. She hadn't seen the car before, and wasn't expecting visitors. Almost everyone she knew who lived on the coast would be recovering from last night's party.

As they walked into the hall, she saw a stack of suitcases and a tall man looming over them. Georgia turned away as Theo Sands walked towards her, his arms outstretched.

She tried to let her hand slip out of Dominic's hold, but he gripped her hard, stroking her shoulder possessively as he stared furiously at the two visitors.

Theo! His clear, bright amber eyes glittered dangerously.

'Georgia, how good of you to ask me down. I take it I'm forgiven.'

'What the hell are you doing here?'

'Is that any way to greet a guest?'

'A guest?'

'Natasha invited me. She said you would be delighted to see me. It appears she was a little over-optimistic.'

And, standing in the shadow behind Theo, Natasha's slight figure stood erect. She moved forward and held out her hand to Georgia.

How she had changed! The long fall of black hair was cropped into the latest bob cut, following the shape of her skull, tracing the delicate outline of her slender neck with tendrils of glossy jet.

Natasha seemed totally unconcerned by Dominic's possessive interest in Georgia. She had a new confidence to go with her changed image. Her violet eyes stared up coolly, and Georgia felt her own gaze drop in the face of the young girl's assurance. It was indeed she who should feel ashamed.

Shaking off Dominic's restraining hand, Georgia took

171

Natasha in her arms. 'Welcome back,' she said. 'It's good to see you.'

But it didn't feel good. She felt cold to the bottom of her stomach. This new Natasha was a very different rival from the naïve young girl who had run away a week ago. And Dominic's whole body showed how aware he was of that. He had tensed at the first sight of Natasha, and now he seemed unable to take his eyes off her.

It was what she had wanted when they first came here, when Georgia first met the girl. Now, with a sickening chill in her stomach, she knew she could not bear to let Dominic go.

And then she saw the contempt in Theo's eyes, and she struggled to control her expression as she held out her hand to him.

'Theo. Thank you for bringing Natasha back to us.' She made no attempt to hide her surprise that they had come together, but neither Theo nor Natasha offered any explanation.

Natasha spoke in her low, cool voice. 'I told Monsieur Sands that I was sure you would like him to stay with us for a few days. I knew you would welcome the opportunity of renewing your acquaintance.'

It was the last thing Georgia wanted. With Theo here, her humiliation would be complete. She tried desperately to think of some excuse, but Dominic stepped forward.

'Since you are already here, it seems we have little choice,' he said rudely. 'Your painting has preceded you. Stay as long as Natasha wants. Perhaps she'll give you further inspiration for your work.' Georgia felt his arm tighten round her waist and he kissed her full on the lips.

'I have been working with Natasha. I find her a fascinating subject.' Theo stroked the delicate down of her cheek. 'Exquisite, isn't she?'

Dominic's back went rigid with rage. Georgia thought

172

that he would explode. Again, it was Natasha who took charge of the situation.

'May we have a drink, Dominic? The road was hot and dusty.' She led the way into the drawing room, wide open at one end to overlook the sea. 'I would love some champagne,' she said coolly.

'Of course.' Dominic's voice was curt.

Natasha took Theo's arm. 'You see. It is as I told you. I was sure you could paint here. Is it not beautiful?'

Theo looked amused now as he smiled down at the girl. Georgia thought he had every reason to be proud of her; she was completely in possession of herself.

Dominic cracked the cork off the bottle. The champagne added an additional sparkle to Natasha's beautiful eyes; it made Georgia feel ill. How long did Theo plan to stay? She couldn't bear the idea of him watching her with Dominic.

Marc was walking towards the open doors, his arms outstretched to welcome Natasha. Catching sight of him, she gave a small cry of pleasure and ran across the room to him. He whirled her into the air like a tiny child.

'*Bienvenue, ma petite.*' He put her down and stood back to admire her. '*C'est bien fait.* You look ravishing. So, to work, huh? This afternoon. We must start right away.' He turned away without a word to Georgia.

'Perhaps you'd like to join us at the rehearsal, Theo?' Dominic spoke softly, but his eyes burned into the older man's face. Georgia watched him, puzzled. Dominic wanted Theo to be there. Was it to prove to Theo that he could dominate Natasha as well as her?

Chapter Twelve

Mathilde bustled Natasha and Theo out on to the terrace for breakfast. Georgia went upstairs with Dominic to change. She tried to think clearly. Why was Theo here with Natasha? What was he doing in her home?

Instead of the sleep she craved, she had to tidy herself up and go back downstairs. She looked in the mirror. In the bright daylight, her crushed dress looked obscene and her hair fell in lank, uncombed tendrils over her shoulders. She took a small sponge and wiped the streaked make-up off her face. Bloodshot eyes, ringed with dark circles, stared at her out of a sallow skin, puffy with tiredness.

No wonder Theo had looked shocked.

She wanted to crawl into her bed and forget the last twelve hours, but she could hear voices out on the terrace. She had to go down. She put on a pair of navy and white beach pyjamas and brushed her hair into some sort of order.

Steam billowed out of the bathroom where Dominic stripped and showered. Naked, and still damp, he sauntered out on to the balcony. 'I see they're making themselves at home.'

'We need to join them.'

'You go ahead, darling. I certainly don't intend to.'

She felt the force of his pent-up anger and frustration like an electric charge between them. His hands gripped the stone balustrade. 'Look at the bitch. How dare she cut her hair!'

'It's wonderful. It really suits her.'

'She didn't ask me if she should do it.'

The terrace was in full sunlight at this time of the morning and the bright light hurt Georgia's eyes. She found a pair of dark glasses and wearily made her way downstairs.

Theo took her half-empty glass of champagne out of her hand and replaced it with a cup of black coffee. 'You look as though you need this,' he said. 'It seems to have been a rough night.'

She sipped cautiously, feeling the hot, bitter liquid burn the back of her throat. Natasha sat in the shade of a mulberry tree at the end of the stone-flagged area, toying with a few berries of the almost ripe fruit. It was the first time Georgia had seen her look truly happy. Thank God the girl obviously did not realise what had happened between her and Dominic.

Theo appeared totally at ease, sitting at the table with his back to the stone wall of the villa. He looked around him at the rocky cliff, the beach below and the broad expanse of turquoise sea, and grinned at Georgia. 'Beautiful. Very beautiful. Natasha said this place would be good to paint.'

Surely he wasn't thinking of staying long enough to work! 'Are you sure you'll have time for that?' she asked.

'Does that mean you want to get rid of me already? I was assured I would be welcome.'

'You know that Dominic isn't happy about it.'

'I understood the invitation came from you. But if he's so important in your life, hadn't we better ask his permission again?'

'My permission for what?' Dominic's voice echoed round the stone walls. He stood on the balcony, bare-chested.

Georgia was sure that if he leant further forward, it would be clearly seen that he was completely naked. And that he was in her bedroom, which he so obviously treated as his own.

Theo shouted up from the terrace.

'Georgia thinks you should be consulted as to whether or not I'm welcome to stay.'

'The house is Georgia's and it's her decision what you do here.'

Theo called up. 'Then I'll stay.'

Marc had joined Natasha under the mulberry tree. Georgia wondered what they were talking about. Natasha was laughing and making extravagant gestures with her arms as if that was the only way she could explain properly. They talked together for a while, then Natasha hugged him and disappeared into the kitchen.

Marc stood hesitantly on the edge of the terrace, staring at Georgia. 'Coffee?' she offered.

'Please. May I sit down?'

'Of course.'

'Natasha has agreed to a rehearsal with the full team this afternoon. She wants you and Dominic to watch. Should I go ahead? Is that all right with you?'

Georgia thought carefully. What could go wrong? If Natasha failed to control the team this time, she would never be able to perform with them again. But what was there to lose? If she couldn't cope she would have to give up anyway. The boys were already dangerously frustrated, sensing that something was wrong, and no doubt disturbed by Natasha's sudden return. Why not give it one last try?

'She wants Dominic to watch? Not to join in?'

'That's what she asked for. Shall I do as she says? The boys are restless.' Marc looked worried. 'She also wants

176

me to arrange for some girls to come up from the perfume factory to look after the boys after the rehearsal.'

'Do whatever she says. This time we'll do it her way.' If Natasha had her own ideas, it might work better. And inviting the girls made sense. They had done that several times before, to make sure that twelve lusty, young men didn't totally disrupt village life. The factory girls were only here for the summer as well, and any broken hearts would be soon mended.

Mathilde placed huge bowls of fruit and plates of hot bread on the table, obviously determined to impress her guest. It was almost lunchtime, and dish after dish of food was brought out. Georgia looked at it all with revulsion, her stomach churning at the thought of eating. When a plate of sardines was served, she refused them and looked away.

Theo's knife sliced through the fish, freshly caught and grilled, and flavoured with herbs. Mathilde had gone to some trouble for him, and she was fussing over him now. Georgia struggled to control her feeling of nausea.

Theo dipped a piece of bread in herb-laden olive oil. 'I look forward to seeing Natasha's performance.'

Dominic appeared in the doorway. 'Why not? She seems to have all our lives planned at the moment. She certainly wants us all to be there.' He gestured languidly at the tanned male bodies exercising on the beach below. 'Are you interested in our work, Theo? They're beautiful, aren't they? Do they excite you as models, or don't you work from life any more?'

'It can sometimes be stimulating. I'd like to see them in action.'

'You promise not to be shocked?'

'I've spent a lot of time in Paris, Dominic.'

'And of course you've seen my stepmother naked. That will be nothing new for you.'

Georgia hid behind her sunglasses as Theo raised an eyebrow.

'Georgia has been training the team while Natasha was away,' Dominic lied. 'I'm sure you'll enjoy her performance.'

'But that won't be today, of course,' Georgia cut in. 'Natasha is practising alone with the team.'

Dominic scowled. 'We can rearrange that.'

'Do as you please, Dominic, but don't expect me to take part.'

Georgia felt tired and ratty. Look what had happened when he had taken the decisions last night! He was not going to persuade her to do anything she didn't want to today.

He scowled at her. 'I'm going for a ride. I'll see you all later.'

Georgia watched Dominic stride away and hoped a long ride on Nimrod might calm his temper. The horse was certainly in need of the exercicse since it had been brought down from Lusigny. Her thoughts quickly returned to Theo.

It had been revenge that had impelled Natasha to invite Theo here, Georgia was sure of it. She watched him across the table, his heavy frame lounging comfortably in his seat, his long fingers twirling his wine glass. She wanted to ask him why he was helping Natasha, but she couldn't find the words.

'That was superb.' Finally, Theo finished eating and pushed back his chair. 'Now, if you will forgive me, I have a little painting to do.'

Georgia was thankful to be left alone at last. She curled up on a hammock stretched beneath the olive trees and swung lazily between the branches. It was such a relief to be on her own. Marc would make sure that everything was prepared for the afternoon, and warn Natasha to be careful with Luc. Wouldn't he?

She wondered what Theo thought he was doing with Natasha. Had he deliberately followed her down to the coast? He had made it clear that he thought she was beautiful when they had first met at the gallery.

Natasha was the same age as Georgia had been when Theo painted her so long ago. Georgia closed her eyes, remembering how she had thought they would be together always.

It seemed only a moment had passed before Marc came to tell her that Natasha was ready. 'It's time. Is Dominic back?'

'I haven't seen him.' She had hoped he was with them, helping them to prepare.

'We'll go ahead anyway, if that's all right with you.'

She felt worse than she had before she fell asleep, with an aching head and eyes that felt sore and sticky. Groping for her shoes, she followed Marc blindly. He walked straight past the barn and out on to the track. Georgia started to ask him where they were going, but he simply smiled at her, and said: 'Follow me.'

He led her along a track into the woods, to a clearing Georgia knew well. 'Natasha asked if we could perform here. She's very positive about it. And you said I was to give her whatever she wanted.'

Theo was already waiting, seated on a fallen tree-trunk. 'Come and sit beside me here, Georgia. It's more comfortable than it looks.' His hands were streaked with thick watercolour paint.

The team was already assembled, lying round the edge of the clearing. Instead of wearing their usual practice clothes they were completely naked, without even the leather thongs that they used in front of the clients. Their tanned, muscled bodies glowed with health and vigour as they waited expectantly.

At a word from Marc, they rose to their feet, moved into the centre of the clearing and lay down on fur rugs that had been placed on the bare earth. Their bodies were in perfect condition from weeks of exercise and sunshine.

At least she had done something right. They were a good team. Georgia had to admit that Luc was magnifi-

179

cent. Natasha had chosen well there. She had an eye for a male body.

Georgia and Theo sat on a stump and waited uneasily. There was no sign of Dominic or Natasha. Georgia bit her lip. Were they going to turn up? Impatiently she picked up a dead twig and snapped it between her fingers.

The boys tensed suddenly and Georgia saw Natasha standing at the edge of the clearing. She wore a cloak of dark violet gauze, the colour of the deepest shadows of the wood. Beneath it, her naked body was painted in swirling shades of mauve and green and black, with great streaks of colour covering every inch of her skin.

So it was Natasha's body that Theo had been so busy painting, not the sea or the sand. Georgia looked at the splashes of black and green staining the pads of his fingers. She imagined him smearing each whorl of colour over Natasha's naked body. He must have loved every moment. Georgia stared angrily at Natasha's violet stained nipples. Whose idea had it been to appear like this, hers or Theo's?

He had done it for her once, a long time ago, for a party and then they had made love before the paint had had a chance to dry, and he had had to start all over again. She wondered if he remembered that as clearly as she did. Her skin tingled now with the memory of the sensation of the brush on her skin.

She shivered. They sat in the shaded edge of the clearing and it was cool under the trees. Theo put his arm around her shoulders, but she pulled away angrily. She didn't want him touching her.

'Afraid I'll stain your smart suit?' he asked. 'Don't worry. It's quite dry.' He took off his jacket and put it over her. 'Natasha seems to be able to keep warm enough.'

Dappled sunlight filtered through the canopy of leaves on to the central area, and the only sound was the crackling of twigs on the forest floor beneath their feet.

Natasha stood completely still, her black kohl-rimmed eyes cast down. She stared at the young men, her expression fierce, unsmiling. She started dancing to the simple beat of a single drum. She took one pace forward, lifted her hand to beckon to Luc with a single imperious gesture, and stood waiting while he padded softly across the rug to stand in front of her.

Georgia frowned. This was not the performance she had expected. But Luc seemed to know exactly what he was doing. Shielding Natasha from the watchers, his hands went to her throat, two massive hams of fists which, with a tender gentleness, unclasped the silk ribbons of the cloak and released its sheer folds so that it fell from Natasha's body. He threw it over a fallen tree-trunk at the edge of the clearing without moving an inch away from her.

Georgia could not see whether his body was touching hers or not. Natasha was partly hidden from them by the powerful back of the young man who towered over her. She looked tiny, feline and dangerous, like an animal, a creature of the woods, her huge eyes dominating the men.

She moved forward at precisely the right moment. Her body brushed softly against Luc, pushing him aside with a tiny movement of her hips as she advanced towards the rest of the team. The boys stared at her, seeming not to recognise in this new figure the girl with whom they had practised before.

Georgia relaxed slightly as Natasha moved away from Luc.

With one curling movement of her body, she lay down on the dark fur and arched her back so that they could watch the suppleness of her body and the glorious, delicate swell of her perfect breasts, each nipple now darkened with colour.

With a deep, throaty purr, Natasha then rose and stepped forward, raising her arms so that the dappled sunlight played on her painted skin, and sparkled on the dark blue depths of her hair.

She moved slowly, so that at times she seemed almost immobile, and yet every eye was fixed on her body, fascinated by her sinewy movements. Above the neat triangle of dark curly hair between her thighs, painted tendrils swirled over her belly, rising and falling as she moved.

Georgia watched the effect on the team. They waited breathlessly for Natasha to choose one of them as her steady, rhythmic movements became more explicit. There was no sign of Dominic. Perhaps that was why she was still so confident.

She paced around the circle of men, standing in front of each one, brushing their tanned chests with her stiffened nipples, sliding her fingers over them until they were fully erect. The tension was unbearable now; Georgia felt the heat flooding through her, the warm moisture of her sex juices trickling into her clothes. She forced herself to remain still. The girl must choose soon.

Steadily, Natasha tested each man, her lips parted now, her pink tongue darting out to sip the sheen of sweat that glistened on their skin. She licked her lips, pressed her pelvis against their cocks, and moved on. The men were agonised, almost unable to move now. Georgia knew that the slightest movement would make them come. She was sure that they could not control themselves any longer. Natasha had gone too far.

And yet the girl continued her relentless circling until she had tasted and felt each man. Natasha bent down in front of Philippe, and stroked his thighs. Her head was level with his pelvis. When his huge organ jerked forward, she opened her mouth and licked it delicately with her tongue, her pink tip darting round the smooth, tumid peak. Philippe groaned and fell beside her as she pulled him to the floor, her mouth never releasing its hold on his penis.

Slowly, she released him and rolled away from him, her tongue the last part of her body to separate from him. She slithered on her stomach towards Pierre and lay in front of him, raising herself by her hands, climbing up his legs as if he were a rope ladder. She rose unbearably slowly, and Pierre's face turned dark with lust as she slid her fingers between his thighs, and continued on and up, trailing her thumbs on the soft flesh below his hip-bones, and stroking the base of his belly. Then she took him by his thick shaft and led him like an animal to join Philippe on the floor.

Natasha teased, taunted, provoked, as powerfully as she had shown herself capable of at first. Only now she had trained until she had learnt all the tricks, the moves. And she had made the performance her own.

She crawled between the eleven men on the ground, her almond-shaped eyes studying them carefully. Then she rose to her feet in one swift supple curve and stood naked in the centre of the clearing. It was a triumph. Her head was bowed, level with the chest of the twelfth man – Luc.

The men lay prone around her. Each man came towards her, bowed, then rose, and disappeared into the forest. Georgia could hear gentle laughter as the factory girls led them away. When they had gone, Natasha lay down in the centre of the fur rug. Only Luc remained.

Georgia wanted to stop this now, but Theo held her hand hard against the ridged bark of the tree trunk. She could feel the lichen scrape beneath her fingernails.

The drum beat a faster rhythm now and Natasha's body curled on the rug as Luc moved towards her. Georgia felt as if the woods were closing in on her as the noises of love-making surrounded them.

Natasha encircled her arms around Luc's neck, buried her face in his chest, pulled him down on to the rug, and then straddled him with her thighs. She grasped his massive shaft with one swift movement, stroking it with her long fingers as she rose slinkily to her knees over him. Luc lay outstretched on the black rug, his penis rearing up into the air, waiting.

Natasha's painted fingers stroked her thighs, trailed over the long curve of one sleek leg, and disappeared between her open thighs. She stretched her spine like a cat, rolled on to her back with one swift movement, and parted her legs, her soft pink lips clearly visible, the black-tipped fingers inserted between them, opening them, allowing full view of her moist entrance.

Then Georgia heard a louder noise, steady, insistent and menacing. It was the fierce crashing of a horse's hooves through the undergrowth.

'Get that horse away.' Marc spoke before Georgia had a chance. 'And come and watch quietly, or get the hell out.'

Dominic's eyes raked the clearing scornfully before resting on the two figures entwined together. Slowly, insolently, he swung out of the saddle, jumped down and knotted Nimrod's reins around a branch.

Georgia looked at Natasha. She lay silent on the bare earth floor, not at all disturbed by Dominic's arrival. She was smiling, contented, and she raised her dark violet eyes up to him and held his gaze.

Georgia relaxed her stiffened muscles. The controlled eroticism of Natasha's performance had affected her as much as the others. If Theo were not here, she might have considered having one of the team. As it was, she would have to look out for Natasha. Dominic looked as if he would murder her.

Georgia was confident that Natasha would be ready and waiting to release Dominic from his pent-up tension if he would accept her. The performance she had just seen had convinced her that the girl was not frigid. Perhaps she had been waiting for the right moment, and it was now. Natasha had been as aroused as Georgia had ever seen a young girl. The juices soaking her dark curls had come from her own body, her own need.

The drum ceased to beat.

* * *

184

Dominic pulled off his gloves and dropped his riding crop on the ground. Natasha lay motionless now, fixed in the centre of the clearing beside Luc's prone figure. Her small figure seemed as still as a leaf. Dominic stared at her smeared body, streaked all over with swirls of paint.

The delicate outline of her skull, poised on her long neck, could have been either male or female. Only the proud thrust of her narrow jutting breasts with their swollen purple nipples and the sweet curve of her long thighs defined her sex. Her high taut buttocks were as firmly rounded as any of the young men who had watched her parade in front of them.

He glanced at Georgia and Theo. They sat motionless beneath an oak tree, apparently as stunned as he was by Natasha's transformation. Then Theo moved. Dominic watched him rise to his feet, take Natasha's wrap in his hands and stride to the centre of the fur rug towards her.

'No, I'll take that.' Dominic snatched the coloured gauze from Theo's grasp and pushed the older man away. 'Cover yourself,' he ordered Natasha, grabbing her wrist and lifting her on to Nimrod's back. He had to get her away from here, away from Luc, and from the lust which he knew would soon break through once more.

He jumped up behind her and rode back through the woods to the villa. He felt her lean forward over the horse's mane, sliding slightly on the saddle, so that she rubbed herself on the smooth leather. It seemed that he had prevented her from satisfying herself with Luc this time. Good. She needed to be taught a lesson. 'Haven't you had enough of that?' he shouted, holding her tightly with one arm, as they cantered along the track.

'What the hell did you think you were doing?' he demanded when they reached the villa, and he lifted her out of the saddle, tightening his grip as she said nothing. He dragged her across the courtyard to the house. She needed to get rid of all this ridiculous paint. How dare she display her body so flagrantly when she had refused to let him touch her?

'I thought I was doing my job,' Natasha said quietly. 'Isn't that why you brought me here?'

'You went too far.'

'Is that possible?'

Dominic pushed her into the house. 'You think letting every man take you like that will excite our clients?'

'Perhaps if you had seen it all, you would know that didn't happen. Not even with Luc. Nor did I intend that it should. And of course at Fleur's I will select carefully. I am sure you will tell me whom I may pump dry and whom leave aching.'

If she thought she could discuss her lover with him, she was wrong! Dominic remained silent as he forced her up the wooden staircase to her room. He saw Mathilde watching anxiously from the hall but he ignored her. Natasha was his business.

She was looking up at him as if nothing had happened. 'You'll excuse me now, Dominic, if I take a rest? The performance was exhausting, you understand?' She rose on tiptoe in front of him, flaunting her body. She reached up and lightly brushed his cheek with her lips. 'Until tonight.'

'You'll stay here until dinner,' he snapped. 'Wash yourself and dress discreetly. I'll decide what is to be done with you later.' He slammed the door shut behind him and leant against it. The slut. The little slut. She had deliberately taunted him, shown him how much she enjoyed having men at her mercy, how much she loved sex. Sex with any man except him.

Slowly he descended the stairs, crossed the hall and went out into the courtyard, increasing his pace as he neared the stable block. Nimrod whinnied as he approached. Dominic jumped up on to the horse's back and set off again into the woods.

Here he could think more clearly. Natasha was beautiful, there was no doubt about that. And she had shown

186

very clearly that she was not the frigid child she had pretended to be. He had seen more of her performance than she realised. Under the trees, as she paraded herself in front of the men, he had desired her almost as much as Georgia. Of course her body lacked the lush ripeness of his stepmother's, and he knew that Georgia's beauty was what he wanted. But Natasha had to learn how to behave, and tonight he would show her who was master in this house.

Natasha was the last one down to dinner. There was an empty place at the table, and they were all waiting for her. Dominic controlled his temper with difficulty, but eased his resentment with the knowledge of what he would do to the girl later. Theo and Georgia were talking stiffly; he was delighted to see that Natasha's plan there did not seem to be working as she had intended. After he had dealt with Natasha, he would return to Georgia's bed and take his pleasure with a real woman.

It surprised him to look up and see Natasha framed in the doorway. Theo and Georgia had become suddenly silent and were staring at the vision in front of them. Natasha wore a long, elegant gown of deep purple shot silk, which looked almost black in the shadows, yet burst into colour as she moved towards them in the candle-light.

At her neck she wore a thin gold chain, which wound round and round her throat. She wore no make-up, but even without the kohl her eyes were enormous in her pale face, and her dark-rose lips looked full and swollen. Silently she took her place at the table.

Theo raised his glass. 'To your future, Natasha. Congratulations.'

Georgia cleared her throat. 'The performance was beautiful. You have succeeded beyond all our hopes. Thank you.'

Dominic knew they were waiting for him to speak. 'The girls at Le Grand Marquis taught you well,' he said insolently. 'You have nothing left to learn.' He was pleased to see a faint colour stain Natasha's chalk-white cheeks, and he felt a surge of excitement as he thought of how he would make her lose her fragile veneer of control later tonight.

He took little part in the conversation at dinner, watching the girl quietly as she blossomed under Georgia and Theo's admiration. Her long white throat excited him, the clear expanse of pale bare flesh above the dark sheen of her silk gown, the faint swell of her breasts rising from the elegant line of her bodice.

When the coffee had been served, he rose abruptly. 'Shall we take a walk, Natasha? Will you come with me?'

He heard her sharp intake of breath and saw her rise to his challenge, her huge violet eyes widening in anticipation. So she knew what he had in mind, and she wanted it. He would make sure that he would provide more than she expected. He was not a rough peasant who could be enthralled by a young girl's beauty. He would take her once, and then send her back to the slums where she belonged.

But first he would show her what she was missing. When she compared his skilled love-making with Luc's rough approach he was sure she would want only him. As he took Natasha's hand and led her along the path to the beach he wondered how she looked when Luc made love to her. Did her breath quicken and her skin flush as he had seen it this afternoon? Had Luc's gigantic penis given her anything like the satisfaction he knew he was capable of?

'A beautiful night.' Dominic pointed to the moon, shining now in the dark night sky, casting a long swathe of bright light over the slate-coloured calm water of the Mediterranean.

'Every night is beautiful here.'

'You like it? I thought you were anxious to leave us.'

'I came back,' Natasha said quietly.

'So you did. Why, I wonder?'

They were on the beach now; Natasha had slipped off

her satin shoes, and now held them in her hand as she walked barefoot on the sand. She turned her face to Dominic and he saw that she was just about to speak, but they were not yet out of sight of the terrace, and he caught hold of her roughly, turning her round and forcing her to walk further.

'You looked like a whore this afternoon.'

'Did that disturb you?'

She shook off his hand and ran along the beach. Dominic thought she looked like an innocent child, but she didn't behave like one, and her dress was that of a full-grown woman. He ran after her and pushed her back against a rock.

'There's no place here for you and Luc.'

'I thought you were employing us both.'

'I'm not employing you so that I must watch you dance with your lover.'

He saw her lift her face towards him, parting her surprisingly full lips. She was laughing at him.

He'd show her what she was missing. He'd show her the difference between a lout like Luc and an experienced lover like himself. And then he'd throw her back in the gutter where she came from.

She was breathing hard. So she wasn't quite as cool as she pretended. He slipped a strap off her shoulder. The silk fell forward, catching on one erect nipple. He pulled the gown further down, exposing her naked belly.

The whore wore nothing except a pair of sheer, lace pants beneath the flimsy silk. She was ready for him, and he would not disappoint her. The dress fell on to the sand in a violet pool. He felt the heat surge through his cock as he looked at her pale, trembling flesh.

She lifted her face up to him and kissed him. How dare she! How many men had she had today? No doubt Theo was her lover as well as Luc. She was completely shameless. He took one nipple between his fingers and squeezed it hard. He heard her gasp. So that was what she wanted. She liked men to be rough with her.

189

Her body was slim and smooth, almost boyish, except for the delicate, tip-tilted breasts. She was all black and white in the moonlight, with her cap of shorn hair crowning her pale face. He looked at her pale, smooth breasts with the dark, swollen buds which had risen into rigid peaks of desire. Her thin lace pants clung to her high, taut buttocks. He slipped one finger inside the sheer lace and stroked her skin. He longed to tear them off her, but fought the instinct.

That was what she wanted, what she was used to in the rough world she came from. Slowly, he slipped them down over her thighs, tracing the edge of her sex lips with the tip of his tongue, as he bent down in front of her.

She looked like a tiny marble statue. How could she seem so pure when her soul was so rotten? She was trembling; her whole body quivered against him. He could feel her hands sliding inside his shirt, rippling over his skin. He felt outraged at her wantonness.

She unbuckled his belt, stripping off his clothes until he was as naked as she was. Was she trying to prove to herself that he was fully aroused?

The bitch was making him lose control. How could he ever have thought she was innocent? She was rising on tiptoe, her thigh sliding up the back of his leg, pressing herself against him. Her skin felt cool and smooth as silk.

She was panting, her eyes like black pools in the moonlight. He wanted to pull her down on to the sand and take her straight away, but he forced himself to wait. He wasn't like Luc, a rough brute whom she could tease into her body.

She was touching him, stroking him, working on him expertly with her tiny hands. She was shameless. He pressed his face again between her thighs, breathing in her hot, sweet, musky scent. He parted her soft sex lips with the tip of his tongue, tasting the honey of her desire flickering inside her.

190

She was moaning now, but he would not take her yet. He must be able to hold on for a few moments longer. And yet the movement of her slim, quivering hips was maddening him. He wanted to drive himself into her, and make her understand that she was his to do with as he chose.

He lowered his body over hers, and looked down at her. Her face was pale in the moonlight, her eyes deeply shadowed. Her flesh had tasted so sweet, how could anything so corrupt be so fragrant?

He straddled her hips, crushing her slim frame with his powerful thighs as he allowed his heavy cock to descend on to the triangle of black curls at the base of her belly. The soft hair caressed his engorged flesh, pumping the blood faster and faster through his veins as his bulging tip pressed against the soft lips of her sex, forcing them apart.

The slut was eager; her tender flesh felt hot and moist on his smooth tightened peak. He felt his control weaken as his urge to enter her overwhelmed him; he could wait no longer.

She had taken so many men into her deceitfully delicate core, that he could not bear her to see how much he wanted her at this moment. He felt her sex lips suck on him, drawing him in, and he cried out as the sweet lips parted beneath his onslaught, enclosing his throbbing flesh with her tender moist sex.

Dominic felt her stiffen and pull back with a small gasp of pain. He stopped as he realised how delicate and slender her tight flesh felt around his penis. This was not the body of an experienced woman enclosing him. He felt a wave of shame as he realised what he had done. He hadn't meant to hurt her. Why hadn't he trusted his first instincts? She was a virgin. Had his insane passion for Georgia blinded him to Natasha's innocence?

Dominic withdrew, horrified, and stared at the frail girl on the sand, trembling beneath him. He bent over her, holding her in his arms, stroking the shorn, black

191

strands of her hair as he brushed her warm skin tenderly with his lips.

She quivered beneath him, raised her arms to draw him back into her, then turned her face aside as he stared at her in dismay. Gently he licked the salt tears from her cheeks, nuzzling his face against her hair. 'My poor darling. Why did you let me do it? Why didn't you tell me? How could you have let me think you wanted any man but me?'

He thought his heart would break as she spoke softly. 'Because I thought it would excite you. With them it was play-acting, pretending.'

'And with me? Was I so terrible that you could not tell me?'

'I was frightened.'

'Frightened? Because you thought I would take you like this if I had known?'

'Because I thought you would not want me.'

He had wanted her from the first moment he saw her, but he had refused to admit it to himself. And because of that, he had almost lost her to Luc. He cradled her in his arms and carried her across the sand, back to the house. Later, in his bed, if she wanted him, he would love her so tenderly that she might forgive him.

Chapter Thirteen

*T*heo painted furiously, his brush dashing over the canvas as fast as Natasha's flying pirouettes. He thought she looked enchanting, dancing barefoot on the sand in the morning sunshine.

Dominic obviously thought so, too. Theo could see him, propped up on his elbows, his habitually languid pose replaced by rapt attention.

Theo felt delighted that Natasha's plan had succeeded. He had not been at all sure that it would work, or even that he wanted it to. When the girl came to see him, he had decided to seduce her himself. Instead, he had to content himself with painting her joyful, dancing figure.

He suspected that neither she nor Dominic had slept much last night, and yet here she was, full of energy, dancing on the sand as if it were the stage at the Opera. He watched as Dominic reached out for her, stroking one flying ankle, as she laughed and twirled faster out of his reach, her bare feet sending a cloud of sand into his face. Theo was sure that she was naked under her short, white tunic. He saw Dominic crawl over the sand towards her, shaking the flying grains out of his eyes as she deliberately teased him.

Theo put down his paintbrush as soon as Natasha

stopped her dance. 'Damn,' he cursed, staring at his brushstrokes of pure white on a background of buff yellow sand. He needed more time to transfer the image of that whirling-dervish figure on to canvas.

Natasha's dancing had exploded with the passion of a woman newly in love, expressing a joy for which she had no words, and he had wanted to portray something of that fresh, unrepeatable moment. With her disappearance behind the rock, Theo was left unfocused and, although he hated to admit it, suddenly jealous.

He had wanted to help the girl when she came to him in trouble. She had intrigued him at first sight, in the gallery in Paris, and of course, he had given her a room in his rented villa when she had asked for it. After all, she had given him Georgia's address, and that had been the reason for him spending the summer down here.

She had proved as fascinating to paint as he had first thought. A week in her company had made him almost fall in love with her, even if she was determined to attract Dominic. Theo was confident enough of his own powers to feel sure that he could divert her, and had been irritated when she had treated him like a favourite uncle, a friend who could be trusted.

He had delayed too long, and taught her too much. After he had sent her off to Paris to see Elsa Schiaparelli, he had seen her return full of confidence, a delicious young woman who knew she could have everything she wanted. And she wanted Dominic.

If Georgia hadn't been so much on his mind, Theo decided, Natasha would have stayed with him and would have felt no need to develop a new style. All the reassurance she needed would have come from him. Except that, with him, she had been a young girl, protected by her own innocence.

Innocence! Theo laughed. He had brought her back here because she had told him she was in love with Dominic. He could understand that; she needed help. And then, in the woods, she had given the most wanton display he had ever seen. A tart from the back streets of Paris could have gone no further. She had used every trace of that so-called innocence to arouse men who, she said, meant nothing to her.

So now here he was, at a disadvantage with Georgia, who had been made miserable by his interference. He could see her out of the corner of his eye, as she sat hunched up on the cliff. She, too, had been watching the young lovers on the beach.

Well, if she was suffering it was her own fault. What had possessed her to take Olivier's son into her bed? Theo was angry with Georgia. She had left him once, and he thought that it was time she came back into his life.

She looked frustrated herself, kicking at the sand now as she walked down the cliff path. She wore a plain, yellow cotton dress, short and sleeveless, showing off her long, tanned limbs. It suited her to be more informal, like this. Even as a young girl, she had been cool and aloof, icily reserved as all English girls seemed to be – until he got them into bed.

He picked up a fresh canvas. 'Over here, Georgia,' he shouted. He saw her look up and frown. He was, however, her guest and Georgia was far too polite a hostess to ignore him. With a fixed smile on her face, she walked towards him.

'Good morning, Theo,' she said stiffly. 'I hope Mathilde gave you breakfast?'

'A splendid one, thank you. How about you? Sleep well?' He was being unfair, he knew. He could see dark circles under her eyes. He put his hand out to touch her, but she drew back instantly. Well, he had asked for that rebuff. 'Sit down,' he said, 'I want to paint you.'

She glared at him. 'Go to hell.'

'Now, that's no way to treat a guest.'

'A guest who invited himself!'

'Not at all. Natasha asked me to come.'

'Why?'

195

'She needed some support,' he said quietly. 'Now, sit still.' This was not the time to explain that Natasha had begged for his help. He picked up his brush.

She was displaying every sign of despair, he thought. Was that an act, too? She had been a wonderful model simply because she could become anything he asked. One word from him, and an instant façade would spring up.

She hesitated, and for a moment he thought she would turn away, but she sat down quietly beside him, and looked at the canvas he had been working on earlier.

'Is that Natasha?' she asked.

'It's how I saw her.'

'Will I recognise myself when you've finished?' Her words were so soft he could scarcely hear her.

He laughed. 'You don't like my new style?'

'It's successful.'

'Oh yes, it sells well. But also, it's what I always aimed for. You know that.' He wanted her to lie down, to relax and throw her arms above her head, but decided she would refuse if he asked her. For the moment he was content that she was here.

He could see Natasha running along the sand, her light tunic fluttering around her. She looked young and carefree as she held out her hands to Dominic.

Theo watched, entranced, as Natasha paused, waited for Dominic to reach her, and then drew him down on the sand beside her. Dominic slid the light covering from the girl's body, exposing her pale skin, rosy now in the early morning sunshine.

They played like two young animals, stroking each other and nuzzling at each other's flesh. Dominic was gentle, Natasha inviting, shy but eager. Dominic bent over her, lifted her gently in his arms and carried her towards the woods, cradling her into his body as if she were the most precious thing in his life.

Theo could see their heads bobbing above the rock as they walked away. He tried to divert Georgia's attention, but she turned her head and held her gaze until they had disappeared far into the distance, two tiny black specks, moulded into one.

'No longer the perfect model, are you?' he said, trying to distract her. 'I thought you knew all about holding a position.'

'Sorry.' She resumed her old pose dutifully, but her eyes were darker now, and full of sadness.

She was a fool to chase after Dominic, he thought angrily, stabbing at the canvas. Her eyes, those great, aquamarine pools of light, were even more luminous now, filling with tears. Damn her, she'd had her fling. There was no need to act the tragic widow. The death of her husband might have hit her hard, he thought, but that was no reason to run after his son.

'Jealous?' he asked, regretting the question immediately.

'Of course not. I'm worried about Natasha.'

'She knows what she wants, and I think she's got it.' Theo concentrated on his painting. 'So what are you going to do now?' He filled in a large patch of blue sky. It was too soon to suggest that she came to him.

'Nothing's changed. As soon as I can leave here, I'll go back to Lusigny, pack up my things and travel.'

'Where will you go? Home to England?'

'I'm not sure I would be accepted there.'

Theo roared with laughter. 'Because I ruined your reputation? That was a long time ago. Madame d'Essange would be welcome in the very best society. Let me take you.'

Georgia's eyes flashed at him. 'I have absolutely no intention of going anywhere with you.'

'I'm an old friend. It might do you good to include me in your plans. What about America? You'd love California.' He kept his voice deliberately casual.

Georgia stood up. 'I'm not going anywhere I might even bump into you, Theo. Now if you'll excuse me, I'm going for a swim.'

197

'Good idea.' Theo put down his brush. 'It's not going well, anyway. You're a fidgety model.'

She rose quietly to her feet, padded across the sand and flung herself into the water without troubling to take off the thin cotton shift she was wearing. Damn. He needed to be careful. She was more hurt than he had realised. Was it possible that she had truly loved Dominic?

He watched Georgia in the water, regretting his earlier harsh words, and let her swim alone, not wanting to crowd her. She was swimming out to sea, with steady, strong, rhythmic strokes. What would she do now? He checked her from time to time. She was not the sort of woman to swim out too far deliberately, but she was tired and might have an accident. It was time she came in.

He thought about going after her, but then she turned towards the shore, and waded up the beach. For a hundred yards, the water was knee-deep. Theo painted furiously as she strode towards him, a tall, majestic, sea-goddess, with dripping cotton clinging to her beautiful breasts. It was exactly how he wanted her.

Sand stuck to her wet legs as she strode defiantly up the beach. She stretched out on a flat rock and closed her eyes. She had changed. He knew that when he had seen her the day before, after the party. He had never seen a woman so burning with love, or so beautiful. The shyness he had known in her as a young girl, the formality she had displayed at the gallery, had both been replaced by an uninhibited passion. And he had helped to destroy her happiness. Had he done it because he wanted her back? It was time he found out, for both their sakes.

Paintbrush in hand, Theo padded across the sand towards Georgia, and stood over her, studying her. He knelt down, holding the brush over her, checking the colour of her flesh tone to ensure he had a perfect match.

'Lift your head,' he ordered. 'Become a water-nymph for me.'

The beautiful black hair lay in damp tendrils around her face, pale now, with those dark violet smudges under her eyes. He would have been only too happy to comfort her, and fill the empty place in her bed. Theo laughed out loud. Georgia had made it very clear that he would not be welcome.

'What's so funny?'

'You are, darling. The beautiful Comtesse, so poised, so chic. If Paris could see you now.'

He had felt insanely jealous when he had returned long ago from New York to find that she had left his studio and married Olivier d'Essange. He had started out to get her back, but his guilt had restrained him. It had been his fault. He had told her that he would be away for a few weeks, but had then returned a whole year later. He had wanted to paint, and had needed no permanent relationship. Georgia had not been good for his work. And by then she was provided for, with a title, a husband and respectability.

Theo had protested that she was too young to be chained to an old man. His friends had laughed. Olivier d'Essange can keep any woman satisfied, they had said. You have no need to worry.

Of course, he had worried more. He had still wanted Georgia; he had missed her, and not simply because she was the best model he had ever had. He had wanted to feel her body in his arms. So, in anger and frustration, he had worked as he had never done before, and the fame that had begun in New York grew until it seemed that anything he painted was a masterpiece. He had only to sign his name to pay a year's rent.

He had wanted to tell Georgia, to lure her back with the money. But by then he knew he had no right. Now he had a second chance.

Theo worked fast. His brush darted across the canvas, swirling flesh tones, a pale shade of topaz, across his canvas. He laughed. Did she know how clearly he saw her naked body in his mind? How well he knew every curve of her body, every line that had burned into his memory for all those years? She looked as if she was almost asleep. Could she really be so relaxed after what she had said earlier? Or had her body finally remembered the perfect discipline of the model?

Theo felt his hand shake as he traced the outline of her buttocks, the full feminine swell outlined by the wet shift that covered her. He needed to see more, to see for himself, again, that faint, apricot sheen on her smooth skin, and the curve of her flesh. Was it really as perfect as he had imagined for so long?

He put down his brush and palette, strode over the sand and gently lifted the hem of Georgia's shift. She didn't move. His hand strayed further, sliding beneath the damp cotton, lifting it to expose the sweet sweep of her thighs, gently curving into a bow of flesh between her legs. His hand hovered an inch away from her, longing to stroke her warm skin. Theo restrained himself with an effort, and contented himself with painting the extra length of naked thigh he had exposed.

He adjusted the beach umbrella so that it cast some shade over the flat rock on which she lay. It was almost midday and the sun blazed down. He put out his hand to stroke the skin he had been absorbed in painting.

Georgia stirred at his touch, her dark lashes fluttering on her cheeks. God, she was so beautiful. He wanted her as much as he had done when she had first walked into his studio.

Her eyes opened. She stared up at him without recognition for a moment, then she stared wildly around her. She sat up and brushed the sand from her body, adjusted the hem of her dress, and glared at him.

'I don't want you to paint me.'

'It's half done. If you move now, it'll be a bad painting, but it will still exist. And I'm a guest. You're supposed to pander to my every whim. How many reasons do you want?'

'Leave me alone.'

'I can't. I care too much. What are you going to do with your life now? Sit around and pick up strangers in bars?' Theo tried to keep his patience, but felt himself failing. 'You want another young man? Try Luc – he's lonely right now.'

'How dare you speak to me like that!'

'You're not a fool, Georgia. Don't behave like one! I'm leaving today. Come back to Paris with me.'

'I have no intention of spending any more time with you. Don't trouble yourself.'

'Georgia, this is ridiculous.'

'I agree. Why don't you leave?'

'Are you sure this is what you want? I sail for the States this week. Come with me.'

'Is that why you came here? I thought it was to help Natasha?'

Theo squirted paint from several tubes on to his palette. 'What's wrong, Georgia? You seem even more unhappy than when we met before.'

'I'm a widow, remember. It's not yet a year since Olivier died.'

Did she think him a fool? Natasha had told him everything. Not that it had been necessary. One look at Georgia and Dominic together made their relationship obvious.

A dark rose flush stained her cheeks and throat. At least she had the grace to know when she was lying. How long had it taken her to seduce Dominic? And how many other men had there been?

'And you miss a man in your bed?'

'I miss Olivier. I don't want anyone else.'

'You found someone pretty fast after me.'

'You left me, Theo. How did you expect me to live?'

'By selling the paintings. Why not?' It had never occurred to him that she would be short of money.

201

'I took one.'

'And what did you do with it? You didn't sell it, I've tried to find it. Did you hide it away somewhere so that your husband wouldn't see it? Anyone with half an eye would have known we were lovers when I painted that.'

Georgia flushed, as if she remembered how that thought had excited Olivier, and Theo knew that the portrait had not been hidden.

He caught her wrist. 'Look at me. That's it, isn't it?' At last he understood. 'That's what Olivier wanted. To think of you with another man? And that's why he ran the club. Olivier d'Essange had no need of money. He wanted to watch you taunting other men, and know that only he could have you.'

'It wasn't like that, Theo. You have no idea.'

'Do you think the society ladies who sit for me don't talk about the thrill of watching you arouse those boys? Do you imagine I don't know what you and Olivier did?'

'I loved him. I still do.'

'He controlled you, don't you understand? He wanted to know that he could possess the creature who was teasing all those men.'

'Olivier is dead. Leave him in peace. And me. Don't destroy the memory I have of him.'

'Don't let him destroy your life. Live a little. Take another lover,' he urged her.

'You're right. I need other men.' She spat the words out at him. 'Lots of them. Get out of my life, Theo. I didn't want you here. You've done what you came to do, haven't you? Now go!'

Theo watched her. She was magnificent, sitting on her rock, flushed with anger. If he could stay here a few more days he might break down her resistance. As it was, he had to sail to New York. He had put back his trip far too long already because of Georgia. He took a step towards her, then turned, picked up his paints and easel, and walked away. It might be better to wait for her to come to him, he thought, and an idea to make her do that had just occurred to him.

Georgia sat under the umbrella and watched him go. How dare he come to her home, uninvited, and talk to her like that? What business was it of his whom she slept with?

She looked down at her shift. It was still damp from her swim, and clung revealingly to her body. She waited until Theo was out of sight, and then clambered up the cliff path. Her foot slipped on a loose stone, and a trickle of blood dripped in to her sandal.

At the top of the path, she pushed open the gate into the garden and stopped. They were still having lunch, all of them, laughing and shouting and having fun.

She took a deep breath and limped across the grass. The voices dropped to a hush and the faces which had looked towards her turned away. The short distance to the house had never seemed so long, nor she so out of control.

When she reached the hall, she crept into its cool, shadowed depths gratefully, hauled herself up the stairs, and breathed a sigh of relief when she closed her bedroom door behind her.

She looked in the mirror. It was worse than she had thought. Lank hair, full of salt and sand, flopped over her shoulders, and her eyes were red and swollen. Her figure was hidden by the shapeless shift, dishevelled and sandy. She was at her best either naked, or in *haute couture*.

Laughter drifted up from the terrace below. Were they all joking about what had happened to her? She could see the gardener, Pedro, sweeping up leaves beneath the olive trees. Over the years he had made the land really beautiful, creating an area of colour and fragrance despite the arid, rocky soil, just as Mathilde always prepared exquisite food with the local ingredients.

Georgia realised that she had never had to lift a finger.

203

Her whole life had been devoted firstly to Theo, then to Olivier and to Fleur's, and then to Dominic. Now there was nothing left. She had never been totally absorbed in anything as Theo was with his painting, shut off from the outside world. Her whole life had revolved around men, exciting them, teasing them, dressing to look good for them. So that now, without a man, she had nothing to occupy her, nothing at all that she wanted to do.

She could hear car doors slamming and voices shouting in the courtyard. So Theo was leaving. Good. She didn't want to hear any more of his opinions about her life.

She flung open her cupboard doors, began lifting out armfuls of clothes and throwing them on to the sofa. It was time to leave here. Theo had been right about that, at least. She would go to Paris first, and then decide her future.

She was startled a little later when the door opened quietly. For a moment she hesitated, not wanting to see anyone, then she heard Mathilde call out, 'Madame, you must eat something. I have brought you a little lunch.'

Mathilde placed a tray of food on a small, painted table and pulled out a chair.

'Come and eat. It will be good for you.' Georgia felt sick. She didn't want food. Mathilde had brought soup, bread and a *salade niçoise*. Right now, she felt that a glass of cognac would have been more use.

But Mathilde insisted. She spooned food on to a plate, and filled a cup. 'Have your consommé while it's hot,' she ordered and Georgia obeyed her.

The salty liquid stung the back of her throat, sending strength through her body, clearing her head a little. She stretched out her arms, and stood a long time in front of the window, watching the sun drop below the surface of the sea, bathing the beach and the olive trees below her in a burst of colour before the darkness fell.

She could see Dominic smoking a cigarette as he leant against the gnarled trunk of an olive tree. Natasha was lying in a hammock strung between two low branches and Georgia saw Dominic bend over her as she stretched out on the gently swinging bed. He threw his cigarette on to the ground and extinguished the glowing stub with his heel. Their soft, loving murmurs seemed to echo through her brain.

When she turned, she saw Mathilde studying her disorganised piles of clothes. 'You're packing. That's good. I'll help you.'

'You're pleased I'm leaving?'

Mathilde nodded.

'You hate me, too?' Georgia's voice was shaky.

'Ah, *non*. But it is what you must do for yourself.'

'Because Dominic no longer wants me?'

Mathilde, folding a dress, said nothing.

'Where Mathilde? Where do I go?'

'That's for you to decide. But you have to leave the two of them alone. He'll be all right now.'

Mathilde's earlier concern for her beloved Dominic seemed to have changed to respect.

'Will you please ask Marc to be ready to drive me to Marseilles?'

Mathilde shook her head. 'You want to take the train? It's too late today. You must go tomorrow.'

Georgia took a grape and ate it slowly, enjoying the fresh taste in her mouth.

What would she do for 24 hours? How would she endure the delay? But Mathilde was right; it was too late to reach Marseilles in time for the night train. She would stay in her room, however, until it was time to go. She undressed slowly and thought about crawling beneath the sheets of her bed and lying there safe until the morning.

A glimmer of moonlight shone in through the open windows. Georgia walked across and looked out again, unable to keep away from the torment of seeing Dominic and Natasha together. Beneath the olive trees they were hidden from the house, except from up here. Either they

205

thought they were totally alone or they had forgotten her existence.

They both lay naked now, enclosed in the soft folds of the gently swinging hammock. She stared down, fascinated, as Dominic bent over Natasha's pale body and covered her with kisses. Georgia ran her fingers over her bare breasts, longing to feel his lips on her skin again. She knew she should move back into her room and leave them to their pleasure, but she stood motionless on the balcony, unable to tear her eyes away from the couple below.

Dominic's dark body covered Natasha now as his head burrowed between her thighs. Georgia felt an ache as she remembered his tongue on her own sex, and she let her fingers fall to her mound as she heard the girl's soft moan and Dominic's tender, loving laughter. Natasha's arms were milk-white against Dominic's dark skin as she raised him up, her fingers lingering over his buttocks as he reared over her. For a moment, Georgia could see the length of his penis outlined in the shadowy moonlight and then she watched as he gently entered Natasha's delicate body.

Georgia longed to escape but felt powerless to move. She wanted to lie motionless in the darkness, to forget what she had seen and shut herself away like an animal in hibernation. She felt hands brush against her shoulders and then watched Marc quietly close her shutters and lead her back towards the bed.

'Forget about them,' he said, wrapping her in the cool sheets. There were bottles on the table beside her and she looked on in amazement as he laid a white lump of crystal sugar in a glass, drenched it in what smelled suspiciously like brandy, and dropped two careful spots of Angostura bitters on top. He stripped the foil off a bottle of Taittinger, and pushed the cork up with his calloused thumbs. The wine foamed into the glass.

She hadn't had a champagne cocktail for a long time – not since her wedding anniversary. For a moment she

206

wanted to throw it in Marc's face. How dare he remind her of Olivier now! She wanted love and comfort, not a memory of a time when she was happier than she would ever be again.

Marc held out a glass, an antique one with a spiral in its stem, of the kind that Olivier had always used for cocktails. She struck out at him, but Marc ducked easily as if he had been expecting her response, and was prepared.

Her hair was still full of sand, and unwashed after her swim. She was dirty and tear-stained and felt ugly. But she needed a friend, and male arms to comfort her, and there was no one she would rather be with than Marc. With one hand he pulled the sheet back so that she was sitting up in bed, completely naked. Then, when she was lost for words, he thrust the glass into her hand. 'Take it,' he insisted.

He took a long drink himself, and waited.

She tasted it – sweet and bitter at the same time – surging through her, giving her life. It was for celebration, for commemoration, for joy, or for pain. She drank deeply.

Marc took the glass gently out of her hand. She let him lead her into the shower. Naked, unashamed, she let him cover her with soap and wash her most intimate parts, without feeling any emotion except the succour of a true friend. When he had shampooed her hair and before he rinsed it off, he pushed the hair away from her damp forehead, kissed her wet cheeks, put the glass again to her lips and let her sip. Then he carefully rinsed the last bubble of shampoo from her hair, until she heard it squeak, and wrapped her in a warm, thick white towel.

Finally, he tipped a few drops from her perfume bottle into the palm of his hand, and stroked the scent over her breasts, belly and thighs. Once more he poured from the flask, running his rough fingers over her back and buttocks, and into the soft creases behind her knees. As he rubbed the oil on her skin, she could feel that he too was excited by his actions, but he continued his soothing progress over his body.

Her hair floated out over her shoulders now, clean and light, rippling in the faint breeze from the sea. She wanted to curl up again in bed, but he led her to a soft armchair and sat her down with the glass once more in her hand. It was kind of him; she was sure she could sleep now. It was what she wanted, sleep and oblivion. She needed to rest, before she started her new life.

Marc held her arm when she tried to put the half-full glass down on the table. 'Drink it all,' he said. 'I have plans for tonight.'

'I'm tired,' she muttered, wanting him to leave her alone now.

He opened the shutters and led her to the window. Georgia could hear the cicadas in the olive trees, and the distant wash of the sea on the shore. She looked out at the clear sky, a dark blue studded with stars, and smelled the tangy scent of eucalyptus. A strong, heady mixture. She breathed in deeply, and leant out of the window, remembering the nights she had spent here with Olivier. The rose coloured bubbles fizzed up to the top of her glass and broke in a fine spray on the tip of her nose.

'Georgia, you've been taking it easy for weeks. You slept alone last night. The last thing you need is sleep.' Marc pressed the glass to her lips again and she felt the champagne trickle down her throat and tiny bubbles bursting on her skin. 'You want stimulation. The boys and I would like to offer you our new programme for the season.'

'Oh Marc, I can't. Please don't ask that of me.' How could he expect her ever to work with them again?

'We're not asking anything of you, Georgia, except that we'll be interested to know what you think. You'll be the first woman to take advantage of our new service. It's guaranteed to relieve stress and make you feel life is worth living.'

Despite her reluctance Georgia was intrigued.

'Trust me,' he said. 'We have a new plan and we want you to be the first to try it out. It will be our present to you. I think you'll like it.' She realised that Marc was wearing the skin-tight, black trousers and full-sleeved white shirt that the team used as a uniform in the evenings, and she could see the line of a leather thong biting into his flesh.

He ran his hands through her hair, fluffing it out over her shoulders. He took an aquamarine kimono from her cupboard and covered her naked body with it. His arms felt good around her and she let her head fall on his chest as they walked out of the room.

Her senses, dazed by the sweet alcohol, responded to the warmth of his arm on her shoulders as he led her down the stairs. Outside, in the courtyard, the air was heavily scented with lavender and pine. It mingled with the brandy, champagne and bitter herbs inside her head, intoxicating her. The villa and the courtyard were dark and silent.

At the barn door, Marc slipped the silk kimono gently off her shoulders. 'You won't need this any more,' he said, holding her upright, with his hand resting on the huge iron latch. He turned her to face him, and put his hand under her chin, lifting it until her drowsy eyes opened to look full into his.

'You are not tired, or alone, or unhappy. You are the most beautiful of women.' He kissed her gently, with closed lips that quivered softly over hers. 'And it is because we love you that we offer you this now, the only reward it is in our power to give you. Enjoy it.'

She heard the door open, but the light was so faint inside the barn that, at first, she struggled to see through the darkness. The space was lit exactly as Olivier had planned it, with thick stubs of candles guttering beneath the stems of the painted lilies.

The team was assembled, in a formal circle, clad only in the leather thongs that they would wear at Fleur's.

They gave no indication of her presence and stood completely still.

She could sense the excitement coursing through the room, could feel it in all the young bodies surging around her. In the corners of the room, she could dimly make out female figures, bending at the knees of the boys and taking their extended cocks into their mouths.

The brandy-soaked sugar still buzzed through her brain, as she took it all in. She turned to Marc; she had no strength, no energy; she felt utterly helpless. He produced a thick swathe of chiffon and tied it over her eyes. 'Don't think, Georgia, just feel.'

The Persian carpet felt smooth beneath her feet as Marc led her to the centre of the room. His arms enveloped her and he kissed her gently, full on the lips. She felt his lips brush the tips of her fingers, and then she was alone.

Soft hands laid her on the rug. She could feel its silky strands brush gently on the small of her back, as a woman's tongue fluttered over her breasts. Long curls of hair, scented with rose and lavender from the perfume factory, fell over her throat as the tiny mouth became more demanding, licking each nipple into a moist erect peak.

She could hear soft movements around her, but the chiffon bandeau blinded her eyes. She could see nothing, as all her senses concentrated on the irresistible stirring of her body.

More hands stroked her, drawing her legs gently apart, and then a dainty finger pushed open the mouth of her sex and slid inside, searching until it found the hard bud of her clitoris. She moaned as her sensitive flesh responded to the increasing pressure. She wanted more, but to her dismay, the finger withdrew as silently as it had come. It was replaced by a delicate, flickering tongue. She felt mouths opening and closing on her flesh now, as two girls sucked with increasing vigour on her

210

breasts, and a third continued her steady progress deep inside her sex.

She heard one of the girls gasp, releasing the pressure from her breast. She wanted to cry out to beg her to continue, but instantly the lips enclosed her again, sucking more fiercely now, and rhythmically, almost as if the girl was in the throes of her own orgasm. The girl's breasts swung against her, forward and back as she sucked, and Georgia realised that one of the men must be taking her from behind.

The thought excited her; she imagined the girl's buttocks rearing high into the air as the man entered her, each thrust pushing the girl against her own body. The second girl, and the third, between her thighs, lost their rhythm and then recaptured it as they, too, experienced pleasure.

Georgia writhed ecstatically beneath the fluttering tongues. She needed more. She, too, wanted one of the massive male organs that she imagined driving into the girls' willing orifices. As each girl neared her climax, their sucking became stronger so that Georgia could feel the full force of their orgasms as they sank down on top of her, covering her with their long perfumed hair.

She moaned as her breasts and sex ached for fulfilment, but heard and felt nothing except the soft drum of bare feet, circling around her.

She wanted to cry out, to beg them to take her, and then she felt strong, male hands slide beneath her, cupping her soft cheeks in large, muscular hands. She felt the smooth head of a swollen penis inserted into her wet and eager opening, filling her as it steadily climbed higher inside her. She felt her muscles quiver uncontrollably around it as the man's fingers kneaded her buttocks, pulling her hard against him. In a swift, irresistible flash, she felt her orgasm flow over him, shuddering with relief as she came. It felt so sweet, so good, lying on the warm rug with the man still hard inside her.

For a moment he remained completely still, letting her

recover, then his mouth found her softened nipple and sucked hard on it, still damp from the girl's tongue. He felt so different from the girl's soft lips. His tongue rasped over her sated buds, teasing them back into life as he steadily moved again inside her.

Every nerve-ending inside her responded to his gentle pressure, waiting until once again she longed for him to drive with greater force. Instead he withdrew, kissing her quivering sex as he released his hold on her. She felt another man lower himself on to her. His body was more muscular, the flesh harder and the penis that pressed into her now was thicker and longer.

Her skin was slippery with sweat as her hips rose to take him, her mind aware of nothing but the pleasure of her body. This time she cried out as she climaxed, and felt him respond to her excitement.

Again and again, male flesh entered her, and withdrew, without her knowing which man was taking her, until a face brushed against her cheek and she felt a long, puckered scar, rough against her skin. She reached up and touched his face, stroking the rough, deep wound with the tips of her fingers. It was Luc. As if angry that she knew him, he thrust harder into her. His penis, unlike the rest of his body, was smooth and silky soft, and it sought out her pleasure like a wild animal inside her. Her senses clouded and blurred as every nerve-ending in her body responded to him.

All the men were new to her except Marc, whom she had worked with at Fleur's. Blindfolded, she recognised him by the callous on his thumb, the result of an accident on a boat. When his scarred hands cupped her buttocks, he lifted her towards him as he drove in the last inches of his massive shaft. She heard him gasp as her sex lips closed around him, and felt the sweet heat of his testicles nestling against her vulva.

When she could take no more and was drifting into the sleep of the sated, unknown hands raised her from the floor and carried her gently out of the barn.

She must have lost consciousness, because she awoke later, in her own bed. There was a bowl of fruit beside her. She ate, suddenly hungry. She bit into the hard, white flesh of an apple, and lay comfortably awake. And alone.

Tomorrow she would leave here, to return to Paris. There she would easily find men to slake the raging passion of her body, men who knew nothing of her past.

Marc had given her the strength to look forward to a fresh beginning. Now she had to go, to get away from here as fast as she could, and start her new life.

Chapter Fourteen

'Stop!'

They were almost at the main road. Now, obediently, Marc drove the Phantom into a lay-by and waited. Georgia looked out of the window at the azure sea and the forest of pine and evergreens. She knew she had to leave today, immediately, before she lost heart and changed her mind. Mathilde was right – this was no place for her any more.

But they were all wrong about Theo. She had not wanted him to come back into her life, and she was glad he was going back to California. She wanted him out of France.

All she needed was one last look at the view she loved so much, at the hills and the brilliant turquoise Mediterranean. 'Do we have time to stay here for a few minutes?' she asked. 'I want to make sure I remember all this.'

'You're not going for ever,' Marc assured her. 'You'll be back.'

She nodded. She would return sometime, but how long would it be before she saw this coastline again, and what was she going to do in the meantime? She closed her eyes, breathing in the sharp tang of the south. 'We'd better drive on. I don't want to miss the train.'

'Are you sure you don't want me to drive you to Paris?' Marc asked when they finally reached the railway station. He looked immaculate in his discreet uniform, but Georgia was all too aware of the powerful body hidden beneath the crisp, grey flannel.

She enjoyed the invitation in his eyes. Did he hope that she would change her mind and stay with him overnight in one of the many pleasurable hotels they knew on the road? After last night, the thought of a whole night with Marc made her shiver with anticipation.

But no. Georgia was determined that her new life would not involve Fleur's in any way, and that included Marc. They would come together again – she was sure about that – but now she needed to cut free, and embark on her new life.

Last night had been wonderful, a perfect present. She reached up, and put her hands on his shoulders. 'Thank you for last night, Marc.'

'It was an honour. You are the best, Georgia. Don't ever forget that. Do you know that Dominic has asked me to run Fleur's for him?

'He's not going to perform with Natasha?'

'No, he doesn't want her involved. I think he wants to keep her to himself.'

'I see.' She tried not to feel hurt, but could not help it.

'Do you think I can make a go of it?' he asked.

Georgia threw her arms around him. 'Darling Marc. If you offer your clients anything like you gave me yesterday, they'll be queuing up. I'll be back myself soon.'

'Any time. We'll all be waiting.'

'You gave me back my sanity. I thought I was helping Dominic, doing what Olivier would have wanted. Instead I nearly destroyed his son.'

'Don't be too hard on yourself. He's a tough kid. And he had his problems before he came to us.'

'Thank you.' Georgia wished she felt as confident as

Marc seemed. 'Anyway, I need to let him live his own life now.'

'He's not on his own, you know.'

'Natasha?'

'She's strong, much stronger than she looks. And she loves him. She'll do anything she can to keep him faithful.' Marc took her hand. 'She'll do what you did for Monsieur le Comte.'

Georgia took a deep breath. 'Olivier helped me, too.' If only he was still with her.

'What will you do now?' Marc sounded concerned.

'I'll spend a couple of days in Paris, then I'll go to Lusigny and pack up my things at the château. I'm leaving France, going right away. But I'm not yet sure where.'

'Why not go back to England?' Marc voiced the thought that kept coming back to her.

'It hasn't been my home for a long time.'

'What about your family?'

'They threw me out.' None of them had made any attempt to contact her in all these years. Was she strong enough to confront them all again?

'Because you married a Frenchman? Or did they know about the club?' Marc grinned, apparently convinced that the sober English would disapprove of the pleasures on offer at Fleur's.

'No, it was before that. I lived with an artist. I was his model.'

'Monsieur Sands?'

Georgia nodded.

'So. You'll go back to him. He would like that.'

'You're quite wrong. He despises me. Maybe I'll just travel around for a while.'

'If you need an escort ...?' Marc's clean young face broke into a grin.

'If I need an escort, I'll let you know right away. But I expect that when I return, you'll be married to Françoise and have a couple of children,' she teased.

Marc grinned. 'You might just be right. I intend to ask her soon.'

'You'll break Mathilde's heart when you do.'

'Mathilde has transferred her affections.'

'Oh?'

'She thinks Luc has a broken heart. As always, she has decided that her cooking will cure him.'

'It probably will.' Georgia had no fears for Luc's future. The ladies at Fleur's would adore him.

'It's time to go.'

Marc nodded and started up the engine. 'OK, please yourself. I'll look after your things at the château whenever you're ready. Take care of yourself. And Georgia – '

'Yes?'

'See Theo again.'

The Marseilles railway station was quiet. She was early for the night train and found a compartment easily. The *chef de train* bustled up, snapped his fingers at a porter to assist Madame with her valise and escorted her himself, settling her comfortably on a plush, velour-covered banquette which would later convert into her bed.

'If there is anything you require, Madame, please do not hesitate to call on me. You will be taking dinner?'

Georgia decided that she could not spend the whole evening shut up in this tiny space, however well appointed. She nodded, slipping a generous tip into his discreetly open palm.

He bowed. 'I will ensure that you have the best table and are not disturbed.'

She did not feel at all hungry, but a meal would help to pass the time. Georgia shook her dress out of its folds of tissue paper and hung it up behind the door.

She looked out of the window as they left the station. Goodbye Antibes. Goodbye Villa d'Essor. She glanced through the newspaper left for her by the guard, but the print seemed to blur in front of her eyes every time she tried to concentrate.

One photograph on the society page caught her eye. 'Famous American artist, Theo Sands, leaves France this week on the *Normandie*. He sails to New York where his latest exhibition is due to open in ten days' time.'

She dropped the newspaper on the seat beside her. At least one of her problems was solved. Theo Sands was out of her life for good.

Georgia breathed a sigh of relief as the train picked up speed. She felt hot and sticky, and opened the small window, grateful for some air now that they were moving fast. Splashing cold water over her hands and face, she changed quickly into her evening dress.

Thanks to Marc, she felt beautiful again. After last night, her body tingled deliciously, feeling smooth and glossy. His idea for Fleur's was brilliant, and she looked forward to taking advantage of it again. But not just yet. Not until she had a clearer idea of her future.

After weeks in the south, it was fun to dress up again in formal clothes, with stockings and suspenders, and soft, kid-leather shoes. And she always enjoyed travelling – just being on a train gave her pleasure.

Sliding one hand along the wooden rail for balance, she made her way through the jolting carriages to the restaurant car. A man stood in the corridor, staring out of the dusty window, smoking a cigarette. He turned round as she squeezed past him. 'I'm so sorry, I'm in your way.'

'Not at all.' She lowered her eyes, sure that he could move closer to the side of the carriage, if he tried. He was good-looking, tall and blonde, and wore an expensive lounge jacket. His hair was long as if he deliberately cultivated an artistic impression.

At another time he might have interested her. Now – she squeezed her thighs together, experiencing again the memory of the previous night – no, she had no need to start on casual encounters yet. She had to be free to think clearly.

The restaurant car was lit by pale pink lamps, and their soft light glowed on tables covered with crisp damask cloths and shining cutlery. Her first glass of champagne revived her, and Georgia began to look forward to her meal. Delicious smells wafted from the tiny galley, and attentive waiters took her order. They stood back discreetly as another passenger walked up to her table. It was the man she had met in the corridor.

'Would you mind if I joined you?'

He gave the appearance of a northerner, Swedish perhaps, or German. He waited courteously for her answer. She hesitated – why not enjoy his company after all? It was a long enough journey, and conversation would help the time pass more pleasantly.

'Please,' she smiled, gesturing to the empty seat opposite her.

'Thank you.' As he sat down she was aware of his quiet appraisal of her body, his pale blue eyes swiftly assessing her as he sipped his cocktail. For the moment he amused her.

He was charming, but a little too attentive, too sure of his attraction. She wondered if he made a habit of picking up lone women on trains.

'There, you are laughing. I am pleased. You seemed so sad that I felt I was intruding.'

'You must forgive me, Monsieur, if I am not responsive. I had expected to dine alone. My mind was on other things.' It would surprise him to learn just what images had been filling her mind.

She had no intention of letting this go any further than dinner; he was not her type, and she objected to being thought of as an easy target. Last night had changed her thinking and, for once, she felt in control. Besides, he was brash, and less sophisticated than he obviously thought he was.

Still, he was excellent company and by the end of the

meal, Georgia was grateful to him for having raised her dull spirits so effectively. As she held out her hand to say goodbye, his fingers curled just a little too firmly in her palm, and his mouth was a touch too close to the back of her hand as he bid her good-night. His lips parted suggestively on her flesh as he lingered over his farewell, making her skin tingle with the heat of his breath.

Georgia could not deny that she felt a strong physical response to his male arrogance, and she was sure that he had no doubt of the effect he had on her. But tonight she preferred to be alone to think.

Her night with Jean at The Ritz had been delightful, and she had every intention of introducing other men into her life. But there was too much to consider, and it was too soon after Dominic; her emotions were still too raw. And for some extraordinary reason, she imagined the scorn in Theo's eyes if he thought she could be had quite so easily.

'Good-night Claude,' she said firmly, looking straight up into his blue eyes to make her decision clear. 'I have enjoyed your company.'

'I hope we will meet again soon.'

'I am sure of it. We have many mutual friends in Paris.'

Negotiating the swaying coaches on her return to her compartment, Georgia wondered if she had been too hasty. Wasn't a night in an attractive man's arms just what she needed to drive Dominic and Theo right out of her mind?

She turned the key and unlocked her door. The tiny space looked cosy and welcoming, with its neat appointments and gleaming wooden walls. For a few hours it was all hers. Was this what her life would be now? Travelling alone from one place to another?

Her bed had been neatly made up with crisp linen and tight, mustard-yellow blankets, with her negligée laid out over the pillow. Like all her night-wear, it was made of exquisite silk and lace, sheer and delicate. Georgia packed the dress she had worn for dinner, and hung up the following day's suit in the narrow, mirror-fronted cupboard.

She fastened the long row of tiny buttons on her gown, enjoying the cool silk on her heated skin. Bracing her legs against the movement of the train, she brushed her teeth in the tiny corner basin, lowered the lid, and laid out her face creams on its surface.

Before she had time to remove her make-up there was a knock at the door. Impatiently, she called out, 'Yes?'

There was no reply, simply another knock. It must be the cup of tea she had ordered. She opened the door a fraction and poked her head out between the gap. It was Claude.

He smiled, his eyes sparkling. 'You are sure you would not welcome some company?'

'You are kind, but no. Another time, perhaps.' She would never see him again, but it seemed more polite to leave the possibility open.

She closed the door gently, leant her back against it and breathed in deeply. However brief it had been, the encounter had aroused her. Her nipples jutted out against the sheer silk negligée; the tingle between her thighs stirred again.

Georgia lay on top of her narrow bed in the small airless compartment. She turned off the main light and drew back the tight sheet and blanket, but her earlier tiredness had gone and there was no chance of sleep. She lifted the corner of the blind, and stared out at the darkened world flashing by outside.

Her skin felt uncomfortably sticky and clammy. She lifted the soft folds of her night-dress, pulling it up over her thighs. She would have preferred to have slept naked, but she felt nervous about doing so on the train. What if there was a crash? She slid her hand in between her legs, comforting herself, rubbing her fingers gently against the hard bud of her clitoris.

221

Maybe she was a fool not to have accepted Claude's invitation. If she had, she would be lying with him now, sharing this narrow bed. Georgia shuddered as her hard-working fingers failed to bring her the satisfaction she craved.

Was Theo right? Was she doomed to be forever alone because she had rejected him? But he had left her first. Surely he was in the wrong? The thought of Theo now overwhelmed her, and her fingers rubbed faster. She wanted Theo here now, taking her as he had done when she was seventeen. But he was far away and, for the second time, she had lost her chance.

Surely other women didn't feel anything like the constant desire that raged through her body now? If they did, how could they control themselves? She had tried celibacy, had maintained her vow for seven long months after Olivier's death. And then her passion for love had returned with double force, leaving her so exposed and vulnerable that she had allowed Dominic to do what he wanted. And, as she had known in her heart that he would, he had left her for a woman of his own. If only she had taken a lover sooner, she might have escaped all this humiliation.

In another six hours they would be in Paris. She planned to spend a day or two at The Ritz while she decided what to do with her life. Maybe she should go to England and see her brother. Would he be prepared to forget the family scandal she had caused by running off to Paris all those years ago? He had been young then, but it must have cast a shadow over his childhood. She wondered if her parents ever mentioned her name.

The train stopped; she wasn't sure where they were. It was too soon for Lyon and the station seemed too small. It was, perhaps, Valence, but it was already quite dark, and the steam from the engine obscured the station's nameplate. She could hear doors slamming and the shrill blast of a guard's whistle.

She faced a long night ahead. The fierce ache inside

her burned with even greater intensity. Involuntarily, her hand strayed again to the damp curls between her thighs and her fingers poked into her open cleft, seeking to assuage her fierce longing for a man.

The constant jolting of the carriage jarred her aching head. After Paris, where could she go? The question rapped through her brain in time to the insistent clatter of wheels on the line. She heard another tap on the door. Impatiently, she called out, 'Go away. Leave me in peace.'

'*Le thé*, Madame?'

She groaned, pulled her gown into place and opened the door. It was terribly late, but she would love a cup of tea. She saw the brown cap of the attendant, with the tray in his hand, and then the door swung fully open and he was inside her compartment, leaning against the polished wood.

'Claude!'

'Your tea, Madame.' The cold blue eyes glittered.

'I said "no",' but she knew that he could see her body giving him an altogether different message.

'I hear your words, but I don't believe you.' He put out his hand and cupped one breast with his long fingers, stroking her hardened nipple through the lace bodice. 'Are you sure you want me to leave?'

His eyes were cool and arrogant, his touch masterly. Once again, she felt his lips on her bare skin, this time more intimately, as his mouth caressed the base of her neck, becoming more confident as her head fell back and she acknowledged her pleasure.

His hands slipped around her waist, pulling her towards him. He was so expert, so sure of himself, so positive that no woman would be able to resist him. He was obviously convinced he was a magnificent lover, and Georgia suspected that he was probably right.

She felt the heat rising between her thighs as he held her tight against the rock-hard shaft inside his pants. She knew her body was responding exactly as he had assumed it would, but maybe, for once in his life, he was not quite aware of her own power, her ability to taunt, tease, and take what she wanted. He had tricked his way into her compartment, but she was delighted to have him here. She would have some fun first. After her previous night, she felt sure again of her power over men.

She felt her nerve endings tingle as his lips fluttered over the soft lobe of her left ear, then she pulled back and held him at arm's length. His previously calm features were eager now; his blue eyes glistened and his breath came hot and fast. Delicately, she brushed his broad shoulders with her fingernails as she smiled up at him.

'You're right, Claude. I want you. Are you sure you are ready for me?'

He laughed out loud as he caught her by the waist again, and pressed against her. She felt the full length of his penis through the thin wool of his elegant slacks as she slipped her hands over his narrow lizard-skin belt.

'Let me see you, Claude,' she breathed. 'I want to know how much you really want me.' Her fingers played with his silver buckle as she loosened the thin strip of leather and started to undo the buttons of his flies. She felt him tremble as she deliberately delayed opening the gusset, then slid her long painted nails inside, down over the taut muscles of his belly, lightly stroking the tip of his engorged penis as she gently slipped his pants and trousers down around his ankles.

He was right to be proud of his manhood. Even Georgia could hardly resist a flash of excitement as she stared at him in admiration. She allowed herself a small, feminine gasp of appreciation, encouraging him to think that she had never seen such a perfect specimen before, that the sheer size and force of the swollen organ before her was reducing her to helpless adoration.

Claude beamed, but, as Georgia had intended, he was at something of a disadvantage, unable to move towards her because of the clutter of clothes wrapped around his ankles. The sight of his elegant, long, black socks, attached to suspenders over his firm calves, was threatening to send bubbles of dangerous laughter up inside her, but Georgia moistened her lips and gazed at him innocently.

Hampered as he was, Claude still heightened the tension in every nerve in her body. She was fully prepared to tease him as much as she could, but she was at least as eager to feel his powerful manhood deep inside her, as he was to thrust it into her. The small moan she gave as she smoothed back his foreskin was not exactly planned.

She watched his eyes fix on her breasts as she slowly unfastened the first of the long row of buttons down the front of her negligée. This was for her; it would be the way she wanted it, for her own pleasure.

Claude stared at her, eagerly watching every movement of her fingers. Mesmerised, he lifted one foot to step out of his trousers, struggling and almost losing his balance as he realised, too late, that his shoes were still on his feet. Inelegantly, he fought his way out of the restricting layers, his eyes still locked on to Georgia as she loosened first one strap of her negligée, and then the other, holding the sheer folds of lace over her full mounds as long as she dared. She slid the gown to the floor, stepped in front of him completely naked, and lay down on the bed.

She watched him strip off his socks, and held out her arms, confident that he would find her teasing as amusing as she had. Claude jumped on the bed beside her. There was no need to hide her eagerness now. She arched her body beneath him and took his swollen penis between her thighs. He groaned out loud as she squeezed his hard flesh with a steady rhythm. Reluctantly, she released him; it had felt too good feeling his strength pressing on her hot sex, and she did not want this to be too quick. Claude was going to have to wait.

She shivered in his arms and murmured softly: 'You are superb.' She watched the swift gleam of triumph in his eyes, felt him thrust against her as her words excited him even more. She pretended to pull back in alarm, and heard a gasp of anger as she slipped away from him. Rolling over on her side until she was on top of him, she took him in her mouth and sucked fiercely. He fought for control. She knew that he would come at any moment if she let him. But she would not. Not yet.

She slid her thigh over his pelvis, straddling him, forcing him down beneath her as she rubbed her vulva up and down the full length of his shaft. He groaned out loud as her breasts swung against his mouth, then she withdrew as his eager lips sought to suckle on her rigid peaks.

Beneath her, Claude's eyes narrowed. She knew just how badly he needed to feel his whole length deep inside her, but her own pleasure was overwhelming as she massaged herself gently on the ridged length of his penis. She could feel the first hot wave of her orgasm rise as she dealt mercilessly with him. His husky groans drove her to even greater excitement as she lowered herself further down on to him, finally taking his full length inside her, until she felt the hard bone of his pelvis against her soft mound, and felt the heat flood through her as wave after wave of pleasure took her beyond all control.

Claude was thrusting now as she straddled over him, her senses reeling as his powerful hips pushed up against her melting sex. She let his harsh tongue suck fiercely as he took her breast into his greedy, open mouth and stroked her finger over his heaving chest as he lay helpless beneath her replete body, tasting the salt sweat on his throat as he climaxed.

Gently, she released him. She would send him on his way as soon as he had recovered. Well, she grinned down at him, perhaps not straightaway.

* * *

Paris was dry and baking hot, the air humid and sultry. At the Gare de Lyon a car was waiting for Georgia as arranged. She slipped thankfully into its roomy interior and sank back on the smooth leather seats. She had decided not to go to The Ritz; in the city heat, she did not feel like dressing up. Instead, she would spend the day at Fleur's, pack up the last of her possessions and spend the evening curled up in a loose gown with her bedroom doors open to the garden. She tapped on the screen isolating the driver.

'101 *Boulevard Berlioz, s'il vous plaît.*' She wanted to say goodbye to Fleur's, to her life there. It would do her good to spend a night or two in the old house, alone with her memories. Another time, when she felt in need of company, she could stay as long as she liked at the hotel.

Heavy drops of rain were just starting to fall as they made their way through the dusty, deserted streets: the languid, full drops of high summer, accompanied by a distant rumble of thunder. Paris was dead in August. Of course there was a dull roar of traffic, but even that was less than usual.

The air was uncannily still and, after Provence, it seemed strange not to hear birds singing. As they turned into the leafy avenue, the trees rustled with a sudden rush of wind as the storm gathered. Georgia sniffed the cooler air appreciatively. Perhaps at last the oppressive heat would break. At the very least the imminent downpour would wash out the dirt from the city streets.

'Thank you. I'll be fine now.'

Quickly she dismissed the driver at the door, after he had deposited her single small suitcase in the hall. It felt strange to be here alone. The house was normally so full of life, but now the old building was quiet and the furniture covered with dust sheets. In a few weeks it would buzz again with the excitement of sexual arousal and fulfilment, with youth and beauty. For the moment it was like a stage set, deserted after the end of a performance.

She had a small suite of rooms downstairs, behind the swimming pool, and she went there now, unbuttoning her jacket. It was still humid and she wanted to be rid of her restricting clothes. Her rooms were all lined with padded beige leather; the furniture was modern glass and chrome, in complete contrast to the Louis XIV style in the rest of the house. The clean contours of this room had always given her pleasure and, with the club empty, she could open the wide, double doors leading to the swimming pool, and look out at the blue, unruffled expanse of water.

In an hour she had packed all the clothes she kept there. There were a few things she wanted from her dressing-room upstairs, but they could wait for the moment. She was longing for a swim.

Quickly she stripped and plunged in. It felt wonderful to have the pool to herself. Georgia swam eight fast lengths, and then sat on the gold mosaic steps, letting the water lap around her feet. She was going to miss this place, especially with Marc's new service.

Right now she felt like lying here, naked as she was, with the boys doing a strong crawl towards her. If she closed her eyes, she could imagine their steady progress, the water rippling as their bodies sent ever more powerful waves to the end of the pool. There was no chance of that tonight. She was alone; the whole house was hers. And, she suddenly realised, she was hungry and thirsty.

She enjoyed the sensation of water dripping off her skin as she slipped a key into the lock of the cellar door. She found a bottle of Krug, and took it upstairs. The air was so warm that she was completely dry before she reached the kitchen. It was mid-afternoon and already as dark as night. She prayed for the storm to break and end this enervating humidity.

She was so hungry that her mouth watered at the thought of the delicious food she might be enjoying at

The Ritz. But it didn't matter, there were always good things to eat in the fridge. She tugged at the door handle and almost fell back. It was open – and empty. There was nothing at all inside. Of course, how stupid of her. No one had been here since June. But there must be something here. She tried the larder and found it full of tins. She took a large tin of beluga caviare and keyed it open.

She unwrapped the foil of the champagne, twisted off the wire, then pushed upwards as Marc had done. Nothing happened. The cork didn't even shift. She was starting to lose her temper. Surely she wasn't this helpless! One night on her own, without a man, and she couldn't even pour herself a drink. Angrily, she thrust upwards with the balls of her thumbs, snapping a nail half-way down, and spraying herself with the spurting foam. At least the champagne had kept cool in the cellar. She filled a glass with the wine and ate a huge spoonful of caviare.

She switched on all the lights in the hall because it was so dark and gloomy. She had never seen this place so empty, nor had she ever stood here stark naked. The staircase was in front of her. With the bottle and a glass in one hand and the caviare in the other, she walked up to the top and opened the salon door. This was your dream, Olivier, she thought, and you made it happen. What would Marc's boys do in here, she wondered. She gave a little twirl. It will be fun, she thought; I shall look forward to returning as a client.

Her glass was empty and she refilled it from the bottle. The curtains were not drawn, but it was dark in the room and no one could see in. The rumbles of thunder were closer together and the rain was starting to fall more steadily. She huddled down on the floor, watching the drops run down the window, washing clean streaks through the summer dust.

She really ought to get dressed; she shouldn't sit here quite naked. There was a robe in the dressing-room. She went to go and get it. The air was much cooler now and the swish of the rain soothed her. There was another flash of lightning and she moved instinctively towards the window. The sky lit up again like a paean to the summer's end and to her life here. And the shaft of light from the doorway died.

She turned and moved on to the landing. She knew that she had left all the lights on, and yet the house was in darkness. She stabbed at the switch on the wall, flicking it back and forth. The rain was falling heavily and the sky was black with thick rain clouds. Georgia peered out of the salon window, but she could see no lights in any of the houses in the street. The main power cable must be down. Only the headlights of a few cars on the street outside lit up the glistening black glass and the streaming rivulets of rainwater.

It didn't matter – this room was full of candles. All she needed was something to light them with. In the dressing-room, there should be a lighter which Dominic had given her. She reached up, took down one of the beeswax candles and held it tightly in her hand.

She groped her way past the heavy, silk curtain covering the dressing-room door, and felt a moment of panic. She was being foolish; it wasn't even late yet, and there was no reason to feel the slightest alarm. If she wished, she could, at any moment, telephone The Ritz and have them send round a car to collect her.

A fire would have been laid in her dressing-room. It was cool enough now to appreciate a little warmth. More importantly, the flames would cheer her.

Dominic was as extravagant as his father had been and the lighter was beautiful, silky, pearl-grey platinum with her name studded on one side in the pale sapphires she loved. She had thought it vulgar, but she had been pleased at his thoughtfulness and, so soon after Olivier's death, it had cheered her as Dominic had said he hoped it would. She flicked it now, relieved to see its steely flame pierce the gloom of the dark room. Perhaps it had not been such a good idea to decide to spend the night here alone, after all.

The red damask on the walls shimmered in the gentle glow of the candle-light, making the room seem even more beautiful to her. She had been happy here. She laughed. What else could she do? With her champagne in one hand and the tin of beluga in the other, Georgia lay back on her chaise longue. At least something was going right; the fire had flared up straight away. Georgia licked the last beads of caviare off her spoon and grinned. If the boys could see her now, they might add this pleasure to their repertoire.

She put the dirty spoon down on the table. Something was wrong. The flickering firelight gave ample light, but there was no answering gleam from the skin-tones of her portrait. She could see the heavy gold frame, but, in place of the glowing flesh of a naked young girl, she saw the dark trunk of an ancient, twisted olive tree, bare of all its leaves. The barren tree mocked her.

Only one man could have painted that.

Only one man would have dared to hang it on her wall.

Theo.

Furious, Georgia jumped to her feet and, taking the candle, she made her way out on to the landing. The light flickered in a sudden draught and went out. She groped her way along the passage, constantly flicking the lighter as the flame wavered and died in sudden draughts. The lighter still shone brightly, but she lit it less often now, feeling her way down the stairs. If the lighter failed she had no idea where to find matches.

She went through the dining room and opened a green baize door leading down to the lower level. Her footsteps echoed eerily round the marble-lined walls surrounding the pool. She dressed hurriedly, grabbed her bag and keys, and opened the garage door. Thank heavens a car had been left here.

She drove madly through the streaming streets, only

slowing down after she took a corner too fast and skidded across the road.

Her portrait would be at the studio. She hadn't been back there since Olivier had taken her away from it, but she knew her way blindfolded. And on this dark night she needed that knowledge. Few of the streetlamps were alight, and there were hardly any cars on the road.

Just what did Theo think he was playing at? Was it some weird form of revenge? Did he plan to display her naked body as the centrepiece of his next exhibition? And how dare he break into Fleur's!

The roads were filthy – weeks worth of dust were splattered up by the rain. The car stuttered once or twice, and then jerked forward erratically. It hadn't been used all summer and the rain was getting to it. Georgia pumped her foot up and down on the accelerator. 'Come on,' she urged, 'we're almost there.'

But, at the end of the next street, the engine gave a final cough and died. Georgia looked up at the road signs and tried to remember how far away she was from the studio. It should only take her a few minutes to walk, but the rain was coming down in sheets. Why hadn't she stayed at Fleur's and gone to bed? She could have retrieved the painting in the morning.

Georgia slammed the car door shut and stepped out into the gutter, already inches deep in fast-running rainwater. Her feet were soaked immediately. She put her jacket over her head and ran through streets that became increasingly familiar. She passed the bakery where she and Theo used to buy their baguettes every morning, and the butcher whose meat they had never been able to afford. All the shops now had their blinds closed, even the café on the corner where she and Theo had eaten whenever he sold a painting.

She was drenched by the time she reached the court-yard. What a fool she was to have come here. What made her think he still kept the old studio? It was dark, but that didn't mean he wasn't there. No one had lights tonight.

The door was locked. She banged on it as hard as she could. She didn't care if he was asleep; so would she have been, if he hadn't started playing stupid games. And then she remembered that he couldn't possibly be there. Theo must be in mid-Atlantic. But, in that case, who had switched the paintings?

There was no sound from inside the studio. Georgia put her hand above the lintel and felt through the dust. Her fingers closed on a heavy iron key. So, Theo still kept it in the same place after all these years.

The key grated in the lock, but it had always been difficult to open. Nothing had changed. The door swung open.

Chapter Fifteen

*I*nside the studio, Georgia lit a stub of candle that she found on the windowsill. She knew this room so well, but it looked unused now, as if it were simply a place for storage.

It had been visited recently though. Even in the dim light she could see scuffed footprints on the dusty, pine floorboards. Stacks of unframed canvases were piled high against the walls, but there was no sign of her portrait. It seemed odd to leave such open access to the place, now that the hundreds of paintings here were valuable. Theo used to be so careful about his work.

With increasing eagerness, Georgia checked through the grimy racks of paintings. She was wasting her time. None of them seemed to have been touched for years, but they were more familiar to her than the modern works she had seen at the gallery. She held the candle up higher and looked around the room. She thought it seemed bigger, as if something was missing, but perhaps it was because the place was so much tidier without the paint-encrusted palettes, dirty glasses and empty wine bottles that used to fill every available surface.

There was an easel at the far end of the studio, covered by a sheet. Tugging at one corner, she exposed a large, familiar painting. Her own eyes stared back at her, out of the face of a young girl in a white débutante's dress, youthful and innocent. Why had he kept that? It should have been burned and the past buried. No one would ever buy it. She felt a million miles away from the girl in the painting.

Behind it, hanging on the wall, was her missing picture. A wave of anger surged up inside her. If Theo was on his way to America, he must have paid someone to break into Fleur's, steal her portrait and replace it with that barren tree. The thought of a stranger creeping into her most private room, enraged her.

Theo was not going to put her naked body on public display! Georgia wrenched her wet shoe off one foot, and wobbled for a moment, off-balance, before she drove the sharp, pointed heel through the canvas, stabbing a ragged-edged hole. She stuck her fingers into the tear, forcing it wider with all the strength in her hands, as she ripped it from side to side. She stepped back, feeling a thrill of pure pleasure. She had lived with that view of herself for too long. It was time to shake off old memories and to look forward.

She turned to go, but the room still had a hold on her. This was where she had lived with Theo during the happiest years of her life. She bit her lip. That couldn't be true – it was just that everything had seemed so simple then. She had loved Theo, and he had loved her, and nothing else had mattered. Until he left her.

Theo obviously didn't work here any more – this was the only easel in the room and the smell of oil paint was faint and stale. The red chair had gone – the one he had kept for mothers to sit on while they chaperoned their daughters. A chair that was deliberately uncomfortable to persuade them not to stay.

All that was left was one old, broken table, splattered with candle grease and stuck in a corner of the room. She ran her hands over its rough surface, remembering the first meal she had eaten sitting here, when she had swallowed her first oyster and sipped her first glass of wine.

She had told her mother she was going to a dance. A friend had covered for her, while she had come to spend an evening with Theo. He had sold a painting, and had wanted to celebrate with her. He had spent every franc he had earnt on that dinner, and on a glorious jade-green silk shawl.

He had already been painting her for a week without her mother present, but that evening she had sat demurely in her ballgown, until, once again, he had slipped it off her shoulders. She was used to that by then, familiar with the way she felt when his fingers touched her naked body. But this time he had wrapped her in the luxurious Chinese silk, carried her over to the bed and asked her if she wanted him to make love to her.

She hadn't known what to say. More than anything else in the world she had wanted to be close to him, to feel his hands caressing her body. She had sat up so that the shawl fell back on the bed, and reached out for him. She had forgotten everything else until the next morning when her parents had broken into the studio. Her friend, tearful and worried, had told them where Georgia had gone.

Sleepy, and deliriously happy, she had announced that she wanted to live with Theo. Her mother had tried to argue with her, but her father had walked straight out of the room. She had heard his harsh voice shouting at her mother in the courtyard. 'Let the slut stay where she is. She'll crawl back when he's had all he wants of her.'

Theo had started painting the second portrait that day. Georgia looked over to the corner of the room where it now lay in shreds. She had watched every movement of his hands on the brushes as he had worked, while she had lain on the bed in which she spent every night in his arms.

Of course – that was why the room looked so different.

The bed was missing: that massive four-poster bed, which Theo had used as a background for all his society portraits, and on which he must have seduced hundreds of young girls since her.

She must go. There was no point in staying here any longer. As soon as the rain slackened, she would run to the bar on the corner of the street and call for a cab.

Her candle flickered and went out. She hadn't closed the door properly, so that now it swung loosely on its hinges. As she watched, the wind blew it fully open and slammed it back against the wall. She walked over to close it, clutching the stub of candle so that she could light it again as soon as she had dealt with the draught.

As she stood in the doorway, Georgia saw a steady light crossing the courtyard. Was the power on again? The storm still seemed as fierce as ever. Quickly she moved back into the shadows. Someone must have noticed the open door and was coming to lock it again. What would happen when they failed to find the key above the lintel?

It would be better to go out and face whoever he was. As long as she could keep the slashed portrait out of sight, a caretaker would decide that she was not a thief, and assume that she was sheltering from the storm. She heard a hand groping for the key, then a deep, familiar laugh.

'Georgia.'

She froze at the sound of Theo's voice. She stared first at the figure looming in the doorway, then at the shredded canvas. He stood holding a lamp, tall and menacing, outlined against a flash of lightning. She backed away as he advanced towards her.

'How did you know I was here?' she asked.

'I saw the door open. I was expecting you. I knew you'd come, if only to ensure that no one else ...' His voice trailed off as the beam of light caught the torn canvas.

She heard him swear under his breath as he strode

across the room, examined the ravaged painting and rounded on her.

'What gave you the right to do that?' he demanded.

Why had she ever come here? She must have been mad. The back of her throat felt dry and constricted, and her voice failed her.

'Well, don't you think I deserve an explanation?' There was a dark threat in Theo's voice that Georgia remembered only too well. No one was ever allowed to touch his work. What would he do now that she had ripped it to pieces?

She would never have come here if he hadn't stolen her portrait. He could answer that first. 'Perhaps you could tell me why you broke into my home?'

Theo gave her a hard look. 'You regard Fleur's as your home? Apart from its obvious unsuitability, I understand that it now belongs to Dominic.'

'That's not the point. You broke in and you stole my painting.'

'So you decided to get even?' Theo bent down, took a piece of torn canvas in his hand and smoothed it out between his fingers.

'As you say, Georgia, the painting was yours, so you were free to do with it as you chose.' He looked sharply at her. 'What did you do to the picture I left with you?'

'Left with me?' Georgia was furious. 'Is that what you call it when you break into someone's property? And don't quibble about whether it's my home or not.' She sidled past him towards the door. 'You needn't worry. It's quite safe. I'll have it sent back to you.'

He was stroking the undamaged portion of the canvas. 'Maybe it's better for both of us to forget that girl. She only existed in the past.'

'I can't forget the past.'

'You haven't tried. You're still living in it.'

She turned to leave but Theo moved swiftly in front of her, an impassable barrier between her and the door. She glared at him.

238

'Don't you dare try to stop me.'

'You're not getting away just yet.' Calmly Theo stepped towards her and took her firmly by the wrist. He turned and pushed her backward out of the studio, closed the door behind him and turned the heavy iron key in the lock. 'You're coming with me.'

'I'm doing no such thing. Let me go. I'm going home.'

'How?'

'What do you mean?' She felt insecure on the slippery stone staircase, with his hand on her wrist. If she tried to pull away she might fall.

'Where's your car? Were you so angry that you walked the whole way?' He touched a strand of her wet hair, still dripping on to her shoulders. 'I wouldn't like to think I made you that angry.'

'The car broke down. I had to walk the last bit.'

Theo turned his face up to the still torrential rain. 'You can't go anywhere in this,' he said, leading her quickly across the courtyard. She felt cold now and shivery in her damp clothes. He stopped in front of a high, arched door. 'At the very least, you can take the time to dry off,' he said. 'Come in.'

'What is this?'

'My new studio. My home, I suppose, when I'm in Paris.'

Georgia was curious to see inside and she wanted to dry her hair and tidy up before she telephoned for a car. She felt perfectly capable of dealing with Theo. The front door was imposing and so was the wide, tiled hall. She hadn't thought of him having a house like this, but when he pushed open a side door and led her into what was obviously his studio, nothing seemed to have changed. Half-completed canvases littered the floor and walls; a huge central table was buried under tubes of paint, jugs, bowls of fruit, and chunks of twisted wood, but what hit her most was the overwhelmingly familiar smell of fresh oil paint.

Like the rest of Paris, the room was in darkness. Theo

cleared a space on the table and put the lamp down amidst the clutter. There was a flash of lightning, brighter than the rest, which seemed to illuminate the whole room. For a moment, Georgia felt as if she were outside, in the full force of the storm. And then she looked up. The ceiling was a single sheet of glass, clear to the sky, and above her she could see a vast expanse of the stormy night.

How different was all this splendour from the old days. Theo seemed able to afford all his fantasies now. As the lightning flashed above her again, she looked around the room. Against the end wall she saw their old bed. So he had kept it. He hadn't thrown it away. She walked instinctively towards it, and then stopped dead. In front of the threadbare, red-gold drapes, there was an unfinished painting on an easel, and behind it, on the bed, she saw two naked girls, entwined in each other's arms.

She felt Theo's hands on her shoulders. 'Don't worry, you aren't disturbing anything. We had to stop when the lights failed,' he said casually.

The power had been cut two hours ago, but it seemed that the girls hadn't made any attempt to leave. Georgia noticed that Theo's shirt was unbuttoned and loosely tucked into his belt, as if he had dressed hurriedly when he was disturbed. She shook off his hands, and turned to go. 'I can see I'm in the way,' she said.

'Nonsense. It's time they went. They enjoy their work far too much.' He slapped one of the tangled bodies on the rump. 'Martine, my love, it's time for you to leave.'

The girls separated their meshed limbs. They stared at Georgia with open-mouthed interest, making her conscious of her soaked dress. Theo put his arm around her and explained to the girls. 'She seems to like being wet. I'm trying to break her of the habit.'

They rose reluctantly to their feet, scrabbled on the floor for their clothes and crossed the room. They draped their arms round Theo's neck and stared resentfully at Georgia, before they walked out into the hall.

Theo's hand caught Georgia's wrist, circling it completely. He led her towards the bed. 'Sit down. We need to talk.'

She had no intention of ever sitting on that bed again. She held firmly on to one of the carved wooden posts in case he should try to force her down on to it.

Theo laughed as he released her and stretched out comfortably on the ancient brocade cover. He looked up at her, his eyes alight with amusement. 'Why don't you tell me why you came here?'

'You broke into Fleur's,' she repeated stubbornly. 'You stole my painting.'

Theo raised one eyebrow. 'I hadn't realised it meant so much to you.'

'It doesn't,' Georgia assured him. 'If you had asked me for it I would have given it back to you at once.'

'Are you sure? Wouldn't you mind the pleasure it gave me? What if I had chosen to display it prominently?'

Georgia flushed uncomfortably. 'You wouldn't have done that.'

'What makes you so sure? I can think of quite a few potential buyers.' He raised himself on one elbow and looked straight into her eyes. 'I wanted it for myself, Georgia, but I don't believe you would have given it to me. And now you've made sure I can't have it.' He shrugged. 'Although now I have the version I prefer. The original.'

Georgia's arm was beginning to ache. She let go of the bedpost. She wanted to sit down, but certainly not beside Theo. She shifted from one foot to the other, then sat primly on a red chair. This conversation was getting nowhere. 'I'll have the painting you left at the club returned to you tomorrow. Now will you please call me a car?'

Theo made no move at all. 'Where to?' he asked.

'Back to Fleur's, of course. Not that it's anything to do with you.'

'You can't go back to that house alone tonight. At least wait until the storm is over, and your hair is dry.'

'As if you cared what happened to me!'

'Is that what you think?' Theo swung his legs off the bed and filled two glasses with brandy. He handed one to her. 'Here, drink this to warm you up.' He pushed open a door. 'Why don't you dry off in there while we talk about this?'

The bathroom was large and uncluttered, all white and chrome, with a huge bath along one wall. Georgia longed to soak in a tub of hot water, but she had no intention of taking her clothes off. She would tidy up a little and then leave.

Theo stood in the doorway. 'I suppose you won't have a bath because I'm here. Very foolish. But you do look a little more comfortable now.' He turned and walked back into the room. 'Don't catch cold, sitting in that wet dress just to spite me,' he called out. 'Here, put this on.' He handed her a model's robe, made of cheap cotton, smelling of sweat, stale wine and sex, like a hundred others. Still, at least it was dry.

She put it on and sat down again on the red chair. Theo laughed and picked up a paintbrush.

'Don't you dare paint me,' she snapped.

'Why not? It'll help to pass the time and you owe me something. No one destroys my work without paying.'

The brandy was soaking into her now, warming her chilled bones and inflaming her temper. There was something she still needed to know. 'How did you get into Fleur's, Theo?' There had been no sign of a forced entry.

'Are you sure you want me to tell you?'

Georgia rubbed her head with a towel. 'Of course I do. Did Natasha help you?'

Theo stopped painting. 'Do you really imagine she would do that? Don't you understand her at all?'

242

Natasha had never been inside Fleur's anyway; she didn't know about the portrait, or the layout of the house. Georgia sipped her brandy, trying not to face the truth. It must have been Dominic then. She had to know.

'It wasn't Dominic either if that's worrying you,' Theo said.

'Then how . . .?'

'One of your clients gave me her key. I guessed that you would keep the painting in the club, and not at Lusigny. And, as there was no one there, I had plenty of time to look for it.'

So her clients talked about her while they sat for Theo. And lent out their keys! But then Theo had always been able to get anything he wanted from a woman, including her. But not any longer.

She looked at him. The broad chest and the lean hips were all as she remembered. He was heavier now, more powerful. Suddenly she wanted him as much as she had when they had made love day after day, night after night, until he had left her. The memory swamped her. She sat up straighter in the chair and sipped her brandy.

Theo smiled at her over the top of the easel. 'Did you think I didn't know how you lived? With the number of women I paint? They come to me with sealed lips, and after one sitting they pour out their hearts.'

Georgia flushed. She was sure that was not all they did for Theo! He put down his brush, walked over to her and adjusted the front of her robe. Angrily she pulled it tighter. 'I thought you no longer painted from life,' she said. 'So why do you use models?'

'I still need the inspiration. And it's convenient for some of your friends if their husbands can't recognise the subjects of their portraits.'

'Subjects? What do you mean?'

'Go and look at the bed. Go on, I promise I'll stay here.'

Dangling between the heavy drapes, Georgia saw narrow, plaited straps of shell-pink leather, exactly the same as the ones she had designed especially for Nadine. Attached to one end was a male thong from Fleur's. She pressed the smooth leather between her fingers as she turned back to face Theo.

'That's right,' he said. 'They often bring their lovers.'

'The boys from Fleur's? My team?' Nadine must have brought Gaston here for Theo to paint the two of them. Involuntarily, Georgia imagined Nadine's wrists and ankles fastened to the four corners of the bed, while Gaston twisted the straps tighter and tighter between her legs.

Theo appeared quite unconcerned. 'I'm sure they're well paid for their time. Is there a problem?'

'But what do they do with the paintings?'

'Nadine hangs a portrait of herself and her lover on her bedroom wall.'

Georgia laughed out loud. 'Don't be ridiculous, Theo. She's happily married.'

'She's respectably married, Georgia. There is a difference. And I think her sex life is a little dull at home. It adds some spice to look up on the wall while her husband is struggling to satisfy her, and see what she knows is a portrait of her with her lover. She even persuaded the count to buy it for her; he prides himself on being a patron of the arts.'

'And is that why your style changed?'

'Absolutely not.' Theo slammed his palette down on the table and came over to her, waving his brush. 'You know I no longer have to compromise my work. Fortunately, it isn't representational. And I enjoy company; I like to talk while I paint. It suits us all.'

Georgia ran the plaited leather strap through her fingers. How many of her friends had enjoyed sex on this bed? And with how many of her young men?

Theo leant against the bedpost. She could smell the strong odour of oil paint, something she always associated with him. She closed her eyes to cut out the sight of

244

his powerful body looming over her, only to find her brain full of memories.

'And what about you?' he asked. 'Do you really believe you can live without a man?'

'It will be easier if . . .'

'If temptation is out of your way? The way you look there will always be temptation.' Theo stretched out his hand; Georgia withdrew. Was he trying to prove how swiftly she reacted to a man's approach?

She twisted the stiff brocade cover between her fingers, remembering the feel of it against her skin and how Theo had draped it over her, only to tear it away from her naked body the first time they had made love.

He was too close to her now. She looked up at him. 'I'm leaving Paris for the time being. Maybe I came here to say goodbye to this part of my life.'

He sat beside her on the bed and held out his arms. 'I want to change your mind,' he said. 'Stay with me now.'

For a moment it felt good to bury her face against the smooth cotton of his shirt and to feel his arms around her. He held her quietly, his head resting on her hair. But she didn't want to be caught in this trap again. 'Why? Why should I stay?' she demanded.

For the first time he looked angry. 'Why? Damn you. How can you ask that? Because I adore you.'

Georgia strained against his grasp. She had to get out of there. She no longer felt safe, no longer in control. All the defences she had so painfully built up after Dominic were crumbling as she felt Theo's hard body pressing against hers. How could she still matter to him? Did he simply resent the idea that any woman might leave him?

'I have to say goodbye,' she insisted. 'Everything we had is long gone.'

'We're not the same, Georgia. Does my hand feel the same as it did then?' Theo stroked the contour of her chin. 'You loved me once. I thought there was a chance that you might forgive me. I know what a fool I was and how much I lost.'

245

'You mean that now that you are successful you have time for me?'

'If you like. I admit I couldn't think beyond my work then. I thought I could have you as well. I was wrong.'

Georgia flushed as she realised how much she still desired Theo, how much her need for him still burned through her. She rose to her feet; she could not stay here. After what he had said, she did not want him to know how much she still wanted him.

Theo pushed her back on to the bed. The sable fur of the paintbrush in his hand caught on her thigh, leaving a long streak of burnt umber. She stared at it, then felt Theo wipe it away with a damp cotton rag, soaked in turpentine. The paint smeared and lifted as he gently rubbed her skin.

She felt the robe part and slip off her shoulders. The soft fur of the brush was stroking the inside of her thighs, edging towards the hem of her knickers. She wanted to shout at him to stop, and yet it was so pleasurable that she waited, moment after moment, until the long, soft tip curled and twisted deep inside the damp silk.

'These are chilling you,' he murmured, as he slipped the pants down over her thighs. He held her in his arms, then bent and caught the hooks of her silk brassière between his strong teeth, teasing it loose until it burst open.

'You have the most perfect breasts I have ever seen. I knew that the first time I painted them.'

With the tip of his brush he darkened her nipples, laughing as the delicate hairs teased them into two stiff, thrusting peaks. The soft tip trailed down over her belly as he worked harder, his fingers following the long wooden shaft.

She lay back on the bed, feeling the delicious sensation of the fur stroking her skin. She closed her eyes as he knelt over her, and combed the dark triangle between her thighs with the tip of his brush. She felt her soft hair spring back as he ran the fur through the little curls, before gently parting her sex lips. She raised her knee slightly off the bed as the brush probed, tantalisingly slowly, between her labia.

She knew that he would understand exactly the pleasure he was giving her. She looked up at the long, thin straps dangling from the four corners of the bed. Had Theo made love to Nadine here, too? Had he tied Nadine with those deceptively delicate, steel-strong plaits of pink leather that left her body marked for hours after they were removed, reminding her deliciously of her enjoyment long after she had returned home in an elegant *couture* gown? And had Nadine, too, enjoyed the exquisite sensation of the sable hairs curling round her clitoris as Theo slipped his brush deep inside her?

Theo's powerful thighs pressed against Georgia's skin as he slowly removed the brush, leaving her poised on the edge of orgasm. She moaned as the subtle teasing ceased, and felt her deprived muscles quiver with frustration.

Theo loomed over her. 'Undress me now,' he ordered.

Georgia's eyes jerked open. She had thought that Theo was the last man she wanted, and yet now she longed to feel him take her again. She raised her crimson nails to his half-open shirt and pressed her thumb against the one button left fastened.

She fought for breath as she felt the familiar, wiry hair on Theo's chest beneath her fingers. His hands clasped her buttocks as she pulled open the fine cotton, exposing a broad expanse of hard, muscled flesh. She ran her nails lightly over his nipples, feeling them harden at her touch. She longed to take them between her lips and feel him respond to the sensation of her tongue flickering over them. She looked into Theo's eyes, the dark amber irises now almost transparent with desire, as she pulled his shirt down over his arms and dropped it to the floor.

She heard him gasp as her fingers hesitated on the zip of his trousers. She pulled the teeth slowly, carefully apart and watched his penis spring forward as he stepped out of the trousers, his muscular thighs golden in a flash of lightning overhead.

Half-buried memories intruded into her mind as Theo stood over her. She was no longer a young girl, overwhelmed by her first vision of a man's naked body. But even now, with all her experience, she knew that he was still as beautiful as she had thought him then. The same fierce need invaded her senses, blinding her to all his faults.

She struggled to keep hold of the anger that she had lived with for so many years. If he would only take her quickly and relieve the physical desire that she could no longer control, she knew that she could walk out of here now and never see him again.

When he pulled back the covers on the bed, she felt the familiar, rough brocade on her skin, and his hands caressing her wrists and ankles as he stroked her skin with Nadine's delicately twisted straps. He was standing over her, letting her see his need for her, waiting for her response. Why couldn't he tie her down with Nadine's plaited leather, and force her to accept his lust without choice? It would be so easy to leave him then.

'We can use these sometime if you like,' he said, 'but now I want to persuade you in my own way to come back to me.'

She watched him lift her hand to his lips, kissing her open palm. Her mouth ached for his touch; her nipples stiffened into rosy peaks waiting for him to take them.

He lay down on the bed beside her, with his breath still on her palm, and stroked the inside of her wrist up to her elbow. The storm had cleared the air only temporarily; now the humidity was building up again. The nerve-endings tingled under her skin as she felt the warmth of his body, inches away from her own. She knew that he must see the rise and fall of her breasts as her breath quickened; and she prayed that he would hold her and make love to her before she was forced to admit her longing for him. She moved her legs nervously, in a useless attempt to hide the moist eagerness between her thighs.

He put his hand on her knee and stroked her skin with the roughened pads of his fingers. Involuntarily, her lips parted and she moaned softly as she felt him lean over her, increasing the pressure of his thumbs on her melting limbs. And still she longed to feel the weight of his body covering hers. She wanted more than the insistent caress of his touch on her inner thighs.

As he knelt over her, Georgia opened her eyes and saw the long, hard line of his erection jutting proudly over her aching mound. She felt she was melting into the golden-brown haven of his body as he covered her with kisses, on her throat, her breasts and the soft lobes of her ears. She no longer wanted to resist the sweet surrender he was demanding. She would give him what he wanted; she would admit that she desired him, if only she could feel him inside her again.

She put out her hands to stroke his shoulders and expose her need, and heard him stifle a sigh as the tips of her fingers touched him. He raised his hand to hers and gazed down at her questioningly as he covered her with his body. She wanted to feel her breasts pressing against his flesh, to let her body mould into his as her arms circled his neck and she pulled his mouth down on to hers.

The rich, sweet flavour of his lips teased her brain with half-buried memories of past nights of pleasure as she kissed him, cradling his head in her fingers as he gently parted her legs and lowered himself on to her. She felt her muscles close around the satisfying bulk of his long, curved penis as he eased deeper inside her with one full, lingering thrust.

All her inner recesses quivered around the hot strength that reached endlessly inside her, seeking out each throbbing pulse with the hard column of his manhood. His firm, ridged flesh rubbed over her swollen bud with the sure, confident rhythm of a master. She lifted her hips, letting him hold the rounded cheeks of her bottom in the palms of his hands as she clasped his hips with her thighs, stroking the soft arches of her feet over his muscular back, sucking him even deeper into her.

She could feel the curl of his folded foreskin slither over her greedy clitoris as his heavy vein swelled with his seed. She came with him in a final, exultant burst of sensation. Slowly he rocked her back and forth in his arms, their bodies locked together, her cheeks damp with tears that she realised had come from his eyes, not hers.

Her response to him was as instinctive as the first time he had made love to her on this bed. She stroked his neck and let the sweetness of his body flow through her as he slept in her arms, his head nestled between her breasts, his strong thighs curving over hers. Her fingers caught in the thick, auburn strands of his hair, their scent as familiar as if he had never left her, as if she had never had other lovers, as if the years between them had never been lost.

When she awoke, the storm had cleared and she could see the first light of dawn through the glass ceiling of the room. Theo stirred in her arms and brushed his lips over her forehead.

'Darling girl, I'm not forcing you to stay. But I'd be a fool if I said I didn't want you now.'

She knew him too well. 'Theo, you want every woman in sight.'

He shrugged. 'It's true that I do if they're willing. But never while you were with me.' He looked deep into her eyes. 'What about you? Do you like sex with other men?'

She would have given a different answer a year ago; now she understood herself better. 'Yes, Theo. Yes, I do.'

'Then perhaps we're more suited than we were. Will you come with me this time?'

She was still unsure. 'Where?'

'New York first. I have an exhibition, and this time I

250

don't want to leave you. After that, England, if you like. We can go wherever you want.'

'Where do you live now? In New York?'

Theo shook his head. 'In California. Will you come and see if you like it? I have a house by the sea. The light is wonderful.'

Georgia nodded. 'One year, Theo. I'll come for one year.'

His mouth twitched with laughter as he looked at her. She wondered if he would agree to do what she wanted. 'I'll come to California with you, but I want total freedom to live as I please. I'm sure you expect the same privilege. After that, I'm going to England.'

'I'll be happy to take you.'

'Oh, no, Theo. I haven't decided that far ahead yet.'

Less than a week later, Georgia stood on the deck of the *Normandie*. Waving crowds lined the quay, but there was no one to see her off. She had said all her goodbyes. Theo was surrounded by a group of eager lady journalists who were far more interested in him than his art. He raised an eyebrow at her, apologetically.

She looked sideways at him. He made an excellent escort. His tawny good looks were a perfect foil for her own. And he was divine in bed.

However, there was a young man travelling alone who had given her a long appreciative look as she had boarded, and several distinguished gentlemen who were accompanying ladies who no longer seemed to interest them.

She turned her attention to the junior officer standing attentively beside her. His crisp, white uniform with its gold-tasselled epaulettes was beautifully tailored to cover his broad chest, and the knife-edge creases in his trousers failed to conceal the bulging thigh muscles beneath the formal clothes. She wondered what the crew's quarters were like.

'Tell me,' she said. 'How many men does it take to run the *Normandie*?'

His answer interested her so much that she hardly noticed Theo's young ladies scampering down the last gangplank, just before it was pulled up.

Theo came to join her on the top deck. He leant against the rail and lit a cigar as he studied the rows of seamen standing to attention. His eyes twinkled. 'Where are you going to start, Georgia?'

BLACK
lace

CONQUERED – Fleur Reynolds
ISBN 0 352 33025 2

DARK OBSESSION – Fredrica Alleyn
ISBN 0 352 33026 0

LED ON BY COMPULSION – Leila James
ISBN 0 352 33032 5

OPAL DARKNESS – Cleo Cordell
ISBN 0 352 33033 3

JEWEL OF XANADU – Roxanne Carr
ISBN 0 352 33037 6

RUDE AWAKENING – Pamela Kyle
ISBN 0 352 33036 8

GOLD FEVER – Louisa Francis
ISBN 0 352 33043 0

EYE OF THE STORM – Georgina Brown
ISBN 0 352 330044 9

WHITE ROSE ENSNARED – Juliet Hastings
ISBN 0 352 33052 X

A SENSE OF ENTITLEMENT – Cheryl Mildenhall
ISBN 0 352 33053 8

ARIA APPASSIONATA – Juliet Hastings
ISBN 0 352 33056 2

THE MISTRESS – Vivienne LaFay
ISBN 0 352 33057 0

ACE OF HEARTS – Lisette Allen
ISBN 0 352 33059 7

DREAMERS IN TIME – Sarah Copeland
ISBN 0 352 33064 3

Published in August

THE HOUSESHARE
Pat O'Brien

When Rupe reveals his most intimate desires over the Internet, he does not know that his electronic confidante is Tine, his landlady. With anonymity guaranteed, steamy encounters in cyberspace are limited only by the bounds of the imagination, but what will happen when Tine attempts to make the virtual real?

ISBN 0 352 33094 5

THE KING'S GIRL
Sylvie Ouellette

The early 1600s. Under the care of the decadent Monsieur and Madame Lampron, Laure, a spirited and sensual young Frenchwoman, is taught much about the darker pleasures of the flesh. Sent to the newly established colony in North America, she tries in vain to behave as a young Catholic girl should, and is soon embarking on a mission of seduction and adventure.

ISBN 0 352 33095 3

Published in September

TO TAKE A QUEEN
Jan Smith

Winter 1314. Lady Blanche McNaghten, the young widow of a Highland chieftain, is rediscovering her taste for sexual pleasures with a variety of new and exciting lovers, when she encounters the Black MacGregor. Proud and dominant, the MacGregror is also a sworn enemy of Blanche's clan. Their lust is instantaneous and mutual, but does nothing to diminish their natural antagonism. In the ensuing struggle for power, neither hesitates to use sex as their primary strategic weapon. Can the conflict ever be resolved?

ISBN 0 352 33098 8

DANCE OF OBSESSION
Olivia Christie

Paris, 1935. Grief-stricken by the sudden death of her husband, Georgia d'Essange wants to be left alone. However, Georgia's stepson, Dominic, has inherited Fleur's – an exclusive club where women of means can indulge their sexual fantasies – and demands her help in running it. Dominic is also eager to take his father's place in Georgia's bed, and further complications arise when Georgia's first lover – now a rich and successful artist – appears on the scene. In an atmosphere of increasing sexual tensions, can everyone's desires be satisfied?

ISBN 0 352 33101 1

Published in October

THE BRACELET
Fredrica Alleyn

Kristina, a successful literary agent may appear to have it all, but her most intimate needs are not being met. She longs for a discreet sexual liaison where – for once – she can relinquish control. Then Kristina is introduced, by her friend Jacqueline, to an elite group devoted to bondage and experimental power games. Soon she is leading a double life – calling the shots at work, but privately wearing the bracelet of bondage.

ISBN 0 352 33110 0

RUNNERS AND RIDERS
Georgina Brown

When a valuable racehorse is stolen from her lover, top showjumper Penny Bennett agrees to infiltrate a syndicate suspected of the theft. As Penny jets between locations as varied and exotic as France, Sri Lanka and Kentucky in an attempt to solve the mystery, she discovers that the members of the syndicate have sophisticated sexual tastes, and are eager for her to participate in their imaginatively kinky fantasies.

ISBN 0 352 33117 8

If you would like a complete list of plot summaries of Black Lace titles, please fill out the questionnaire overleaf or send a stamped addressed envelope to:-

Black Lace
332 Ladbroke Grove
London W10 5AH

BLACK
lace

WE NEED YOUR HELP . . .
to plan the future of women's erotic fiction –

– and no stamp required!

Yours are the only opinions that matter.

Black Lace is the first series of books devoted to erotic fiction by women for women.

We intend to keep providing the best-written, sexiest books you can buy. And we'd appreciate your help and valued opinion of the books so far. Tell us what you want to read.

THE BLACK LACE QUESTIONNAIRE

SECTION ONE: ABOUT YOU

1.1 Sex (*we presume you are female, but so as not to discriminate*)
Are you?

Male ☐
Female ☐

1.2 Age

under 21 ☐ 21–30 ☐
31–40 ☐ 41–50 ☐
51–60 ☐ over 60 ☐

1.3 At what age did you leave full-time education?

still in education ☐ 16 or younger ☐
17–19 ☐ 20 or older ☐

1.4 Occupation _____

1.5 Annual household income

under £10,000	☐	£10–£20,000	☐
£20–£30,000	☐	£30–£40,000	☐
over £40,000	☐		

1.6 We are perfectly happy for you to remain anonymous; but if you would like to receive information on other publications available, please insert your name and address

_____

_____

_____

_____

SECTION TWO: ABOUT BUYING BLACK LACE BOOKS

2.1 How did you acquire this copy of *Dance of Obsession*?

| I bought it myself | ☐ | My partner bought it | ☐ |
| I borrowed/found it | ☐ | | |

2.2 How did you find out about Black Lace books?

I saw them in a shop	☐
I saw them advertised in a magazine	☐
I saw the London Underground posters	☐

I read about them in _____

Other _____

2.3 Please tick the following statements you agree with:

I would be less embarrassed about buying Black Lace books if the cover pictures were less explicit	☐
I think that in general the pictures on Black Lace books are about right	☐
I think Black Lace cover pictures should be as explicit as possible	☐

2.4 Would you read a Black Lace book in a public place – on a train for instance?

| Yes | ☐ | No | ☐ |

SECTION THREE: ABOUT THIS BLACK LACE BOOK

3.1 Do you think the sex content in this book is:
        Too much   ☐   About right   ☐
        Not enough   ☐

3.2 Do you think the writing style in this book is:
        Too unreal/escapist ☐   About right   ☐
        Too down to earth   ☐

3.3 Do you think the story in this book is:
        Too complicated   ☐   About right   ☐
        Too boring/simple   ☐

3.4 Do you think the cover of this book is:
        Too explicit   ☐   About right   ☐
        Not explicit enough ☐

Here's a space for any other comments:

SECTION FOUR: ABOUT OTHER BLACK LACE BOOKS

4.1 How many Black Lace books have you read?   ☐

4.2 If more than one, which one did you prefer?

4.3 Why?

SECTION FIVE: ABOUT YOUR IDEAL EROTIC NOVEL

We want to publish the books you want to read – so this is
your chance to tell us exactly what your ideal erotic novel
would be like.

5.1 Using a scale of 1 to 5 (1 = no interest at all, 5 = your
ideal), please rate the following possible settings for an
erotic novel:

Medieval/barbarian/sword 'n' sorcery ☐
Renaissance/Elizabethan/Restoration ☐
Victorian/Edwardian ☐
1920s & 1930s – the Jazz Age ☐
Present day ☐
Future/Science Fiction ☐

5.2 Using the same scale of 1 to 5, please rate the following
themes you may find in an erotic novel:

Submissive male/dominant female ☐
Submissive female/dominant male ☐
Lesbianism ☐
Bondage/fetishism ☐
Romantic love ☐
Experimental sex e.g. anal/watersports/sex toys ☐
Gay male sex ☐
Group sex ☐

Using the same scale of 1 to 5, please rate the following
styles in which an erotic novel could be written:

Realistic, down to earth, set in real life ☐
Escapist fantasy, but just about believable ☐
Completely unreal, impressionistic, dreamlike ☐

5.3 Would you prefer your ideal erotic novel to be written
from the viewpoint of the main male characters or the
main female characters?

Male ☐ Female ☐
Both ☐

5.4   What would your ideal Black Lace heroine be like? Tick
      as many as you like:

Dominant	☐	Glamorous	☐
Extroverted	☐	Contemporary	☐
Independent	☐	Bisexual	☐
Adventurous	☐	Naive	☐
Intellectual	☐	Introverted	☐
Professional	☐	Kinky	☐
Submissive	☐	Anything else?	☐
Ordinary	☐	_____	

5.5   What would your ideal male lead character be like?
      Again, tick as many as you like:

Rugged	☐		
Athletic	☐	Caring	☐
Sophisticated	☐	Cruel	☐
Retiring	☐	Debonair	☐
Outdoor-type	☐	Naive	☐
Executive-type	☐	Intellectual	☐
Ordinary	☐	Professional	☐
Kinky	☐	Romantic	☐
Hunky	☐		
Sexually dominant	☐	Anything else?	☐
Sexually submissive	☐	_____	

5.6   Is there one particular setting or subject matter that your
      ideal erotic novel would contain?

_____

SECTION SIX: LAST WORDS

6.1   What do you like best about Black Lace books?

_____

6.2   What do you most dislike about Black Lace books?

_____

6.3   In what way, if any, would you like to change Black Lace
      covers?

_____

6.4   Here's a space for any other comments:

_____
_____
_____
_____

Thank you for completing this questionnaire. Now tear it out of the book – carefully! – put it in an envelope and send it to:

Black Lace
FREEPOST
London
W10 5BR

No stamp is required if you are resident in the U.K.